A CAUSE

AND

MANNER

A CAUSE AND MANNER

a medical noir thriller

by PETER TINITS MD

Dying Medium Press

Name: Tinits, Peter, author
Title: *A CAUSE and MANNER*
Description: a sleep-deprived, morally ambivalent doctor looks to his circle of close friends for help in dealing severely with his wife's lover.
Subject: fiction/thrillers/domestic,medical,psychological
BISAC: FIC 031100, FIC031040, FIC031080
ISBN: 978-1-7771904-1-5 (softcover)
ISBN: 978-1-7771904-9-1 (hardcover)

Print edition cover art by Eric Beddows
Operating room illustration by Scott O'Neill
Cover design by Ted Glaszewski

Thanks to my best beta-reader wife Nijole and
my editor Ken Nutt

PART 1

And our little life is rounded with a sleep —William Shakespeare, The Tempest.

Chapter 1

Our little lives are rounded with a sleep. I had been called out overnight to examine a massively obese, naked corpse. He was lounging on a sofa in a Coventry public housing unit, surrounded by pills, potato chips, beer cans, cigarette butts and wide-screen porn. How to choose a cause and manner of death. Gluttony, sloth, lust and poverty of purpose are all deadly sins. I try not to be judgemental or play favourites.

It is a 90-minute drive from Coventry to Toronto. I was sleep deprived and driving. This was to interview for a new job that Katya said we wanted. My destination wasn't far from the suburban street I grew up on, so I detoured down from the highway. Cruising tentatively, I experienced a mixture of apprehension and curiosity. I thought I would never want to see it again. I didn't want to see how the new owners had changed my childhood home.

Each house was more familiar, and I was only a block from mine, when I heard the drone of an under-muffled motor and changing gears. A motorcyclist was approaching from 50 yards ahead. He kept a steady pace and didn't decelerate until we collided. His bulk flew in an arc over my windshield, blocking the light. I heard the thud behind me a few seconds later.

Well, that sucked. I turned off my engine and went looking for him. He was dressed in black leathers and a black helmet, face down, not moving. There were no gang insignia on the jacket. Why would the idiot steer straight at me. Drunk, high or suicidal. Most likely insane.

It flashed through my mind that if his neck were broken, it would from a legal perspective be bad for me to move his head. He had nothing to lose, since I had probably already killed him. Reaching under one hip and shoulder, I log rolled him onto his side. If he was alive, his position might otherwise obstruct his breathing. His face was bloody. His lips were puffy and split by broken teeth. I elevated his jaw like they teach on mannequins in life support courses, and he took a shallow breath.

A few neighbours stood on their front steps, silhouetted against the setting sun. It wasn't long before I heard the cacophony of wailing sirens. A policeman asked me to tell what happened. My throat felt dry. A small crowd gathered in a circle around the accident scene. The paramedics tried to insert a breathing tube, which went better when I helped them.

I watched while they loaded him up. He could have been a local, but I didn't know him. His chest was moving in an exaggerated mechanical way. They were bagging oxygen into his lungs, so maybe he was still alive. I gave the officers my name and address and told them I was a doctor. That made them relax a little. They took my driver's licence and said I should stay at the scene until the technical accident investigator arrived to measure skid marks and put little red cones on the pavement.

"There won't be any skid marks. He came right at me without braking."

"Hopefully you made some."

"No." I was distracted by forgotten familiar houses.

I walked over to see if there was any damage to my car and had a look at the bike. It was a big Harley with saddlebags on the sides. The cop came up behind me and told me not to touch anything. My

4

car had a gaping crack in the front bumper moulding but looked still driveable.

A group of gawkers had gathered around the bike. A thin older woman was scrutinizing me. She came closer. "You used to live on this street, didn't ya?"

"Yes. I'm Matt. You're Mrs. Gaffney, right?"

"No. Mrs. Wattle. You look a little banged up. You've got a cut on your forehead. Why don't you come over and I'll get you a Band-Aid?"

I touched my forehead. My hand came back wet and red. "Okay, thanks. Can I go across the street to her house, officer?"

"Sure he can," she said. "He can wait with me until the accident detection cops or whatever come."

We walked over to her bungalow, a yellow brick, one-story, two-bedroom affair with a lawn chair on the front porch. Our house was red brick but otherwise identical. Most of the houses on the street looked the same. Her kitchen was furnished with a Formica table and vinyl-upholstered chrome chairs.

"Your dad died about five years ago, wasn't it, Matt? You want a cup of tea? Have a seat."

"My dad used to make me tea as soon as I walked in the door. Do you live by yourself, Mrs. Wattle?"

"Call me Dolly. Yes, I'm afraid so. Francis passed on two years ago now." She lit a cigarette and took a long drag making the tip glow. "Didn't you used to buy me smokes at the corner store?"

"Maybe. I don't think so." I might have told her smoking was bad for her, but she probably already knew.

There was a knock and Dolly got up. I followed her to the front door. A policeman was waiting. I could see over his shoulder that a tow truck was hoisting the Harley into the back of a pickup truck. He handed me my driver's licence. "The technical collision investigators say that if there are no marks on the pavement, there's no point in

5

them coming out. We'll do some measurements and then you can move your vehicle off the road. Where's the best place to reach you? Do you have a cell number?"

The officer followed us back into the kitchen to record my information. We all sat down and drank tea. Dolly said, "You look a little rattled, Matthew. You shouldn't drive anywhere. I got a spare bedroom you can use."

"I have a hotel room booked."

"Well you can cancel that. You shouldn't drive tonight. You probably got a concussion."

"She might be right there, Matthew," the cop said. "You wanna go to the hospital?"

I said I was fine but accepted the offer to stay. It was getting late. Dolly watched through the window while I moved my car around bits of motorcycle and sport utility bumper into her driveway. She let me back in and gave me some toiletries. I could hear her padding around in her slippers in the hallway on the other side of the locked bathroom door.

The nightmarish last night I had spent five years earlier, alone in my old house, danced before my eyes as I lay in Dolly's guest bedroom. I was picking through the contents after my father died. My sister had told me whatever I didn't take was going to the dump. I chose a few things from the detritus—a painting, a glass candy dish, some old laundered pillow cases with the distinctive odour of the home I knew. The guns had already been removed.

My cell phone jarred me awake. "Hi. It's Officer Potvin from the accident scene. Would you mind coming to Station 43 tomorrow morning at 9 a.m., Doctor? It turns out you knew the other driver. The detectives would like a word with you."

"How is he?"

"Sorry. I can't discuss it until we locate his next of kin... It's not looking too good."

"What was his name?"

"Can't tell you that either until we find his next of kin and notify them."

"Okay. Well, what's the address of the station?"

"Don't you know it? It's the same one your dad used to work at."

"No. I've been there once, but give it to me again."

It dawned on me that I hadn't called Katya to tell her what had happened. I hadn't even thought of it. It was too late to call or text her and upset her now. I would call her tomorrow and tell her the whack in the head I got caused brain damage.

I encountered Dolly again in the morning. She was standing in the kitchen, dressed in a faded pink bathrobe. She didn't seem to be a morning person. She might have been 65 or 70, but she looked older. "Would you like some breakfast?" Her tone was a little dour.

"No thanks. Thanks for putting me up. I have to go to the police station. They want to talk to me some more. And I've got a job interview at Scarborough Health Sciences Centre. I'm a doctor—an anesthesiologist and a coroner. That's why I'm here."

She looked at me dubiously. Then she had a new idea. "Would you like a cocktail?" She was already reaching for a bottle in the liquor cabinet.

"No thanks. I'm serious. I have to go to the cop-shop to answer questions about the accident. And I have a job interview."

"But it's Sunday! Well, you can stay here tonight if you like. Just come back when you're done."

"Dolly, did you know the guy I hit on the bike?"

"Sure I knew him. That was Wayney."

"Wayney. Wayney who? Not Wayney Delaney?"

"Yeah. Wayney Delaney. I wouldn't tell the cops, because I'm an unreliable witness, and I'm not going to court with any bikers. Let them find out on their own. That's what they get paid for." She said *unreliable* like it needed air quotes.

7

"Wayney was in a bike gang?"

"Oh, I don't know. He might have been."

Dolly watched as I packed my stuff and continued my interrupted drive down the street, past my old house. I didn't like what they had done with the place. It made my heart ache a little.

Chapter 2

I was the gas man in the gynecology operating room, half-sitting, half-lying in my imitation leather swivel chair, my legs slung over the footrest of the gas machine. Mondays are for misgivings and contemplation. I was home after my lost weekend in Toronto.

Our head nurse Eve came in and announced: "We're really short-staffed today. Three nurses called in sick. I can help you get started, but you'll all have to break for lunch together. There is no one to relieve."

"They must have the Friday-Monday flu," I remarked.

"I think Christina's grandmother died," Joanie said. She was the scrub nurse, the oldest and most experienced nurse in the O.R.

"Second time she died this month." Adam was the surgeon. He was a gynecologist, originally from Barbados, who had competed for Canada in the Olympics in two track events. He was streamlined—six feet, four inches, head shaved bald. He wore the latest fashion-forward eyeglasses. You could hear a trace of West Indies in his voice.

"What about a signup sheet so that not too many people are sick the same day? Hey Sara, you never miss work," I said. "How many times have you got your picture put up as employee of the month at Coventry General Hospital?"

9

"None." Sara was the circulating nurse. She had a cute triangular face, with blonde hair and luminous green eyes. She was still in her thirties and assuredly photogenic.

"No way! You would crawl through broken glass. You would skip your lunch to help your sisters and brothers in the operating room."

"Yes, but I would still have lunch." She was blushing a little.

Adam leaned over to speak with me confidentially. "Matthew, be careful of this first patient. She makes me uncomfortable." I had seen from the day list that she was a 45-year-old woman scheduled for a hysterectomy.

"In the office, I told her I would leave while she took off her clothes, including her underwear, and to put on an examination gown," he continued. "She told me that she never wears underwear. I always have a nurse with me in the room whenever I see her. She wanted me to help diagnose her husband's condition, so she showed me a picture of his thigh rash on her phone, with his penis prominently in the frame."

"Not another one! Flaccid or erect?" Simon, the surgical assistant, had just entered the room and the conversation. He was a retired English family doctor with a rosy complexion and profuse hoary beard, which he pointed at whomever he was addressing.

There is normally a surgeon and a physician assistant in Canadian operating rooms. There is also a gas man slash anesthesiologist, a scrub nurse who hands instruments to the surgeon and a circulating nurse, who assists the anesthesiologist and brings equipment to the scrub nurse. That comes to five people, six if you include the patient.

"She wants to have a threesome with you, Adam. It's not cheating if her husband is there too." I made a rude gesture with one of my syringes.

Anesthesiologists are medical doctors who anesthetize patients for operations that surgeons perform. We are a dysfunctional family.

Surgeons want to get operating, and they see anesthesiologists as impediments to this. In fact, surgeons even have an acronym for the time taken by anesthesiologists to do their questionnaires with patients, set up their drugs and monitoring equipment and get the patients asleep—OAFAT. This stands for obligatory anesthesia fuck-around time.

Surgeons like to point out that no one was ever cured by an anesthetic. Surgeons heal with steel. When in doubt, cut it out. When the performance of my duties, as I saw them, resulted in Angelo Amodeo, a general surgeon at our hospital, being delayed, he barked that I was passive-aggressive. My practiced answer was that he was aggressive-aggressive. His next move would be to say that only faggots wear their stethoscopes draped around their necks as I was doing.

A standard operating room is outfitted with a mechanical steel table that patients lie on, a gas machine for ventilating patients' lungs with inhaled anesthetics, and various carts and cupboards filled with drugs and equipment. Our operating rooms were older, so they had windows. They were built in a time when the mental health of staff trumped any privacy concerns of patients. They had rubberized flooring and green ceramic tile walls. The theory was that blue walls might cast a confusing cyanotic pall over patients and that pink walls wouldn't show blood splatter to advantage.

Soon after the surgery had begun, I heard Adam complaining to Sara. "Rass! I think the tubing is clogged. Check dee suction, mon." He could turn the Rasta on and off. There was a loud slurping sound as the tubing was changed and the suction returned. "Only two things sound like that," Adam said, looking directly at Joanie.

"Ha ha. Isn't there a word for a blow job when the woman has no teeth?" she asked.

"I don't know. Is there a word?" I joined in.

"Hey Sara, what's the word?" Joanie called. This set her off on a bout of laughing and coughing. The loose smoker's phlegm rattled in her bronchi.

"It's called a 'hummer.' I wish I wasn't the only one who knew that." Sara had an angel's face and a devil's smile. She was a nice distraction from recent events.

It wasn't long before Adam was closing. "How much blood do you think she's lost, Matthew?" he asked. This was a sensitive question. A high estimate could be interpreted by a surgeon to reflect on his skill and wound his ego.

"Not much."

"Purr-fect," he said, surveying his work. He said that after most operations.

Our next case was an elective Cesarean section. We had to trek to the operating room on the obstetric ward, one floor below us. I did a spinal anesthetic, which meant the patient would be frozen from the chest down and would be awake to see her baby born. Sara was assisting me.

I liked working with Sara. She was very attentive. She didn't get flustered. Whenever there was trouble, she could be relied upon to be right there by my side with exactly the right piece of equipment in her hand. A vigorous, screaming baby was soon pulled from the patient's abdomen, through a gush of blood and amniotic fluid.

"That's the first time I've ever heard a baby make more noise than you, Joanie," Simon said. Then to the mother, "What's the baby's name?" His beard, which overflowed his surgical mask, was bobbing as he spoke.

"Delilah," she answered.

"Very Biblical. She was a temptress or a whore, I think." Simon didn't practice self-censorship. "What would you do if the surgeon accidentally cut the ureter?" He was directing this question to the medical student who had been allowed to scrub in. Coventry General

12

is a community, not a teaching hospital, but we still get our share of students rotating through.

"I would scratch my name off the chart. Are you a resident in obstetrics?" I asked the student across the large drape separating surgery from anesthesia. A resident is a postgraduate trainee in a medical specialty. This was meant as a compliment because she was actually doing useful things.

There was a chorus of answers. "No, a third-year medical student."

"You're assisting very well. You have a brilliant future in obstetrics," I said. "Of course, you may not want that. The on-call responsibilities are the worst of any specialty—even worse than anesthesia. There is a lot of night work. Obstetrics is also the most sued specialty."

"How often do anesthesiologists get sued?" she asked timidly.

"We're in maybe fifth place."

"Yes, obstetric night call is a young man's game. I used to do it of course, as well as anesthesia and general surgery. I was quite busy as a family doctor." Simon liked to self-aggrandize. It is true that many family doctors in a bygone era did do all these things.

"Anesthesia call is worse than general surgery call," I insisted.

I was on call that night. Once a week, I have to carry a pager for twenty-four hours and respond promptly if it alarms. I am Pavlov's dog, but instead of salivating, I get a visceral startle response when I hear it. I am the rat in a psychology experiment, where the floor of its cage is intermittently electrified. It feels like everybody wants a piece of me. I resent being disturbed and curse myself for not sleeping sufficiently in preparation.

We completed the remainder of our day with a few more hysterectomies back in the main operating room. Taking out uteruses is the primary way gynecologists make a living. Just as the dressing was being put on the incision of the last patient, one of the orthopedic surgeons, Joshua Smith, poked his head through the door to our room. "Como estas, bitches?"

"What do you want?" everyone groaned in unison.

"Bone broke. Me fix!"

Orthopedic surgeons almost always have a hip fracture they would like to do after hours. This has to do with the epidemic of aging and old people falling over in a pre-terminal way. A chance to cut is a chance to cure.

Angelo Amodeo followed the hip fracture with a bowel obstruction and an appendix. He was pissy because he had to wait while I did an epidural anesthetic for a woman in labour. As he was closing our last emergency case of the evening, the operating room nurses asked me who was still in labour and whether they were likely to deliver vaginally. The majority of anesthesia late night work has to do with obstetrics—epidurals and Cesarean sections.

"Just one that I know of," I answered. "But alas, her pelvis is as yet unproven." This meant it was her first baby and we might get called back for a Cesarean section. Some anesthesiologists go to the obstetric ward before leaving to check what's there. I never do, because I believe it's bad luck. Work, like the devil, could be summoned by speaking its name. The obstetric nurses might mistake my visit for being interested.

Since everyone lived close to the hospital, we didn't have an on-call room for anesthesiologists to sleep. I go home to sleep. If I didn't get a change of scenery and some fresh air, you might find me swinging at the end of a rope. I personally knew of two anesthesiologists who had committed suicide. One hung himself from a girder in his garage on a Good Friday after a fight with his wife. It was dramatic when she found him, but selfish because he was on call. It meant someone else would be forced to cover his Easter long weekend.

Before I left at midnight there was the usual refrain of, "See you later—much, much later." Despite receiving call-back pay, no one wanted to return. As I was leaving the hospital, I had some trouble getting through the exit to the parking lot. I was so tired that I had been repetitively pushing on the hinge side of the door.

Chapter 3

After a night on call, I feel shell-shocked. There were two epidurals to do for women in labour—one at 2 and one at 4 a.m. I get called through the night about half the time. I take the next day off to recover. Even if I don't get called, I don't sleep well.

I wandered to the kitchen past the stack of mail in the hallway without looking at it. Doctors get a lot of mail—mostly drug company adverts, once-in-a-lifetime investment opportunities and solicitations from charities. I downed a glass of orange juice and stared dumbly at the coffee maker. We have a low-end espresso machine that makes pretty good cappuccino. I turned it on, listening for the pump to start chugging. Taking a seat, I scanned the newspaper, luxuriating in the knowledge that I wasn't obligated to speak with anyone. There was nothing about Wayney.

The phone rang, but I didn't respond. I let the answering machine get it. Grampa never answered the phone either. My 90-year-old Polish father-in-law lives with us. If he came into the kitchen, I would have to acknowledge him, but I didn't have the energy to shout conversation into his good ear. I grabbed my pager and turned it off. Pagers are relics used by doctors who want to keep their cell phone numbers secret. Only my wife and the coroners' answering service have my cell number.

I had become a coroner five years ago because it promised some variety. There were only a couple of calls per month. Being an anesthesiologist means that one is confined all day with surgeons. Surgeons are alpha males, and occasionally females, who want to dominate the pack. They might accord you more respect if they think that someday you will be the one investigating their mishaps.

If police call me to examine a death scene, I would be in charge of whether to order an autopsy and assigning a cause and manner of death. Cause means medical cause, like exsanguination or a heart attack. Manner means whether it was natural, accident, suicide or homicide, with murder being a subtype as defined by law. I suppose it's appropriate I do some police work because I look like a cop. My father and his father before him were cops. I am six feet two, two hundred pounds. When I travel to a different city and put on a black baseball cap and sunglasses, cops on the street nod to me fraternally.

We live on the older doctors' street in Coventry. We have a nice house, but not the nicest one. It used to be *the* doctors' street, but a few years ago newer younger doctors started their own street. Because of my cop heritage, the first thing I did after moving in was install a burglar alarm. The Coventry police are at my door within five minutes of the false alarms. Crime is rare here.

I took my coffee to my study to start in on some billing. I had to enter patient data and fee codes into a computer software program. It was work I could do without being fully awake. It is relatively easy to scam the public healthcare system if you don't have a conscience. I have mixed feelings about "creative billing," meaning an aggressive interpretation of the wording in the fee schedule. My parents taught me it was wrong to steal.

Old Order Mennonites in our area refuse free medical coverage as conscientious objectors. They pay but try to make you feel guilty about taking their money. They usually say that their community church will take up a collection for them. I charge them a little more for being a pain—for making me print a bill, stamp a letter and go to the mailbox. I can sympathize with their pacifist moral code without donating my time to support it. This code is not freely chosen. Church elders posing as wise men dictate it to them.

When I moved to Coventry twenty years ago, my father gave me a shotgun as a housewarming present. It wasn't a joke. That was the way he was. After he died, his cop friends came and removed three loaded handguns he had secreted around the house. He was a reverse Mennonite. He said it was to scare off criminals and relatives of any patients I might accidentally harm. He believed that a weapon guaranteed the necessities of life. I took it and put it away because he meant well. In a situation where social norms have broken down, it seems now that he was right.

I was napping on the living room couch when Katya got home from work. My wife is a pretty, young thing, five years my junior. When we met, she was a statuesque, svelte redhead with freckles. She is currently a blonde with pink fringes. Her cheekbones make her look feline, like the actress Cate Blanchett or Sara in the operating room. One grandmother was Japanese. I'm not sure how that happened.

She surveyed the mail basket in the hall. "It's all for Dr. M. Kork. We should get an unlisted address. Do you know any lonely people who would like more mail?"

"I wonder how long it would take to get deleted from the advertisers' databases if I dropped dead—years probably."

"I haven't seen you for three days. How was your night on call, Matthias?" I had slept in the spare bedroom the last two nights. Only my mother ever called me Matthias. Katya must have seen it on a letter.

"I didn't want to disturb you. I had to get up twice."

"I don't know how you do that job, Matthew."

"It's not like they ask me if I would like to come in. It's a command performance."

"I suppose the patients can't really plan when they are going to get sick."

"I prefer to blame surgeons. They are up, so they think I should be too."

Katya addressed the elephant in the room. "How did your job interview in Toronto go? You got home so late. I didn't get a chance to talk to you."

"I didn't go."

"Why not? You spent all that time setting it up, and you drove all the way there. Where were you then?"

"I couldn't do it."

"Matthew, we went all through this. We agreed that it would be good for us to have a fresh start."

"And I got into a car accident. I spent half of Sunday at the police station."

"What! Why didn't you call me?"

"A guy died. Katya, I just can't live there. It's all the things I don't want."

"Okay. I understand. Never mind, Matthew. We can make it work here. Now tell me what happened."

"A motorcycle drove into me. The guy died. He used to live on my street."

"What guy? Did you know him?"

"Wayney Delaney. We played together when we were little. He was a mild-mannered kid. He became an impulsive class clown as a teenager to improve his social status. I didn't recognize him."

"Are they trying to blame you for the accident?"

"No. I don't think so. They measured everything. He hit square in the middle of my bumper on my side of the road."

"Did you tell them you are a coroner?"

"Yeah. It may have helped."

"I am so sorry that had to happen, Matthew."

"I could have told you I was too distraught from the accident to go to the interview. I wasn't going anyway."

"Okay Matthew. Let's try to forget about it. Let's make some dinner."

It used to be a bone of contention as to whose turn it was to cook. Katya didn't really enjoy it. The resolution we came to was to do it together. I took a cooking course, which was probably cheaper and more effective than marriage counselling.

We moved to the kitchen. I surveyed the contents of the refrigerator speculatively. "Looks like you've been shopping."

"You have to put in to take out, honey." She reached past me, behind the newly minted sushi, to grab some raw chicken breasts. She plopped these into a frying pan and covered them with peanut sauce.

"The sushi is good, dear," I said, sampling a piece.

The sushi was good, but the epithets were our inside joke. Our parents never said "honey" or "dear," as they did in TV families. They were immigrants from Eastern Europe and wouldn't have known the words.

I started making a salad. "Did you take Grampa to the supermarket with you?"

"Yes. He likes to push the cart. It's like walking with a walker without admitting you need one."

"You should ride alongside in one of those motorized carts they have for fat people. You would make a comical pair—not that you're fat of course."

"Watch it buster. Tell dad dinner is ready please." Grampa had drifted into the laundry room so as not to be in the way.

Grampa happily tucked in. He wouldn't eat when he was alone but had a marvellous appetite for cooked meals. He had probably gained ten pounds since moving in with us.

"Finish your food. Don't make the baby Jesus cry," Katya teased me.

Religious references came naturally to Katya because, as a Catholic high school teacher, she heard them every day at work. She doesn't go to church except to occasionally take her father. It could have been the whacking she got with a splintered ruler at the hands of the nuns for talking in class when she was six years old. It could also be my influence as I am not religious. Grampa likes to attend because he has to think about the hereafter.

"Jesus served fish, not chicken," I said.

"Okay then. What should we do after supper?"

"How about belly up on the couch, Home and Garden Channel, House Hunters International?" I suggested. Katya loves home improvement and shopping shows. She lives for the reveal, the dramatic unveiling of the final product.

She took Grampa to walk on the indoor track surrounding the hockey arena instead. Grampa needed an outing. I was sitting on the couch watching television in the living room when they returned. I cranked the sound up to eleven out of ten, so Grampa could hear.

"We should go to bed early tonight," Katya said, standing behind me.

"Good idea. You've been looking so disappointed in the mornings."

She put her two arms around my neck and her cheek against the side of my head. It was touching because it was spontaneous and heartfelt. "Just tired, not disappointed. Matthew, I'm not sure why there is this barrier between us. How can we make it right?"

"It's just the ebb and flow of a marriage, Katya. Everything's fine."

Her embrace went slack. "I'm going to bed. Aren't you coming?"

21

"I might stay up and watch some TV. My diurnal rhythm is screwed up from being on call. Can I record any late-night programs for you? You could view them for your viewing pleasure tomorrow." I also had Wayney on my conscience.

"Okay then, good night honey bunch."

"Good night, bunches of honey."

By the time I got to bed, Katya was snoring lightly.

Chapter 4

Some of the same staff were assigned to work with me again on Wednesday. It was just another day ending in day. Joanie was scrubbed and Sara was circulating. Simon was assisting. We greeted each other with an exchange of the phrase, "Dare to care." It was intended ironically. This was a slogan that our paternalistic hospital administrators had introduced to encourage attitude correctness.

Our surgeon, Dr. Angelo Amodeo, was last to enter the O.R. There are happy and unhappy rooms to work in. His was an unhappy one. He was a man in his forties, of average height, with a broad hairy chest and a fleshy circular face that bore the vestiges of teenage acne. He liked to intimidate the staff around him with angry outbursts and silences. Angelo wasn't my favourite person, but he was a good technical surgeon.

The day started with two hernia repairs. After the second hernia, I went to the bathroom and then to my locker to cram a muffin into my face. I was hungry because I never ate breakfast. There were no breaks for anesthesiologists built into the schedule. When I ushered the next patient into the operating room, Angelo was seated inside waiting.

"Where were you so long?" His tone was petulant.

"I was in the bathroom. I accumulated some urine during the first two cases."

"You should have a urinary catheter inserted."

"Okay. Would you mind doing it? I wouldn't trust anyone else."

"I'll ask my student to do it. We'll get the operating microscope." He was advertising my challenged penis to the O.R. staff.

Our third case was a cholecystectomy. Angelo was earnestly complaining to Simon about fucking ophthalmologists making too much money. Then he fell silent as he began to have difficulty freeing the gallbladder. No one spoke as the surgery wore on. Angelo's head glowed beet red. He eventually broke the silence with, "You know, it's not difficult. Scheduling depends on people arriving on time and turning the room over quickly." He was still thinking about my bathroom and muffin break.

"Soup start overturned quickly?" I asked.

"You start on time and turn the room over quickly."

"I don't understand what those words mean. Is it Klingon?"

"You know, we were discussing what to do about obstructionist, passive-aggressive anesthesiologists at our last general surgery departmental meeting. Don't make me angrier. I won't be able to operate. This is gonna screw up my whole day. It's all these fucking delays."

Joanie interrupted. "Angelo, get back to work. You know the difference between you and a puppy? The puppy stops whining after three months."

Everyone in the room held their breath, waiting to see how he would respond. He was freshly back from a second round of anger management classes. Angelo's neck muscles bulged, but his answer verged on benign. "Okay, you only get one insult and one dropped instrument per day." I had heard one clanking to the floor earlier and noticed it now by his feet.

"What instrument did you ask for, princess?" She seemed to be testing his resolve. No one else would have dared.

"What did you say!"

"What did you say?"

Angelo's complexion changed to the colour of rusted iron, but he didn't respond. Either his reprogramming had worked, or even he was wary of Joanie. She worked part time as the nurse at the Coventry jail. She might have connections in the underworld.

"He said pass me the fork'n knife. How about we break for lunch after this case." I was still hungry.

Sara returned from her break and said that the next patient was refusing to sign his consent. She wondered whether Angelo could speak with him. He didn't acknowledge her. We weren't that far behind, so as soon as we finished, I followed my own suggestion and went to the lunchroom. On busy days, I was sometimes forced to save time by eating my lunch clandestinely while standing at the urinal.

Angelo came in a few minutes later. "I thought I'd find you in here."

"Nice detective work. I'm eating my lunch passive-aggressively."

He sat down and began munching a big crusty white bread sandwich. Angelo was one of the few surgeons who ate lunch, although quickly. The others didn't want to set a poor example. Most surgeons want to work through, to maximize their dollars.

Just like at home, in the lunchroom the Home and Garden channel, with its steady stream of home and self-improvement advice, was always on. The nurses were sitting there, zombie-eyed, hypnotized by the show. Most of the nurses were female and they far outnumbered the doctors. Sara came in and melodiously proclaimed over the TV noise that the next patient still would not sign his consent. "He says he wants to speak to the aesthetician." She was looking at me.

"Hair and nails in rough shape?" I asked.

"No worse than any of the other clients," she said.

"Don't say client! Hospital administrators babble about stake-holders and clients." Angelo was spitting bits of sandwich. "We look after fucking patients, not clients!"

"Tell that client to be patient," I said to Sara.

"I spent half an hour with him in the office," Angelo complained. "He probably wants to ask you a lot of fucking questions now. He said he was nauseated after his last anesthetic."

"Angelo, I could just sit here and listen to you swear all day."

"What about the patient?" Sara asked.

"Cancelled for excessive curiosity."

I wasn't serious of course. Our patient with the weak stomach was having a skin melanoma excised and a lymph node biopsy to check for spread. Melanoma is potentially lethal, so I was sympa-thetic and promised him several antiemetic drugs. After he was asleep, I settled into my pleather swivel chair beside the gas machine and monitors to do my charting. Things seemed to be going well, when I heard the voice of one of my anesthesia colleagues over my shoulder.

"What did you do with Mr. B.?" It was Zack White. He was leaning in close to my ear. I hadn't heard him enter the room. Although he had only been at the hospital a year, Zack was the new chief of my department. He was twenty years my junior and trying to establish his authority.

"What are you talking about?" I asked. "Who the hell is Mr. B.?"

"Mr. Basciuseson. You gave him an anesthetic four years ago. I heard that his ex-wife's upset and has hired a lawyer."

I felt my heart descend deep into my abdomen. I experienced a moment of recognition—hazy outlines, far away, like someone else's dream.

"What has that got to do with me?" I protested.

26

"Well, he died after he left hospital. The Chief of Staff told me that a lawyer came in person to the Medical Records Department with warrants for old paper charts. He must think he's onto something. I know it's probably nothing to do with you."

"Thanks a lot," I said facetiously. "I guess I should find out what's going on—or maybe I'll just wait to be served with a subpoena."

"The ex-wife is alleging that you used drugs during his anesthetic that suppressed his immunity and made him get a recurrence of cancer. Also, he was depressed, and you should have known the drugs you used could exacerbate depression. You were also the coroner who certified his death, and you had a conflict of interest in not mentioning it."

There actually was some recent evidence that general anesthetic agents could suppress immunity. This was thought to be true for all general anesthetic agents, even the newest ones that Zack liked. I looked wistfully through the window of the operating room at the anonymous houses across the street, with their doors locked and curtains drawn. I had been Chief of Anesthesia for a few years a decade ago. I wasn't fond of attending endless committee meetings in my free time. The position carried with it no real power. "How the fuck do you know all that?"

"The Chief of Staff told me unofficially. Maybe you should call the CDDA." The CDDA is the Canadian Doctors' Defence Association, the primary company that defends doctors in Canada against malpractice claims.

"You're kidding, right? I probably gave the same anesthetic most people were using then."

"I guess back in the day, that would have been one of those dinosaur anesthetics that suppressed immune responsiveness," Zack said. There is a lot of competitiveness and one-upmanship in the medical field.

"Thanks," I said for lack of anything better and to make him go away. The eyes told me that the face behind his surgical mask didn't look too unhappy that this was happening. He looked like he was thinking better me than him. Everyone in the room was party to our conversation. Their own conversations had tailed off to concentrate on ours. Angelo already knew the case because he was involved.

I went through the motions of work for the rest of the day, making an extra effort to stay focused on what I was doing. All my cockiness was gone. I did know who Mr. Basciuseson was. I had managed to repress that part of my life like a dream you forget as soon as the alarm clock rings. Zack was talking about Jesus. I had thought that he was gone and forgotten—Jesus and his associates Matthew, Mark, Luke and Sean.

When the operating list was done, I went down to the doctors' lounge to pick up my mail on my way out. As I entered the room, the telephone was ringing. Thinking that the recovery room might be trying to reach me about my last patient, I picked up. A male voice said, "May I speak with Dr. Kork please?"

"Speaking." I didn't recognize the caller.

He continued in a somewhat exited, more breathless tone: "Is it true you were both the anesthesiologist and the coroner who looked after Mr. Basciuseson when he died four years ago?"

Was this a new hospital administrator? "Yes, it's true. May I ask who is speaking?"

"Isn't that a conflict of interest, Doctor?"

"What are you talking about? They aren't related. It was just a coincidence." I was trying to explain the situation in a reasonable way, but the words weren't making sense. I was allowing myself to become flustered.

"What about the allegation that the drugs you used cause cancer?"

"Who am I speaking with please?"

"This is Tim McIsaac from the Coventry Herald. I would like you to explain what really happened, Doctor. This is your opportunity to explain your side of things to help clear up any misconceptions." He sounded like he couldn't believe his luck in actually being able to get me on the phone.

I should have known better, but life is full of hard lessons. Thinking that I would help him out of his confusion, I explained that this was sometimes unavoidable in a smaller city. The anesthetic I had given was for a minor procedure and the death, which occurred much later, was completely unrelated to the surgery.

When I got home, I called the CDDA in Ottawa. They are known for fighting every lawsuit to discourage frivolous actions. After being routed to a counselor who introduced herself as doctor something, I recounted what had happened. Her response was that it sounded frivolous.

"Don't worry about it too much for now. Make notes of everything you remember about the case. If you get a subpoena, we'll open a file. Don't worry if you don't tell me everything right now. Of course, anesthesiologists aren't used to speaking, are they. Send us a written summary of everything you remember. Call us if you get a subpoena."

I didn't like her condescension but accepted it. I needed her help.

Chapter 5

I went to work at the hospital on Thursday as if nothing had happened, but clearly something had. People were averting their eyes or looking at me too hard. Mark Vandermeer, a fundamentalist Christian family doctor with ten children, stopped me in the hallway and asked me if I would like to pray with him. I politely declined. The operating room nurses expressed their condolences over an article they had seen or heard about on the front page of the morning newspaper. I hadn't seen it.

Simon, who was assisting, came into the room as I was setting up for the first case. "Cor blimey mate, you're all over the news! You're in a bit of hot water, aren't you. I mean, I support you, but others may not. You may not be able to find work much longer."

I didn't know how to answer without making the situation worse. Simon is insensitive but not malicious. I looked around the room and wondered what I would do if all this went south. I depended on a good reputation for employment. If this got out of hand, patients might start refusing to let me administer their anesthetics.

No one else seemed eager to speak with me that morning, so I just did my thing with my gas machine and my charting. As we were breaking for lunch, Eve, the head nurse, came in and told me that there was a call for me from hospital switchboard that sounded urgent. I dialled the number and the receptionist said, "There is a policeman here who would like to speak with you. I am putting him on now."

I heard the phone changing hands. "Could you come down to the lobby please, Doctor? I don't want to embarrass you by serving you with a subpoena in front of your colleagues."

I complied immediately and exited the operating room in my scrub suit covered by a white laboratory coat. I nodded to various people who greeted me in the hallway, most of whom I knew only by sight because I had never made the effort to learn their names. When I reached the lobby, I saw that it was crowded. People were milling around and asking directions. Others were lined up for service at the coffee shop and sitting at tables that spilled over into the reception area, pseudo-alfresco.

A large family of Mennonites in traditional dress was sitting awkwardly at one of the tables. The men and boys all wore identical blue shirts, black pants with suspenders and wide-brimmed straw hats. The females wore identical long frilly dresses and bonnets. They were self-consciously eating candy bars and drinking soft drinks that they could never get at home.

There was a uniformed cop waiting nonchalantly, just away from a crowd of people coming in the front entrance. I didn't know him, but I caught his eye and he recognized me immediately. He presented me formally and almost apologetically with a thick white envelope and had me sign for it. The whole transaction was over in seconds. I shoved the envelope into my lab coat pocket before anyone could notice.

The heavy envelope bobbled awkwardly as I walked and slapped against my thigh as I climbed the stairs that led back to the operating room. I saw Dr. Jeremiah Chang, our Chinese Buddhist pediatrician, at the top of the staircase. He was a short, thin, middle-aged man in a dark grey suit and white shirt with a narrow necktie. Most doctors don't wear suits any more. He was waiting for me.

"How are you, Matthew," he asked.

"Good."

He looked at me piercingly with some concern evident in his eyes. "Don't let the bastards get to you." His English was quite good.

"I will try to not let them do that."

"Matthew, you may have some difficult times ahead of you. I want you to know that I have also experienced this pain."

"Do you mean in this life Jeremiah?"

"Yes of course in this life."

"Why? What happened to you?"

"Your adversaries are interested only in financial gain. They see you as a parasite sees a passing beast—an opportunity for a meal. They are jackals and vultures who will take advantage of weakness. They are calculating that you will lose your serenity. You must not allow this to happen."

"Yes. Thanks Jeremiah. They could make it difficult for me to work."

"Do you love or need a lot of material luxuries?"

We were still eerily alone in the stairwell.

"No. I don't refuse them. I am lucky that I practice a trade that is valued by society, but I am not my job. Quite honestly, I don't give a shit. I could be happy doing something else."

"That is why they cannot harm you. You will still have every-thing that is important—your family, your health, your spirit. Your spirit is strong."

Jeremiah could not know the story behind the story. "When one door closes, another one opens," I said.

"Be aware of your reactions. They will affect what is happening around you. Control them or they will cause you misery. All of this is temporary."

32

"Okay. I don't need misery."

"I think you are secretly a Buddhist."

"You flatter me. Thanks Jeremiah."

"There is no disgrace in being sued. It is an obstacle no doctor can avoid forever. Call me if you want to talk."

I carried the envelope back to the operating room and stuck it in my briefcase at the first opportunity. I couldn't really bear to look at it until later. I couldn't let it impair my concentration.

When I got home that evening, Katya showed me the newspaper. The headline read, "Doctor Claims 'Coincidence.' " Underneath, in smaller boldface, a sub-headline read, "Doctor Both Administered Anesthetic that Led to Death of Mr. B. and Acted as Coroner Investigating Himself!" The insinuations were given the ring of truth because the reporter used words I had actually spoken to him, in quotations, omitting context. This was bad.

I took the subpoena from its envelope and read it: "The plaintiffs allege that the anesthetic given by Dr. Kork to Mr. James Jesus Basciuseson was of the type that was known or should have been known to cause immune suppression. This caused Mr. Basciuseson's lymphoma and prostate cancer to progress, which in turn resulted in a deterioration of his mental state and in his committing suicide. Alternatively, if it did not cause Mr. Basciuseson's cancers to progress, it caused an exacerbation of the depressive phase of his bipolar affective disorder, which led to his suicide. Dr. Kork had a conflict of interest in acting as the coroner investigating Mr. Basciuseson's death in that he both gave the anesthetic that led to his death and was in a position to cover up the actual cause of the death."

It was good that I waited to open the subpoena. This was my first time being sued. As I was reading it, my face was hot, my heart racing and my guts churning. It would have been difficult to stay composed at work after reading it. I took this very personally. I had heard that lawyers use a shotgun approach when launching a lawsuit,

33

alleging every kind of wrongdoing even if the acts are mutually contradictory, and naming everyone in the vicinity as a defendant. They discharge a blast of excrement, hoping some of it will stick to the wall. Unfortunately, there was enough truth there that some of it might.

I called the CDDA the next day to tell them I had been served and that I was in the newspaper. I was given a new person who said he hadn't seen the story. So far, it was a local event only. "Didn't we tell you not to speak with the media?" he demanded crossly. I tried to explain how this had happened accidentally and that I had been naive. He answered that if I did not do exactly what I was told in future, they would be within their rights to refuse to defend me. I would be left to pay any settlements out of my own pocket.

He finished by saying: "The plaintiff's attorney is being very aggressive. He has obviously called up several media outlets to embarrass you and to try to get you publicly explaining yourself. It is important that you not say anything. You can't take things back later. We have to be the sole source of all information. Write down exactly what happened while it is still fresh in your mind and submit it to us. Make notes right away. Include everything you remember. If you wait, you will forget details." These details were already four years old.

I didn't have much appetite for dinner, so I went to the gym to clear my head. When I got home, Katya told me that there had been a phone call for me. Someone named Maryanne McAndrews had called and asked to speak with Matthew. I wasn't sure who that was, but Katya recognized the name. She was a young attractive local television reporter. She was posing as someone who was on a first name basis with me. She had left a number where she could be reached. I wasn't foolish enough to call back. The jackals and vultures were circling.

My counselor at the CDDA called me back the following week. He had received my report. His voice was solemn. He reiterated his previous advice: "Do not speak to anyone about the case. Follow our instructions exactly. Refer all questions to us. Don't talk to reporters. If you say anything or fail to follow instructions, we have grounds to not cover you."

"Can I talk to the hospital administration? They want to meet with me."

"No. Their interests are not aligned with ours. They have their own representation. If you collaborate with them, they can turn around and use information you give them to sue you to recover their losses." After a pause for effect, he added, "You will be hearing from the firm that does our legal work. The lawyer handling your case will be Mr. Richard Chrétien." None of this interaction was friendly.

Three weeks later, I got a telephone call from a lady with a pleasant voice, who identified herself as Mr. Chrétien's secretary. She wondered whether it would be convenient for me to meet with Mr. Chrétien at the downtown Sheraton hotel in Coventry next week. She sounded really nice, as people without real power often are. I agreed to the date and time she proposed and then she told me not to worry. She said you have to expect one of these every few years. I must have sounded worried.

I Googled Richard Chrétien. He was a senior associate at the legal firm of Solomon Hankey that had offices in Vancouver, Toronto and Montreal and 450 lawyers on staff. There was a picture and brief curriculum vitae. He had been practicing for seven years and had litigation experience. I wondered why they had selected him. There were biographies for another 449 lawyers, some of whom were partners and senior partners. Mr. Chrétien hadn't gotten there yet, but the mug shot made him look hungry.

"What did you do with Mr. B?" Zack had wanted to know. My contention is that he basically committed suicide. I did what had to

35

be done to make him disappear from everyone's memory. I did what I did to stop Katya's ennui. Of course there would be consequences. I was foolish to think he would just disappear. Being served with the subpoena was the beginning of a dead man's vengeance. It was him screaming through the newspaper headline, "Doctor Claims Coincidence!"

Chapter 6

Since my fall from grace, I have had a recurring dream. Luke comes to me late at night for help. I have to shield him in my house. He can't go out of course, because he would be arrested. He will have to hide here for a few weeks before I can risk moving him to a country where he can live incognito. I am thinking Brazil or South Africa.

In another version, Luke has returned to Canada under an assumed name and identity. He doesn't go out much because he is keeping a low profile. He moves purposefully around his dark house like a mole in a burrow. It's a miserable life, but he is clearly unrepentant. He doesn't say anything because he is in fact possibly dead.

In high school, Luke referred to us tongue-in-cheek as "the team," as in you don't let the team down. Being nearly two years younger than my classmates, I looked like a well-scrubbed baby. I think he befriended me because he admired my academic success. We accumulated some more team members, but he reserved an older brother's style of tribal loyalty for me. The others were subversive types like him, although one later became a bank manager. Exceptions prove a rule.

I remember vignettes. One summer evening, he instructed three of us to hide behind a tree while he hitched a ride. Luke knew that drivers would be more likely to stop for a single passenger. When a car did stop, he motioned for us to all pile in. Before long, he was climbing the slippery precipices of Scarborough Bluffs, high cliffs overlooking Lake Ontario, five kilometers south of where we lived. After watching for a few minutes, we followed him over the guard-rail.

Luke and I swam lengths in our high school pool on public nights. In their bathing suits, it was easy to see who amongst the girls was developing womanly features. He would extract a promise from his favourite to meet on the warm air vent behind the pool and to bring a friend. The friend, who was to be my introduction to necking, would not have won any beauty contests. I wouldn't have recognized her in daylight, but he pointed her out the next week, gleefully asking me how I liked my prize, Doris Delaney.

He probably had a screw loose. Luke's parents had a cherry tree in their backyard. In summer, birds would strip the tree of its fruit. He told me that he had hidden under his porch and shot starlings with a pellet rifle as they were feeding. The ground under the tree was blanketed with corpses. After this tale of carnage, he looked at me uncertainly for my reaction. I considered saying those birds had it coming, but I stayed mute. If he had said lawyers, I would have had no objection.

Later, I moved onto the university campus in downtown Toronto but came home frequently on weekends. I could study without being reminded that I was missing out on campus social life. Luke bought a muscle car and would roar up my driveway those weekend mornings shouting, "Hey Mutt Corgi, let's go play some tennis!" We thought that tennis was what well-adjusted, successful people played. We would drive to a private club before it opened and climb over the locked gate, or go to the Catholic seminary on Kingston Road where they forgave us our trespassing.

A growth spurt caused me to shoot up five inches past Luke. I put on twenty pounds pumping iron and tried my hand at boxing. I enjoyed the physical training and the self-confidence of knowing I could assert myself. If you have a weapon you are going to want to use it. After provoking a bar fight, I threw a combination of left jabs and a right cross I had been practicing, landing my adversary quickly on his ass.

I was surprised at how easy this was. In the ring, against better trained opponents, I discovered I didn't enjoy being on the receiving end of a punch or delivering one without good reason. This is how moral codes evolve. The sting of a remembered punch in the face can keep one from needlessly inviting or inflicting one.

We lost touch after I got into medical school. The antiseptic smell of hospitals used to make me nauseous, but you can get used to anything. I remember it from sitting at my mother's bedside as a teenager when she was in hospital dying. I remember sitting there for hours, holding her hand. I remember Luke's grim face and his tears when I told him she was dead.

My mother was always nice to Luke, but I had no idea why he took her death so hard—possibly because he didn't have a real one of his own. Luke was adopted by an older childless couple. I hadn't known that. I only knew that his parents were a lot older than mine. He first mentioned it in Muskoka. At our high school class reunion, someone commented on how we were fast friends but so different from one another. I answered that Luke had helped me bury the body that one time.

He left his wife and children on an impulse. He used his remaining money to buy a house close to the water in Scarborough and fill it with furniture and appliances. Luke used the ruses available to a middle-aged man to attract a young woman—lavish spending and feigned sophistication. Despite the fact that Luke was my friend, an accurate assessment is that this would have been especially necessary for him.

Of course, every man has likely experienced temptations similar to Luke's. I had always stepped back from the brink, maybe because of timidity, maybe because I love my wife. Sara told me that we worked so much together that she spent more time with me than she did with her husband. She said that she had dreamt about me. I resisted the temptation to ask the contents of the dream. Then she leaned in close and whispered that if she ever needed an operation, she would want me to do her anesthetic. We both knew she was making a veiled invitation. It was one I would ignore for now.

This wasn't the first time a nurse had told me these kinds of things. It happened more frequently twenty years ago of course, but I never worried Katya by telling her. After seeing me buying meals at the hospital, nurses sometimes asked why my wife hadn't packed something and told me disingenuously how much they loved cooking and cleaning. A nurse told me that she was in the early stages of considering the possibility of leaving her husband, so it would be okay if I wanted to see her outside of work.

I am not sure if men and women can ever be close friends without one of them indulging in romantic fantasies. An affair with a co-worker would be life changing because it would logically have to progress to changing your wife or your job. Rather than responding directly, I pretended not to understand. We could continue to work together without embarrassment and inaction would be its own answer. I suppose that this strategy also left the door open a crack.

In some versions of the dream, *I* am the man on the run. The reasons aren't clear. Perhaps I have been a bad husband, a bad debtor or a bad doctor. When I travel on holiday, I look at locales I am passing through for their potential as hiding spots—for disappearing to in a hurry if necessary, if a worst-case scenario came to pass. I think many men do this.

PART 2

Five Years Earlier

"And hast thou slain the Jabberwock? Come to my arms my beamish boy! O frabjous day! Callou! Callay!" He chortled in his joy. —Lewis Carroll, Jabberwocky.

Chapter 7

My cell phone rang at midnight. I read the message glaring on its call display—Aug 2, Coroners' Answering Service. I hesitated before answering. I had to work in the morning. There were three coroners for our area, but we didn't have a call schedule. It was just whoever would pick up the phone. Someone else could do it. I picked up reluctantly and left the bedroom.

"It's the coroners' office calling, Doctor. Can you take a case? We have a death at home of a 75-year-old with some medical problems. You might be able to get the family doctor to go."

This was going to be another death of an old person from natural causes. Age is the primary determinant in deciding whether a death is natural. Aside from advising old people to stop allowing their health to deteriorate, there are really no useful recommendations for a coroner to make. A family doctor could certify the death. Finding one who would answer the phone at this time of night would be difficult. If there was no family doctor, I would be obligated to attend.

"Where is it? Is it in Coventry?" A thick fog was rolling in as the temperature fell. I looked nervously out the window of my study at pea soup.

"The address is 2437 Line 42, near Warwick. Can I give you the information, Doctor?"

This was a remote country address and exactly what I didn't need. I didn't much feel like driving for half an hour somewhere so late at night looking for a farm, in the fog, in the dark. Country addresses don't show up on GPS devices. I would be hung over in the operating room in the morning. On the other hand, I was now almost obligated because I had let the dispatcher talk for so long.

"Okay give me the information."

The dispatcher gave me the name and date of birth of the newly dead person and the phone number of the policeman at the scene. I logged onto the hospital server from my computer and typed in the decedent's name. Luckily, there was some information about him. I was looking for any potentially lethal illnesses, plausible causes of death to obviate the need for an investigation and save me a trip. And I needed the name of a family doctor to take responsibility for the paperwork.

The decedent, Mr. Anderson, had had a probable transient ischemic attack one week before. This is a mild stroke from which the patient recovers quickly, so that minimal damage is done to the brain. It can be a harbinger of a future, more serious stroke. It wasn't as compelling a cause of death as cancer or a heart attack. I would have preferred he had one of those.

He had had computerized tomography or a CT scan of his head in Coventry. I pulled up the report. It was unfortunately normal, so there was no smoking gun. He might have had a new stroke. The family doctor in Warwick was Mark Vandermeer. This was a positive development. Mark was the fundamentalist Christian with eight children. He might feel morally obligated to answer his phone. I couldn't compel him to take responsibility, but he might not know that.

I called the cop at the scene to get a description. Mr. Anderson lived with his daughter and her fiancé on the family farm, which they worked together. He was last seen alive by the fiancé at 1 p.m. and was found by his daughter at 9 p.m. He was sitting on a toilet, slumped over, his head resting on the edge of a bathtub.

Dying on the toilet is not uncommon for old people. Old people get constipated. Straining causes a slowing of the heart, which can lead to fainting or a malignant cardiac arrhythmia. The fiancé had called emergency medical services, but it was too late. The policeman said that Mr. Anderson was already in full rigor mortis when they arrived, which meant he had been dead for hours.

"Are there any medications around?" I asked. I could deduce his medical history if I knew what he was being treated for.

"There's one prescription," the cop answered. He spelled out the name from the label on the bottle. It was a blood pressure pill. Mr. Anderson, like almost everyone his age, was being treated for hypertension. Ninety pills were dispensed two months ago, and he took one each evening.

"Did you count the number of pills left in the bottle? Does it look like the right amount is missing?"

"Yeah, it looks about right..."

I didn't say anything. I was waiting him out.

"Okay, hold on," the cop said. I listened to him counting. "Twenty-five left. There is also a big bottle of aspirin."

"The aspirin must be to prevent a stroke. Four or five BP pills unaccounted for. He didn't overdose, or he would have taken them all."

I called the Coventry Hospital switchboard, identified myself and got Mark Vandermeer's home phone and pager numbers. His home number went to an answering machine. I called the pager number, hung up and waited for a few minutes. Nothing happened, so I started filling out the necessary forms in preparation for having to go. Ten minutes later, a sleepy Dr. Vandermeer called me back. His conscience must have nagged him awake.

Mark knew the family well. I told him that his patient had died of natural causes. It wasn't a coroner's case. Could he please drive out and complete a Medical Certificate of Death? It was his final responsibility to his patient. I sweetened this with, I could have the body released to the local funeral home now, and he could go in the morning to fill out the form there. His voice brightened at this suggestion. I called the policeman back and everything was settled.

As I came back to bed Katya asked, "Who was that calling so late?"

"Mark Vandermeer, the Seventh Day Adventist with fifteen children." I didn't really know what branch of Christianity Mark subscribed to.

"What did he want?"

"I asked him to take a coroner's case for me. What do Seventh Day Adventists believe?"

"They think that Saturday, not Sunday, is the holiest day of the week."

"That's it? That's what sets them apart? Is it still, step on a crack, break your mother's back, like the 'Cat-licks'?"

"Yes."

At work in the operating room the next day, I got a message to call Dr. Vandermeer. By the end of the day, I also had two voicemail messages on my cell phone—one to call the Ontario Provincial Police and one for a funeral home in Coventry. There were two more messages on my home answering machine. These were from an anxious sounding Mark.

I called the police first. Apparently, a neighbour had left a message on the Ontario Provincial Police Warwick division answering machine that if anything ever happened to Mr. Anderson, they should suspect the daughter's boyfriend. He and Mr. Anderson had been witnessed arguing loudly in a bank in Warwick, with mutual name-calling and threats.

I asked the policeman on the phone if it was an anonymous message. "No, we interviewed the neighbour who made the call," he replied. I wrote down the neighbour's name and phone number.

"What do you want to do, Doctor?" He wanted to cover himself by putting the onus on me.

"I'll let you know."

I called Mark back and got the same breathless message. Shit! This was embarrassing. I should have attended to the matter myself after all and not imposed on his good nature. My thinking was that no one would take the trouble to murder a 75-year-old.

Mark had actually driven out to the farm through the fog the previous night. It turned out that the daughter and fiancé were friends with a funeral home staff member in Coventry, and that the body had been shipped here. It was more convenient for him to visit the residence than to drive all the way to Coventry the next day.

"Well, what did you see when you visited the house?" I asked. "What position was the body in?"

"He was sitting on the toilet slumped over, with his head on the rim of the bathtub."

"Were there any signs of trauma to the body?"

"No, no trauma. Well—I'm not sure. There might have been a mark where his head hit the bathtub— nothing to write home about."

"What colour was the bruise? Was it fresh?" If it was an old yellow bruise, he might have been beaten. Alternatively, he might have hit his head in an earlier fall and developed intracranial bleeding, which gradually put pressure on his brain and caused him to collapse.

"I don't remember for sure."

"Was he in rigor?"

"Oh yes. He was stiff all over." That meant he had been dead at least five hours.

"Was he stiffly draped over the bathtub? I mean, was there a limb sticking up out of place?" If there was an awkwardly projecting airborne limb, he might have been moved onto the toilet after rigor had set in.

"He was kind of leaning to the right, half off the toilet with his knees set in a sitting position. He looked like he was still sitting on the toilet, only he wasn't."

That meant he had stayed balanced on the toilet for hours. "Was there urine or feces in the toilet bowl?"

"Yes."

"So, he hadn't been placed on the toilet—unless some one had the foresight to have a dump there first. Okay, who was there? Did they look appropriately sad?"

"Several family members were there, including the estranged wife," he replied. "She's remarried and lives in Toronto. Maybe she stood to inherit back the farm if Mr. Anderson died. It would be worth quite a lot."

"The wife had remarried? Was her new husband there—or the fiancé?" Men are more likely to commit violent acts.

"Yes. There were a lot of people there. I don't know if one of them was her husband."

"And the fiancé?"

"He was there. He lives there. He told me it was their one-month anniversary. He's a home renovator."

"Great. Very romantic. You said you knew the family. Were they quarrelling?"

"Never when I saw them together. They seemed pretty normal. The daughter was a little wild when she was younger—tattoos and piercings. The old man had promised to retire and hand the farm over to his daughter and her boyfriend. He may have been just stringing them along to get them to live with him and help with the work."

Everyone had a motive. I needed some guidance. I telephoned the Regional Supervising Coroner on call. It was the supervisor for Central Ontario region. I had never met him, but I knew his voice from previous calls. He listened silently to the story and then said, "You have to pull the body, Matt."

"What do you mean—send it for an autopsy?"

"Yes. You have to pull it."

"Okay thanks."

I telephoned the funeral home director to let him know I was coming over. "But the body's already been embalmed!" he objected.

"I see. Nevertheless, I have to come."

"—But, we have a visitation tomorrow!"

"Sorry about that."

I rang the doorbell at Christobel's Funeral Home twenty minutes later. A fresh-faced junior mortician unlocked the door. "Hello Doctor. We close at 5 o'clock." His stomach growled and he looked down at it.

"Sorry for making you miss your dinner."

He didn't answer.

"Did you know Mr. Anderson?"

He said he knew the decedent and had in fact recently been at his house for his daughter's engagement party. They had been class-mates growing up. He had never witnessed any family arguments. He led me down a hall past some new-looking, modern décor to their embalming parlor. The air was thick with acrid chemicals.

"Hello Dr. Kork." Jacob Christobel was hunched over a corpse on a steel gurney. Jacob was a gangly man in his sixties. Business was good. There were two more corpses on gurneys in the room—naked, yellow and staring straight up at nothing. "I was thinking of taking an Alaskan cruise. I heard you went there. How was it?"

"Picturesque. I recommend it highly."

"How was the food on board? Pretty good?"

"Yes."

"I love fresh Alaskan king crab. That's Mr. Anderson over there." Jacob's vinyl-gloved hand gestured toward the body closest to me.

He was thin, old and cold. He was out of rigor now because he was lying flat, no longer on an imaginary toilet. His limbs were stiffened by formaldehyde and his jaw was clenched. Other than a small wound on his abdomen and one under his right clavicle, there were no marks on him.

"You've never seen what we do here, have you, Matthew," Jacob said. "Well, we inject pressurized embalming fluid into the common carotid artery, and then we push this in through the abdominal wall." He held up a two-foot length of thin metal pipe that looked like a liposuction device and smiled like he was trying to shock me. "Then, we attach it to suction and fan it out in every direction clearing out body fluids."

So, in effect, he suctioned blood and faeces and traumatized every abdominal and chest organ. I said, "Can I use your business office to make some calls?"

"It's down the hall. Thank you for your patronage, Matthew."

The Coventry Hospital switchboard operator connected me to the pathologist on call. It was Rachel Weinstein. She answered after a few rings. In case she didn't have caller ID, I introduced myself. I heard chewing and swallowing.

"Hey Matt. How's the coroner gig working out for you?"

"Sorry for bothering you at home, Rachel. It's okay—a little embarrassing at the moment though. That's actually why I'm calling. Are you interested in doing a coroner's autopsy?"

"I thought so... I suppose. What have you got?"

I explained the situation to her and heard more chewing followed by silence. Then she said, "Well, we'll do what we can. I'll get back to you after the initial autopsy results tomorrow. Are you going to be in the O.R.?" Pathologists are obligated by law to call coroners with a verbal result on the day of the autopsy. Their final reports can take months or years to come back.

"Yeah. Will you still be able to tell anything?"

"Well, we might see something interesting in his head if he had a stroke. We could look at his coronary arteries. I don't know about the rest."

"Thanks. Are you still out jogging every day?" I had seen Rachel out running at noon hour through my car window. She had a physique like a greyhound.

"Mostly. How about you?"

"A little. I don't have the same spring in my step."

"That sucks."

"Just a few aches and pains."

"You have to work through the pain, Matt. Talk to you tomorrow."

I noticed the junior mortician loitering in the doorway. He hadn't had time to develop the gravitas or professional veneer of sadness of his boss. He appeared to be eaves dropping. There was no polite way to eject him from his own office. I wanted some privacy, so I went home.

There was still another task to complete. I had to speak with the next of kin. This is repetitively emphasized at the training course for new coroners and typed boldface in the coroners' manual. Supervising coroners are worried about public relations. In this case, the closest relative was also one of the prime suspects.

I called up the daughter, Raven, and listened carefully for signs of attitude. She had discovered the body after returning home from work at a chicken processing plant. She was a little resentful, but cooperative. I could tell that she already knew what had transpired. The junior mortician must have called her the moment I left. Everyone knows everybody else in small towns. There was another person on the line. After an initial period of hearing him breathe in the background, I asked, "Is there someone on the extension?"

A male baritone answered, "Yes, hi. I am the late Mr. Anderson's son-in-law." I thought he was only a fiancé. He seemed more mature than the daughter.

"What's your name please?"

"Jim."

"Jim. What can you tell me about what happened yesterday? I understand you last saw Mr. Anderson at one in the afternoon."

"Yes. As I told the police, I left around that time to do some work around the farm. Then I drove into Coventry to run some errands there. I got back late."

I presumed the police had checked his alibi. "Were you home when Raven found her dad?"

"Well, we actually found him together. She went to look for him, and there he was. He didn't lock the bathroom door."

"Do either of you know whether he was good with taking his blood pressure pills?"

"Jimmy and I had to keep reminding him," Raven said. "Jimmy had to make him take one yesterday morning because he forgot the night before."

Old people can't remember two minutes after the fact whether they just took a pill or was it yesterday. That's why they need the plastic pill organizers with hatches for the days and times.

"Were you on pretty good terms with Raven's dad, Jim?"

"Yeah, we were great. I loved the old guy."

Okay, this was surely hyperbole. I couldn't challenge it without seeming mean spirited, and that wasn't really my role. There wasn't anything else suspicious about them. They might have been consummate actors, but I didn't think so. I didn't ask Jim his date of birth, although I was curious about what their age discrepancy might be.

The autopsy, which was done the following day, showed there had been no stroke. There was no occult skull fracture or intracranial bleeding, so no one had bashed him over the head. The coronary arteries were narrowed, as might be expected from the decedent's age, but no heart attack either. There were no significant findings. The majority of autopsies do not provide a definitive cause of death. He had probably had a heart rhythm disturbance provoked by bearing down to empty his bowels.

I tried to get hold of the policeman with whom I had spoken the day before, but he was off duty. The policewoman who took my call told me that they were not at all concerned about this case. The neighbour who had made the complaint had recanted. She seemed surprised that I would disrupt everyone's life by requiring an autopsy. I was glad to wash my hands of the affair. At the time, I took it as confirmation that first impressions are usually correct.

Chapter 8

My childhood friend Luke called me out of the blue suggesting that our families do a joint holiday. He told me that after a stint in the armed forces, which included a tour of duty in Afghanistan, he had attended college and become an operating room nurse. Katya agreed and we went to a resort in Muskoka. This was a plush place, with water sports and fine dining.

Luke had come into some money. He had inherited and sold his parents' house, which had appreciated in value with the Toronto real estate boom. He had accumulated some new toys, arriving with his wife Pam in a new black muscle car, towing a new mega-horsepower boat for waterskiing. I didn't hear about anything special for Pam, except for her share of the wine. At the resort, they ordered the most expensive bottles on the menu. They showed me a scrapbook showcasing the labels from expensive bottles they had consumed together.

We went waterskiing in Luke's boat. I'd never tried it before and he gave me some lessons. Luke was doing jumps over a ramp and skiing barefoot. Pam was driving. She was a good person for putting up with him. She had put on some weight since I had seen her last. She looked like a round lump crouched beside the motor. We had a good time, and Luke seemed content. I was surprised to learn that he left his wife for a divorced veterinary technician, ten years his junior, a month later. I had witnessed one of the last happy times they had together.

I had shared my little life with Katya for twenty-five years, and we still liked each other. Activities of daily living seemed to consume most of our time, so we didn't actually spend a lot of time together. This can be a good thing for some couples. We got together to cook a meal or to watch a movie. We probably should have made an effort to find more things.

It was the second of November and pumpkins were being recycled from porches. Grampa had methodically doled out treats to the little Halloweeners who came to our door. Our family had recently expanded when Grampa, Katya's dad, moved in with us. His wife had died. He got bowel cancer and expected to die himself. He sold his house and gave half the proceeds to the church. He distributed most of the rest amongst his three children. However, he did not die and consequently needed a place to live.

Grampa was 86 years old and still had his wits. He had high cheekbones like Katya and a full head of snow-white hair, acquired through perseverance, not peroxide. He was tall but had suffered some shrinkage. Grampa generally wore pants with a razor-sharp crease draped onto meticulously polished patent leather shoes, a dress shirt covered by a wool vest, plus a cardigan or two. He arrived with all of his belongings stuffed into what looked like a large gym bag.

Katya initially told me he was coming for a two-week visit. He had been living with her brother. Grampa was a nice man, but her brother's wife needed a break. Grampa was sitting at the kitchen table with his back to the wall, affording him a commanding view of the room. I was at home with him as I was post call. Katya was at work.

"How are you today, Grampa?" I shouted.

"Good."

"How did you sleep last night?" I was casting around for a topic of mutual interest.

There was usually a long period of silence after I addressed him. He hadn't heard me, he had heard me and was still thinking of an answer, or he had heard me, thought about it and had decided not to respond.

"How did you sleep?" I repeated.

"Good. I took my pill. I voke up at five. That's all what I can sleep."

Grampa napped a lot and was getting his days and nights mixed up. I decided to make some scrambled eggs. He sat at the kitchen table, pretending to read the morning newspaper, watching me. I was his entertainment.

"Would you like some scrambled eggs, Grampa?"

"Hah? Scrambl-ED eggs?" Grampa speaks English phonetically as it is written.

"Yes."

"Okay."

I ate quickly. Grampa's watching was making me self-conscious. I went into the living room and put the television speakers into head-phone mode. Otherwise, he might be blasting the decibels soon after I settled in to do some work. I had a coroner's report to write up. A psychiatric patient had committed suicide a few hours after being discharged from hospital. He was angry about having to leave and wanted to embarrass his psychiatrist. He hung himself from a door-knob. He could have saved himself by standing up.

The psychiatrist had written, "This patient demonstrates split-ting, externalization, projective identification, impulsivity, affective instability and does not make effective use of our time together." The suicide note read, "I hope your happy. I am NOT. Stupit!" I am no fan of psychiatrists either. I suspect that they choose the specialty to diagnose themselves. Their patients however are ticking time bombs, who sooner or later do have to be discharged.

Hospital administrators are terrified by the possibility of law suits. A coroner is not allowed to find fault or impose penalties. Nevertheless, assigning a cause and manner of death could lead relatives to infer blame and lawyer up. No one wants that. I used only my diplomatic words.

I was napping on the sofa when Katya got home. I never used to do that. Grampas do that. It's another milestone on the path to the big sleep. I heard dishes clanking in the kitchen, so I ambled in to be sociable. Katya was making herself a cup of tea to decompress. Grampa was sitting quietly at his vantage point at the kitchen table, with his head pointed at a dog-eared Polish magazine.

"How was your work-a-day?" I asked.

Katya turned her freckled cheeks to face me. Katya is tall. She is just under six feet, and a bit ungainly in her body, as if she didn't expect to grow that high. This little vulnerability is endearing.

"Okay. How was your coroner visit? Were they still dead?"

"Yes. It was a suicide."

"You like those, right?"

"No. I want taxpayers to get value for their money, which they don't with deaths from natural causes. Coroners are supposed to investigate accident, suicide or homicide."

I had been to a car accident with eight fatalities. The most dramatic suicide I'd seen had only a hollow, craggy eggshell cradle of a lower skull after evacuating his brain with a high-power rifle. He would have made a convincing Halloween prop. I hadn't heard of a murder during my sixteen years in Coventry.

Katya took a seat, arranging her chair closely beside Grampa's and began to peruse the newspaper. Reading is Katya's favourite pastime. She reads voraciously. She discusses books at a book club with her friends over glasses of wine, before moving on to home renovations and their children's accomplishments.

"What do you think of all those organs being retained by the coroner's office?" The scandal was in the newspaper open in front of Katya.

"They were probably retained for archiving evidence or maybe for someone's collection. It's a very sensitive subject. We are not allowed to comment. I refer all questions to the Regional Supervising Coroner. I'll give you his number."

"I have to go for a haircut in Pickering on Saturday."

Her hair looked good already. She thought I didn't notice, but I can confidently say it was currently shortish, auburn with blonde highlights and sprayed into place to frame her head on three sides. My wife loves haircuts. She loves to think about and talk about hair but has no one living at our house who is willing to reciprocate. She has her twin sister Magda for that. Magda lives in Pickering, a satellite of Toronto.

Katya and her sister are very close. They talk to or text every day. They wear each other's clothes and hairstyles and adopt each other's mode of speech. They confide almost everything to one another. If we see Magda at a family gathering, she asks innocent sounding questions that betray her intimate knowledge of our affairs. Magda is five minutes older than Katya and feels like her protector.

" 'Hairscut.' In French, you say hairscut because you cut all of them. You could try the place I go to in Coventry. It's a lot closer. They do a great job on Madame Fifi."

I was taking a French course. I had seen an interesting job advertisement for the CDDA in Ottawa, listing French as an asset. No night work.

"Ottawa is too far from our relatives." Katya said. She meant her sister of course.

"Inquiring minds want to know what we should have for supper."

"What do *you* think we should have for supper?"

I put some hummus on crackers for appetizers. Katya dutifully got up to contribute. She heated up a new type of soup in a plastic bag. "Broccoli and cheese. You want some?"

"I'll have a taste." I ladled a tiny amount of cholesterol from the pot.

"Chase it down with grapefruit juice." She was reading my mind.

"Grapefruit juice and Drano. Hey, is there gluten in rice? If you recall, my friend Ingrid, the local Green Party candidate, is coming for dinner Saturday. She emailed me that she was eating gluten and dairy free. Someone wrote a book about gluten being bad for you."

"You're the doctor aren't you dammit, Bones? You should be up on all this nutritional trend stuff."

"Also, Luke emailed me today. Do you think we should invite him for the same night?"

"He's going to get drunk and want to drive back to Toronto—like he did in Muskoka. He was drunk when we went waterskiing."

"Well, he can stay the night here, can't he?"

"You know he won't want to. And do you think he would get along with Ingrid?"

"Probably not."

"Do you think he's an alcoholic?"

"An alcoholic is anyone who drinks more than you do. We do have a lot of history..."

"One of my teacher friends said it was ironic that we have a weed control company's sign next to a Green Party sign on our lawn." She was redirecting the conversation away from Luke.

"Ordinary conventions don't apply to me, and I don't see the contradiction. Toxic chemicals aren't going to spray themselves just because there is an election imminent."

"Ask Ingrid if she wants a ride in your SUV, honey." Katya said honey for comic effect. We were above plebeian endearments, but I did like the sound of it.

I walked over to Grampa who was still holding his magazine to offer him some crackers and hummus. His eyes were shut.

"We should go to bed early tonight, hon," I said.

"Great idea. I was waking up every two hours last night. My hip was hurting, and my thigh was hurting, hon."

"Those bones are connected to the head bone, hon." Sympathy is hard to come by for the spouse of a doctor.

"I think I'm getting arthritis. Feel the lumps on these two fingers." Katya showed me some fingers and I felt the lumps.

"Yeah, that's a bit of osteoarthritic lipping."

Grampa held up his gnarled hands. He had surreptitiously been following the conversation. "Oh, that's not even fair," I said. "You're going to win that contest every time."

Despite the best of intentions, it was almost midnight before I made it to bed. It was the being on call and daytime napping. Katya was in bed ahead of me. She always said she couldn't sleep well without me, but she was being nice. I think the noise I made getting ready disturbed her. Our sleeping patterns were never that compatible. We couldn't agree on how much windows should be open or blankets should be thick.

"Did you let Madame Fifi out?" she asked from the darkness.

"Yes. She's downstairs eating her treat. If you want to see canine moral outrage, try not giving her one." Our bichon frise and I had an agreement that she would urinate outdoors rather than on the rug, in exchange for a biscuit.

I slipped into bed. After a few minutes, Katya said, "My hip hurts." I was nearly asleep, so I didn't answer.

"What does it mean if your hip hurts after you've been jogging?"

I considered saying, what does it mean if you stub your toe and your toe hurts. "Heating pad, Tylenol, sleep on the non-sore side, pillow between your legs, switch to swimming."

"It's a thought."

"You still need weight bearing exercise to keep your bones mineralized. Sex with me on top could be a fun way to achieve that. I'm awake now anyway."

"Sleeping is the most fun you can have in bed," she countered and passed out.

I wasn't serious anyway.

Chapter 9

Despite being something of a sleep expert, my difficulties with sleeping worsened. Caffeine and alcohol disturb your normal sleep cycle. I didn't drink caffeinated beverages after 3 p.m. and cut out alcohol almost completely. You can't drink when you are on call, so I just generalized and found I didn't miss it. I used a blindfold because light and dark are also important biologic cues. I tried earplugs but was bothered by the sound of blood pulsing in my head, so I turned on a fan for white noise.

I slept on my side, the way I positioned patients on the operating table. There were three pillows under my head, two between my legs and a folded one to support my upper arm. I used the adhesive nasal strips that flare your nostrils. My problem sleeping was probably because of screwed up diurnal rhythms and some stress at work, but also because Katya was becoming a noisy sleeper.

I know that everyone's body changes as they age and that women don't snore—they purr. Of course, Katya was still attractive, but she may have put on a tiny bit of weight. I innocently said that I had read an article about how exercise and sleeping on your side with multiple strategic pillows, perhaps as many as six, and eliminating alcohol before bed could improve purring. She didn't disagree, if that's what silence implies. I suspected I would not likely be able to talk her out of her evening glass of wine.

Stress relief is important in promoting sleep. I swam four nights a week at the Coventry Recreation Complex. Katya used to belong to a running club but stopped when her hips began to ache. After dinner, I asked her whether she wanted to come with me to the pool.

"I hate swimming. I'm going to the drug store. Do you want anything?" She was taking Tylenol and ibuprofen for her hips.

"Just a big bag of drugs that make you feel like you should," I replied, although I am anti-drug. "If you take a shopping bag you can shop lift."

"I'm going to walk." She pronounced the "L" in walk. That's how Grampa would have said it.

"You're walking all the way to the drug store. Is that your new deal? You were born from water. You are descended from fish that crawled out of the water. If you come, you can sit with the lesbian ladies in the steam room," I said enticingly.

"I have evolved. When I die, I will return to dust, not water."

"Well, me too but—"

"I think you must be the most dedicated swimmer in Coventry."

"Not even close. There are guys at the 'Rec' who swim a hundred lengths every night. I didn't even do that in my prime."

"Speaking of water, I have another problem. It's a little embarrassing. When I sneeze, I lose a little bit of water into my panties," she confided.

"Use a liner and change your panties more frequently. It's part of the physiology of aging."

"Don't they have an operation for that?"

"They have an operation, but the lawyers have found out about it. Haven't you seen the advertisement where you can call a number to join a class action suit if you had mesh inserted for an incontinence procedure?"

"A teacher at work had that operation, and she is younger than I am."

"It is a very common operation. They keep changing and improving it. I won't tell anyone if you pee a little bit in the pool."

There was a fairly regular group who trained together at the Recreation Complex for triathlons—swimming, running and biking. The Rec wasn't luxurious, but it served our needs. We were called the Masters' Club. The coterie of swimmers met on weeknights at 9 p.m. I knew most of them by name. That evening, I heard a mellifluous baritone radio announcer's voice projecting through the change room. It belonged to a new arrival, James.

Though we'd never met, James greeted me as Matt, a familiarity that I thought was unwarranted. He was tall, fifty-ish like me, athletic but with a small potbelly. He had olive skin, an aquiline nose and a full head of dark curly hair, greying at the temples—a handsome specimen. I resolved to ignore his friendly advances. By age fifty, most people have accumulated a full quota of friends. I didn't especially need another one. Seinfeld says age thirty, but I'm not that extreme.

After a few weeks, I began to understand that James would become a new regular in our group. The other swimmers seemed to engage easily with him. After swimming, he took long, un-self-conscious showers across from Theo, who is gay. They had detailed conversations about design and furnishings to make spaces more inviting, which were amplified by the tile walls of the shower room. James was jovial and gregarious. He always called hello from across the change room before I noticed him. Despite some reservations, I decided to adopt him too.

James was free with details of his life. He had moved to Coventry from Toronto and was growing his interior decorating business. He had a degree in architecture and contributed free-lance articles to home style magazines. He dabbled in real estate and also did home inspections to make ends meet. I didn't share what I did for a living, but I think he already knew.

James' full name was James Jesus Basciuseson, but I could call him James, or Mister B. He said his mother had chosen his given names. His mother was Latino and loved Jesus—his father not so much. His father had been a diplomat, but after retiring had worked in the armaments industry. The family had moved frequently when he was growing up.

"I guess husbands must hate to see you coming," I told him. "Interior decorators are generally bad news for husbands who are trying to rein in their wives' champagne dreams."

"No, not really," he said, looking at me levelly with the practiced look he gave cheapskate spouses.

"Basciuseson is an interesting surname. It sounds vaguely North African or Middle Eastern, something like Balthazar in the Lawrence Durrell novel." I was flaunting my knowledge of a book I had never read. James' long face and Roman nose made it seem possible. "Where is your last name from?"

"Toronto Canada, Matt," he answered. "All of God's children from 'round the world gather there."

"You know what, James? I think we may have met before on the telephone. Aren't you engaged to Raven Anderson?" It was his voice on the extension at the farm house I didn't go to a few months ago.

"Yes, I wondered that too. We aren't engaged anymore."

"I'm sorry. What happened?"

"Well, it's for the best, Matt. Her mother moved back onto the farm and didn't seem to take a shine to me."

I was right to have had misgivings. As a rule, I avoid associating with people I have dealt with professionally. It wasn't always possible. Who knows? Maybe he and his fiancée did off old Mr. Anderson after all.

"We might have another connection, Matt."

"Oh yeah? How's that?"

"Wayne Delaney. He's a friend of yours, isn't he?"

"Wayney Delaney? He lived a few blocks away in Scarborough, where I grew up. Not really a friend. I didn't know him that well."

"Well, he knows you."

"How do *you* know him?"

"We met briefly through some mutual friends—a very interesting fellow."

"How so?"

"Artistic, with an appreciation for the finer things."

"It's a small world after all."

James was competitive. When I arrived at the pool after he did and occupied the lane next to his, he would alter his pace to keep up or pass me. It was remarkable that he always knew when I was there, but I guess he was observant. Naturally, I didn't want to be outdone and these recreational swims turned into competitions. After each swim, he asked how many lengths I had done. He had done one hundred. I said I hadn't kept track. I might have done fifty.

James had played competitive mixed doubles tennis in university and married his playing partner. He was making some changes. These included trading competitive tennis for triathlon training and divorcing his wife. They had had one daughter together. His wife was engaged to be re-married. He said that on the advice of his lawyer he had given her the family home and more than half of their joint possessions. James told me he was taking the high road.

He didn't mind sharing information about his romantic preferences. He said, "I am very particular about my women. I love vintage Tuesday Weld, and Cate Blanchett really gets me excited. I needed a little more excitement than my wife could offer, if you know what I mean."

We had surprisingly similar tastes in movie starlets. James also waxed poetic about female lifeguards at the pool who were younger than his own daughter. They had a touch of Tuesday Weld.

One night after swimming, I found myself showering across from James. "Hey Matt," he said. "I sent some video recordings to Toronto. It's all hush-hush, but I think they really like me."

"What recordings do you mean, James?"

"I'm interviewing for a new home improvement show on the Home and Garden channel."

"I should buy stock in that channel. Can I say I know you when you become famous? What kind of show is it?"

"Well, the format is going to be a panel of experts in interior design pitching a homeowner on their design plans. The homeowner evaluates them and picks their favourite, and then the winning designer coordinates the makeover."

"Like 'Makeover Mavens'? That show got cancelled, didn't it?" This tidbit had stayed in my mind because it had been one of Katya's favourites.

"Yes, but the hook is that we compete for the work and the lady of the house gets to go shopping with me! The homeowners get a discount of course. I've been to Toronto twice about it. I'm keeping my fingers crossed."

James seemed to have every attribute on most women's laundry list of desirable male attributes. He was outgoing, athletic, self-confident and had a full head of curly hair. He was a professional architect. He was a writer. He was a shopper, a metrosexual and an almost star on TV. What woman could resist that? I had a weird flash forward—an apparition of James in my slippers, living in domestic bliss in my house with my wife, enjoying home improvement shows on my widescreen television.

At home, the snoring continued. It wasn't loud, but after years of being on call and listening for a pager, I was sensitized to noises at night-time. Katya might need better muscle tone. When she said that we should do more things together, I said well then why not swimming. To my surprise, she offered to come with me the following evening.

I cleared the assortment of cups, pens, sweaters and umbrellas into the back seat of my SUV with the hockey sticks. There was an odour of stale coffee mingled with under seat drier sheet that I used as an air freshener. Katya climbed in beside me and we drove to the Rec Complex. Cruising through the empty streets, she was oddly silent, as if contemplating a distasteful chore.

I had a pretend shower in the change room as usual, sprinkling just enough water on my head to get my hair wet. Showers were mandatory, but I didn't like the chill from walking soaking wet down the hall to the pool. It would have been embarrassing for a doctor such as myself to be challenged by teenaged lifeguards, so I gave them an excuse not to. Katya, dripping from her shower, met me on the pool deck. It was halfway through the hour reserved for the lengths swim. James and Theo were in a lane together and in full swing.

I could see James was doing his best to stay ahead of Theo, who was the stronger swimmer. We slipped into the water in the adjacent lane when they were in mid-pool. I led the way and swam hard with my head down to give Katya some space. After a while, James and Theo stopped to rest. As I approached the wall, they said hello, but I didn't stop to chat.

Katya swam impressively well for someone who hates swimming. We finished after James and Theo had left and arranged to meet in the lobby. In the car on the way home, Katya asked me who the two men in the next lane were. I didn't think that she had noticed them. I answered that they were a gay couple who swam there most nights, and she immediately lost interest.

I returned to the Rec alone to swim a couple of days later. Katya had lost her enthusiasm for swimming there because it didn't meet her standards of hygiene. It was clean enough for me, but I didn't argue. As I entered the change room, James approached me earnestly to inquire who the woman swimming in the lane with me had been. His question seemed to verge on romantic longing. At first, I pretended not to understand. Then I responded that that was no woman; that was my wife. There was still an element of unabated eagerness in his eyes.

I determined that he must never meet Katya. I didn't have enough working years left to share half my worldly possessions with him. I supposed that if James did get his own TV show, Katya would inevitably become aware of him. She knew every show of that description. She normally capped her evening off at 10:00 p.m. with a glass of wine and whatever home improvement show was on.

I seemed to be toying with some sort of possible future that was trying to manifest itself. I resolved not to promote the idea of swimming with Katya any further. Brisk walking might be a good thing. I knew that my concern was fatuous. I am not normally the jealous type, but for some reason this seemed to be a special situation.

Chapter 10

It was the beginning of December and the annual round of Christmas parties had started. Initially, I had resisted the Christmas spirit because I thought it was too early. The yuletide shop window decorations and television advertising had started the day after Halloween. When November became December and frost formed on our front windows, I warmed to the idea.

We were invited to two events on the first Saturday evening of December, the doctors' and the swimmers' parties. The doctors' featured dinner and dancing at a fancy hotel. The women all wore evening gowns. Some of the men wore tuxedos. I opted for a dark business suit with the top shirt button undone behind my tie, so I could breathe.

Katya enjoyed dressing up. She wore a sleeveless low-cut dress of silver satin with an off-white brocade jacket and silver high heels. She had a white gold chain necklace suspending a pendant with some light and dark stones glittering in the middle. It contrasted nicely on her pale skin. The stones weren't real, but because she was a doctor's wife, people assumed they were.

Katya and I arrived at the hotel foyer and surveyed the room. We were looking for prospective dining companions. I helped her off with her coat, and we went to the bar to get our two free drinks. I handed one to her.

"You're a gentleman, hon," she said.

"I would hold your hair if you were puking."

Katya leaned in close and whispered in my ear, "Do I look like a big doctor's wife?"

"Do I look like the husband of a big doctor's wife?"

She leaned in close again. "You'll do." I felt her wet tongue in my ear.

We found a seat at a table beside Adam, the obstetrician-gynecologist, and Simon, the retired English family doctor, and their wives. I considered this lucky because with open seating I might have been forced into an uncomfortable chair beside Angelo Amodeo and his allies. Adam and Simon were both sporting tuxedos, Adam's the more fashionable. Adam described his formative years in an English style boarding school in Jamaica, and Simon said he preferred his martinis shaken not stirred, nicely avoiding a discussion of caning and sodomy.

After dinner, all conversation was forced to a halt when a disco band took the stage. They performed at the party every year. They belted out a wall of sound to encourage people to shake their booty. Adam got up to get down with his bad self. Katya and I had taken several dance lessons together but always had selective amnesia for the steps. Neither of us really had a sense of rhythm.

I had secured an advance agreement that we would leave the doctors' party right after dinner to catch the end of the swimmers' soirée. I noticed Adam showing off his boogaloo moves and Simon adopting a ballroom stance, each with his respective wife. The alternatives were silent drinking or spastic dancing. I told my wife she looked terrific, that her hair was perfect and would she please now honour our agreement to leave? It was starting to snow as we made our way back to the car.

71

Traditionally, there was a "Secret Santa" gift exchange at the swimmers' party. It involved people exchanging or stealing each other's gifts according to some arcane rules I didn't want to learn. We had forgotten to bring our present, so we had to detour home to get it. I saw Katya yawning as we pulled into the garage.

Once inside the warm house, Katya started stripping off layers of clothing. I could see she had lost all interest in going out again. I could understand why. She wasn't a regular swimmer and wasn't really close with anyone there. She had been to one of these events before when the gift announcements had lasted for hours. I was secretly relieved. James might be there, and I was serious about her not meeting him. I had had my déjà vu.

As I backed out of the garage alone, I noticed it was nearly 11 p.m. Wet snow was clinging to the boughs of trees hanging low to the streets. The wind drove snowflakes nearly horizontally at my windshield, like asteroids bombarding the Starship Enterprise. I leaned forward in my seat and gripped the wheel tightly with both hands. Luckily, nothing is far in Coventry.

The house was in an upscale subdivision that was only a few years old. It had the hardwood floors, the kitchen island and stain-less-steel appliances that people pined for on home renovation shows, but not a lot of furniture. The owners must have exhausted their budget after they signed the purchase and sale agreement. The party was well underway.

A large living room that opened into a dining room and kitchen was full of Masters' Club members discussing swimming, running and cycling minutiae. The event was being hosted by a runner-biker couple. I didn't know them because they didn't swim. Scanning the room, I didn't know more than a few people. Some of the more ava-ricious were still forcing others to relinquish desirable presents for inferior ones. I saw James standing by himself, so I approached.

"Hey Matt, how are you?" he crooned in his smooth baritone,

giving me a sweet smile. He was wearing a crisp shiny shirt with the two top buttons undone. His hair had been coiffed into salt-and-pepper waves.

"I'm great. Merry Christmas," I said, extending my hand for shaking. "Have you been here long?"

He attempted to pulverize my hand in his own. "No, I arrived an hour ago. I saw you just arrived."

"Second Christmas party of the night," I bragged. "Nice house. Do you know the owners?"

"Not really. So, where's your wife tonight?"

"She begged off. She was feeling a little sick. Worn out from Christmas shopping."

"That's too bad. Are you done your shopping, Matt? Are you giving me the keys to my new Mercedes this year?" He wanted to lock eyes with me.

"You know, I would. I'm getting away from all that though. It was too much of a chore buying everyone cars. I'm just giving Christmas tree ornaments this year. Are you here alone?"

"Yes, the woman I am really passionate about lives in Toronto."

"I suppose that's a little far to come," I supposed. "Are you spending Christmas together?"

"No, I don't think so. She has a very responsible position in Toronto. She doesn't have a lot of free time."

"Absence makes the heart grow fonder." I was going to say, "dick grow longer," but resisted the temptation. "What does she do?"

"She is an executive vice-president at an auction house. I think she has a very busy social life and is having trouble fitting me in."

She didn't sound anything like the farm girl he was courting before. "Well, you're a good-looking guy James. Maybe she's afraid you're a gigolo."

"Yeah, thanks Matt. She's being a little non-committal. I've been looking at this really exquisite present for her. It's an expensive piece of antique jewellery she said she liked. I was actually in Toronto today looking at it."

"What woman wouldn't like that? So, you can spend Christmas with your daughter."

"She's going to her mother's house that day."

"So, you'll see her Boxing Day. Most girls like shopping."

"Yes," he said.

"Well, that's not all bad. My wife's sister is coming to my house for Christmas."

"Wayne Delaney says hello."

"What? Are you two close?"

"No. I saw him at a wine and cheese my friend in Toronto organized. He was with one of the wealthier clients."

"That so?"

We spoke for another few minutes until we ran out of things to say. I advised him to try internet dating. Neither of us had much interest in mixing with the other guests. We drifted toward the door, as most of the rest of the guests were doing and went our separate ways.

The day before our son Michael came home from university for Christmas, Katya and I put up decorations and a few outdoor lights so that it would be homey. I was pleased with the result, but Katya complained that the number of Christmas cards we had on the mantelpiece was less each year. I told her you have to send some to get some. She could write some cards to herself and display them, or recycle the ones from last year. They aren't usually dated. Consequently, who would know the difference?

The three of us were going to church on Christmas Eve. Because of Katya's job, this had become our family custom. I like the carols and the ceremony. I like the warm fuzzy feelings of brotherly love, even though they are short lived. We were going with another couple, Sean and Sinead, and their youngest daughter who was still in high school. I knew Sean Feeney through Katya, and he had become my close friend and mentor.

Sean taught at the same school as my wife. He was a Catholic educator, who put the existence of God at 50-50. He was tall, with a steel grey brush cut, focused blue eyes and bristly eyebrows trimmed like hedges to a uniform length. He was five years older than me, but looked more. His love of the outdoors had weathered his pink Irish skin. Sinead and Sean ran a bed and breakfast hotel out of their stately home. They had traded an average house in Toronto for a giant one in Coventry that cost about the same.

If Sean verged on burly, Sinead was somewhat delicate. She had classic Celtic features with dark straight hair and pale skin. She had more free time, so she ran the business end of the hotel, taking bookings and chatting up the guests. Sean didn't waste time on that. He kept the building up and dreamt up heroic exploits. His next scheme was to buy a sailboat and cross the Atlantic.

We usually went to Coventry's Catholic church, but Sean said the United church would have the better show. It was favoured by Coventry's artistic community. It was also walking distance from his house. I was leery. My parents had sent me to Baptist Sunday school for some religious training because it was the closest.

I was ten years old and sitting in a pew on a Sunday morning. Between Bible drills, during group prayer with your eyes closed, the minister asked for anyone with secret doubts about being born again in Christ to raise their hand. When I did, a flock of suburban Sunday school teachers joyously descended to do battle with the infidel in me. Their cause was weak to need so many reinforcements. I noticed Luke's arm go up to join mine, although we weren't friends yet.

The United church program that night featured professional singers and musicians in full Christmas regalia. This Protestant show was good, but the service at the one true Catholic Church would have been more traditional and packed to the rafters. There was a feeling of community there, which I enjoyed.

After church, the six of us marched up a cold suburban street to Moira's Christmas Eve party. Moira was another of Katya's teacher friends. She came from an Irish Catholic family, so her parents, seven sisters, two brothers, their families and her closest friends were there. When Sean walked in the door, the brothers threw their arms around him and bellowed, "Happy Christmas ya crazy koont!" It was obvious they had some history.

Sean's father had been an Irish republican who collected tithes for the Irish Republican Army after immigrating to Canada. He had had a trucking business operating on both sides of the American border. Sean, as a teenager, had to drive back and forth delivering satchels of money to support the cause of Irish reunification. While growing up, he was made aware by clicks on the line that their telephone at home was being monitored.

Moira's clan had been to the Catholic service and were full of communal cheer. There was a Christmas tree with multicoloured lights, delirious children still running at midnight and patriotic brands of whiskey. This was a night for mingling and drinking. Moira's dad, being the patriarch, was the paragon of this. We were invited to a small supper, and Moira asked Sean to say grace.

"Heavenly father, we would just like to thank you so much for giving us this beautiful day, for building this gorgeous house for Moira and Michael, providing all the lovely Christmas decorations and preparing this fine repast. Amen." Moira regarded Sean suspiciously, but then she smiled.

I admitted to Moira that we had been to a pagan church but weren't proud of it. Sean had forced us to go. Everyone knew Sean was a leftist libertarian and that there was no reforming him. He was still his father's son and an Irish patriot. Moira's dad proposed a toast to Sean senior and we all joined in, although most of us had never met him.

Chapter 11

Other than working, there is not much else to do in Coventry in winter. There is no downhill skiing. The countryside is as flat as a pancake, which makes it good for farming and snowmobiling, which the yokels enjoy. Snow blows through the open fields and across the highways, making it difficult to drive anywhere. Florida beckons, but getting to the airport in Toronto can be a problem. Most of the new doctors who moved here bought themselves four-wheel drive vehicles so they could get to the hospital in an emergency. Many of the surgeons had giant pickup trucks to transport their oversized egos.

This was the last day of the Christmas break and I was back on call. We had had a major blizzard overnight. I went out to shovel the berm that the snowplow had left at the end of my driveway. I could have gotten out in my SUV, but it was my job to ensure Katya could get her car out too. Snowplows leave obnoxious, compressed, non-shovel-sized boulders. Everyone on the street was outside with their snow blowers. I didn't want one because I was tougher than that. Thankfully, a good Samaritan neighbour eventually came over to help.

Only one operating room was open for elective surgery. We had a half list with Adam until noon, doing some gynecology cases. Joanie and Kristiaan were in the O.R. lounge having coffee. Joanie was talking in earnest. It sounded like gossip because it stopped as soon as I sat down at their table. A student nurse in the corner of the room was focused on her smartphone and oblivious. I didn't want the CIA always knowing where I was, or balls' cancer, so I only carried my phone when I had to.

Kristiaan was the most caring-sharing nurse in the O.R. "Hi Matt! Did you have a good New Year's Eve?" he asked in an upbeat way.

"Yes thanks. I stayed home. Did you have to work?"

"No, we just came on," Kristiaan said. "And did you attend a big, fancy New Year's Eve party, Joanie?"

"I don't really go to a lot of bother," Joanie said. "Just finish off the best part of a bottle of wine at home, two actually."

"Puke, masturbate and go to bed," I suggested. Joanie was a divorcée and lived alone.

"Yes, except the puking," she said dryly.

"So, what's the gossip?"

Joanie and Kristiaan looked at each other uncertainly. Joanie was the first to speak. "Adam's been caught cheating."

"Do you mean like sex?"

"Of course sex. He's been dipping his wick in skank wax."

"Don't tell me he followed up with that dame with her husband's rash-on-the-penis pic."

"Maybe the same one. Anyway, just the dame, not the husband. He called Adam's wife to tell on him. If Adam had invited the husband too, there might not have been a problem."

"No shit. I'm sorry. He has been looking stressed lately. Is his wife still with him?"

Adam came into the lounge looking for us.

"Did you have to work over Christmas?" Kristiaan asked quickly. "We heard you were in last night at 2 a.m. for a section."

"Yes mon. I delivered a mother with twins."

"Oooh, what did she get?" Kris always wanted to know.

"Good question."

"Did you sleep after that?" Kris asked sympathetically.

"I'm a'ight. I got two hours. I'm on call today too. My colleagues flocked off with the birdies to Wally World or some shite."

Nobody mentioned Adam's problems at home. We chugged our coffees so he could get his list started. The first hour was punctuated by his fussy requests to raise the bed, lower the bed or place the bed in a head down position. There was also, "The patient is moving. Could she be light? The patient is bleeding. What's the blood pressure?" The surgery was taking a long time.

"Yeah, the blood pressure was a little high. It's coming down now."

"Ya-mon. I can always tell." He finished up and sank onto a chair in the corner of the room.

"Hey diddle-de-dee. A surgeon's life for me." I walked around the O.R. table looking at wet sponges to tally blood loss. It was higher than usual.

Adam was watching. "How much blood do you think she's lost?"

"Maybe 500 mils. Order her a steak for dinner tonight to replenish her iron stores."

"We didn't lose any blood. I know where it all is."

"You should go home and shut them bloodshot peepers."

"Ya-mammy."

There were no more cases. I set up the anesthesia equipment for any emergencies that might materialize and then drove home. As soon as I had pulled my car into the garage, I got a call from Kristiaan to tell me that Angelo Amodeo had a case to do. Angelo was covering for general surgery. He liked to be busy when he was on call. I avoided his daytime lists whenever possible, but we had to work together whenever our on-call days coincided.

Most surgeons would call me directly to explain the details of an emergency case. Angelo thought it was beneath his dignity to have to discuss this type of thing with an anesthesiologist. I surmised it might cause flashbacks to when he was humiliated as a trainee reporting clinical findings to a critical senior surgeon, which he now considered himself to be.

Traditionally, general surgeons are brutalized in their residency training. They develop Stockholm syndrome and sometimes spend their working lives returning the favour. General surgery used to encompass everything, but with sub-specialization that era has passed. They have been left with bowel, breast and diminished prestige.

A few minutes later, the phone rang again. It doesn't rain unless it pours. It was Adam requesting an epidural for a woman in labour. I drove back to the hospital and went up to the operating room to change my clothes. Angelo was pacing in the corridor.

"I have to do an epidural," I informed him.

"Bullshit! Adam dee-mon can call me directly and ask permission if he wants to bump. Why is every epidural automatically an 'A' case? Why is his case more important than mine?"

"I don't care who goes first. Sort it out between yourselves."

"Just inject the white shit and get on with it," he demanded. The white shit was propofol, the standard anesthetic induction agent that Michael Jackson liked.

I pulled out my phone and called the obstetric ward. "May I speak with Adam please?" I heard the sound of a phone changing hands. "Angelo wants to talk to you," I told him.

"She cannot wait. Shite. A'ight. Nuf bare foolishness. Put on dee baby, bumboclot, fassyhole general surgeon who tink he a real general."

I handed the phone to Angelo. He said, "You have to call me if you want to bump."

There was a period of silence while he listened and then he said, "No... No... It is a problem. No. What's a fassyhole?" Then he handed me back the phone.

"So, am I going?" I asked him.

"Do whatever the fuck you like." He stormed off proclaiming that I was passive-aggressive. Originality wasn't his strength. He had copied this epithet from Isaiah, an older, higher in pack order, general surgeon. Isaiah could operate the longest without urinating, eating or sleeping and farted regally and unapologetically in public. Isaiah had probably in turn copied the epithet from his own mentors.

When I got back from the epidural half an hour later, a 40-year-old, 400-pound woman was waiting on a stretcher outside the operating room. She was a willing casualty of the North American obesity epidemic. Her chart said she had an incarcerated hernia. There was a patch of redness overlying her groin, but her pannus obscured whatever swelling there might otherwise have been. The novice nurse and Angelo were with her. He was scowling and pacing.

I went into the room to set up, and the nurse walked the patient in soon afterward. She ported her 400 pounds with her feet widely apart, most of the way to the operating table. As she raised one foot to the stepstool beside it, she wavered, hesitated and descended, coming to rest sitting perilously on her haunches. Then she did a pirouette and sank, wedging her backside between the base of the table and the floor, unable to rise.

In retrospect, the student nurse should have brought the patient in on her stretcher and had her shuffle horizontally from bed to bed. The student tugged on the patient's arms to stand her up again, but she didn't budge. Kristiaan came over to help. Rather than chastising his inexperienced colleague, he acted like a cheerleader counting down to liftoff as the two of them tried to get her up again. Despite Kris' "ra-ra" enthusiasm, it seemed more likely that they would disconnect her arms from her shoulders than raise her.

I went over to see what could be done. I placed an arm under the patient's shoulder and indented her fat. She was too fatigued to pretend to help. I made a mental calculation that if I applied more force, my arm would sink further into her armpit fat, but her frame would remain at rest.

Angelo sat immobile at the computer terminal in the corner regarding the scene. I looked over at him hopelessly. He didn't move or offer to help, so we were at an impasse. Joanie, our scrub nurse, sat blithely on her stool and didn't un-scrub. I sat back down on the pleather chair beside my gas machine. The patient sat on the floor. There was only silence in the room. This situation persisted for about five minutes, after which Angelo stood up and left.

Suddenly, Kristiaan had a eureka moment. "I think there is a Hoyer lifter over on the chronic care unit." He was a part-timer and worked on other wards whenever they called him in. It is O.R. mythology that male nurses are either lazy or gay. Kristiaan was definitely not lazy. He dashed out the door and returned ten minutes later with a large apparatus that looked like a hammock strung on metal uprights. We got the hammock under the floor sitter and used the hand crank to get her airborne.

The hammock trembled ominously. There was some urgency to getting her moved off of it. The tines of the lifting device wouldn't fit under the operating table, so the newbie nurse and I got her swinging like a pendulum in larger and larger arcs trying to centre her over it. One tine lifted off the floor, and Kristiaan released the crank sinking her onto the vinyl mattress.

When we had all the monitors attached, and the patient asleep and intubated, Angelo re-entered the room. He never inquired how we had gotten her onto the table. He performed his operation without speaking a word.

After he was done, Kristiaan asked, "Angelo, have you met Char, our new student nurse?"

"No. I thought she was the patient's lawyer."

"Did I snore?" the patient slurred. "My husband says that I snore." It is not possible to snore with a tube in the trachea because it splints the airway open.

"You didn't snore. Your husband's a fucking liar," Angelo said.

"Thank you, Dr. Amodeo. I knew I liked you." Patients allow their surgeons a lot of leeway. Then she remembered her surgery and started complaining of pain.

I heard Angelo mumble, "You're wrong. It doesn't hurt, because I just fixed it."

"What's your pain out of ten?" Kristiaan asked.

"Ten out of ten."

"Take this knife, put it in your eye and work it around," Angelo said. "Take a rusty saw and cut off your leg. That's ten out of ten. You're maybe a two."

"You're going to get a bad review on Rate Your MD dot com," I said.

"You can suck my dick."

"Okay, thank you, Doctor. I knew I liked you, Doctor," the patient slurred again.

Josh Smith, the orthopedic surgeon, appeared in the doorway. "What time can I start my emergency hip fracture?" he asked. The term "emergency" was open to interpretation. Hip fractures could wait a day or two if necessary and we didn't do them after 11 p.m.

"We have to have supper first—union rules," I answered.

"So 5:30 then?" It was now 5 o'clock.

"We have to get this one off the table first, have a leisurely four-course meal, and set up for the next one...so, no."

"Why don't you just do my case first and then have supper?" he asked half-heartedly.

This was a classic surgeons' ploy. A real emergency could intervene and prevent us from ever having dinner. He knew this of course but wanted to get his case done before a more urgent case from a different surgeon could bump him.

"How about we try for five minutes to six and don't answer the phone to anyone between now and then."

"You suck," was his answer.

Josh and two large pizzas were waiting in the lounge when we arrived.

"Thanks for the pizza," I said. "That's very generous. Is this to get us back to work faster?"

"Maybe... Angelo was just here trying to get me to sign a letter of complaint against you for being slow and intentionally holding up cases. He was telling me about a fat-lady hernia."

"Did you sign?"

"No."

"Thanks. How many signatures did he have?"

"Just his own so far. He was vewy, vewy angwy."

As we were eating, Josh sat there trying not to stare at us, but covertly urging the mouthfuls and the mastication on with his eyes. Surgeons don't seem to need to eat at work.

"So... What's the patient like?" I asked him.

"She's 90, but you'll like her."

"I mean medically."

"Good." That meant he probably didn't know.

"How did she break her hip?" I asked.

"I don't know. Maybe she stepped on her cat."

"They all use that excuse after they get tanked up."

The patient with the hip fracture was mostly demented. I tried asking her the routine questions about heart or breathing problems. She made sense for a while but then stopped. She was from a nursing home, so she wouldn't have stepped on a cat nor had access to alcohol. She responded to kind words.

"Just inject her with the big syringe and then the little syringe." Josh was standing beside me, holding a big and little syringe he had taken from my cart. This was his stock joke, mocking the complexities of anesthesia.

"Okay. That's fine," I said. "Just inject them yourself," and he backed off.

The patient looked up and stared at me venomously. "Yes, I bought it and hid it!" she hissed. This was unconcealed white-hot hatred. She had obviously mistaken me for a long-dead husband.

"Being in this specialty is a constant reminder to me of how much it sucks to get old," Josh said.

After the hip, we did an appendix with Angelo and then it looked like we could go home. I didn't speak to him. I was wondering what I should do about him.

"You have the day off tomorrow don't you, Matt. Have a nice day!" Kris said enthusiastically. "I hope that everyone has a nice day tomorrow. Does anyone know the weather for tomorrow? I think I heard that it's going to be really nice!" He was trying to cheer us up, forgetting that we still had all night to be on call.

"More snow all week, I think," Char ventured, pulling out her phone to check. She was becoming part of the team.

"Angelo," I said, "Use your powers as general surgeon for good, and give us nice weather for the weekend."

"I'll give you something different."

I changed and went down the back stairs out of the O.R. Exiting the building, I inhaled with pleasure. I had forgotten what fresh air smelled like.

Sometime after midnight, I got a call from Adam to come do another epidural. I thought of telling him to try doing it himself since he was up, or the woman to deliver it like they do on Discovery Channel, or to leave me the fuck alone. I remembered that his problems might be worse than mine and said that I would be right there.

Chapter 12

The Rec Complex re-opened for the new year on January 2. I had to stop to wipe my fogged-up glasses as I came in from the cold to the lobby. The humidity in the change room hit me like a wet blanket fogging them up again. There were a lot of people inside. They had a lot of holiday eating to atone for.

I walked onto the pool deck and surveyed the scene. The water was packed. After New Year's, there is usually an influx of resolvers clogging up the swim lanes. This year was no exception. This would last about three weeks. After January passed its zenith, a lot of people would give up and decide to try again next year.

An unfortunate man sharing a lane with James was receiving a tongue lashing for not asking permission to enter. As James did flip turns at the walls, this would have been difficult to do unless he waited for James to get tired and stop. Aside from a sign suggesting lanes designated for fast and slow swimmers, there really was no such convention. The guy was too uncoordinated to get any closer to the buoy line and occupied more than half the lane as they passed.

Luckily, just as I was despairing of getting a spot, one opened up in the lane next to James. In my younger days, I would have created some space by swimming over people until they changed lanes or left. I wasn't the strongest swimmer in the pool anymore, and a lot of people knew I was a doctor—two good reasons not to do that today.

I got in and swam for a few minutes. When James stopped, I paused to briefly say hello.

"I thought I recognized your stroke, Matt."

"Yes, I've been practicing in the bathtub. Have you been here a while?"

"I started at 24 minutes to." It was now 24 minutes after the hour.

"So, you didn't quite swim an hour," I observed.

"I meant 34 minutes to."

"You're still two minutes shy." I was taunting him to amuse myself. I knew he was competitive.

"I swam a hundred lengths."

"What proof do I really have of that, James?" I asked with pretend seriousness.

"Very funny." He turned and swam hard for another two minutes before getting out of the water.

I overheard him talking to the teenaged lifeguard. "I don't want to tell you your job, but slower swimmers should stay in their designated lane."

"Jeff's mentally challenged," he replied uncomfortably. "I noticed him in your lane, but the pool was pretty full."

"We-tah-dad. You should tell the challengers to get in the far-left lane with the belugas." James smiled nicely and exited to the showers.

I swam for another half hour before returning to the change room. As I was getting dressed, I heard James call, "So how's your lovely wife, Matt?"

"Good."

"Say Matt, I've had this cold for a week that I haven't been able to shake." James was standing at my shoulder. "Would you mind having a look at my throat?" He leaned in close, mouth gaping, tonsils exposed for me to admire.

People are always asking about colds and postnasal drips as if doctors had a cure they weren't divulging. I took a step backwards, dodging viruses. "Don't see anything too bad in there, James."

"Yeah, I visited my doctor, but he didn't see anything either. He said my glands were swollen. I don't want to be sick too long. Last time, I left it too long before going, and I was sick for a month."

People often say this too, as if coming earlier meant the cure for the cold could be put to work sooner. He actually looked surprisingly well, as hypochondriacs frequently do.

"How about we go out for a late lunch, Matt?"

"Well, today's not good. I have about ten minutes more work to do. I'm trying a shower first, then swim, then gym sequence to break up the monotony of gym-swim-shower."

He seemed disappointed but didn't persist. Something about him made me uneasy.

"I'm in the final interview stage of that TV show I was telling you about. I think they really like me. I'm very excited about it."

"It sounds wonderful."

It did sound like a great job for him. He would be using all of his skill sets. I wondered whether, if he got hired, he would be leaving Coventry to live in Toronto. That might be a good thing.

I watched him sneeze into a tissue and then examine it thoughtfully. I left him preening in front of the mirror, calling over my shoulder, "See you later, handsome James."

I saw James again a week later as I was putting on my swim trunks in the Rec Complex change room. He approached me with a broad smile. "Hey Matt. You're going to be giving me an anesthetic."

"What do you mean, James?"

"Oh, I'm having a bit of surgery in February, and I requested you."

"What operation are you having, James?"

"Oh, I've been having a bit of trouble with a hernia."

"That's not a big operation." I was trying to sound reassuring. "Who is the surgeon?"

"Dr. Amodeo."

"Yeah, he's good," I said half-heartedly.

"I told him and the hospital staff at the preoperative visit that I wanted you to be my anesthesiologist." His eyes shone at me widely like a trusting child.

"But I may not be the one giving your anesthetic," I hastened to inform him. "We don't guarantee because there are six anesthesiologists on staff. The first choice of operating room list goes to the person who is on call, and then there is a hierarchy of choice depending on when your next on-call day is. The room assignations are only made one week in advance."

"It was my good fortune to meet you on the phone when you called the farm. I liked your self-assurance and attention to detail when you were investigating me."

The adulation was a little disturbing. I liked James, but I wasn't sure that I wanted to be involved in his care. I didn't want to progress to the next level of intimacy that being responsible for his life implied. He was a peculiar mix of insecurities, disarming friendliness and competitiveness. He was being led by a destiny that was attempting to intersect mine.

Chapter 13

On the morning of February 14, Katya asked me whether I knew what day it was. I answered that it would have to be the anniversary of that infamous Chicago massacre. We should fire off a few celebratory rounds. She said that was funny and was I buying her a bobble or a supermarket flower bouquet for Valentine's? Supermarket bouquets are cheaper than florists', but they have the telltale store logo on the wrapper.

"I don't want to ruin the surprise," I said, "but I can tell you that many homemakers would consider a shiny new flour sifter more durable."

Katya left for work early. Grampa was clearing a path in the deep snow behind the back door for Madame Fifi to walk. I was getting into my truck in the garage, when I heard a volley of barking. This was how the dog signalled a full bowel or bladder. It could also mean that she wanted an unearned doggy treat. There was another volley. I went back inside because I didn't want to call her bluff.

Grampa was lying in a snow bank behind the house and struggling like a tortoise to right himself. Madame Fifi had saved Grampa. He would have become a tragic popsicle before long. Fun fact from the coroners' manual: if its owner dies, a dog will guard the body until it is nearly starving. A cat will begin dining on the face before the body is cold. Grampa couldn't be allowed out by himself any more in winter.

I was scheduled to work in the plastic surgery room. Eve, the head nurse, was rhapsodizing about something she had seen on television the night before. Eve was in her early fifties. She was tall, slender and energetic. One lock of her dark curly hair protruded artfully from under her operating room cap. She was attractive, but not in any conventional way. She actually did "dare to care," as the administrators' slogan du jour exhorted us. She was a happy person and made you feel like a co-conspirator in her positivity.

"Did you see that David Beckham commercial where his robe gets caught in a car door and then he runs after the car in his underwear and scores a goal as he passes some kids playing soccer and then his underwear gets pulled down and you see a little bit of his bum? It's been on for a few weeks." She was enthralled to the point of losing track of what she was doing. I felt her joy in this recitation.

"Eve, that is a beautiful story," I said. "You make the world a better place."

"Thanks Matthew. You're doing that for some other people today."

"More or less beautiful, depending on what they prefer." Our first patient was having a breast augmentation, the second one a reduction.

Eve did some more busy work around the room to make sure we were set for the day. Simon was assisting again. As soon as Eve had closed the door behind herself, he asked, "Have you seen Evelyn's daughter? She has really blossomed." His eyes were sparkling and his silver beard was bobbing enthusiastically. Simon considered himself a ladies' man. There didn't seem to be a lower age limit.

"How is your wife doing, Simon?" I asked.

"Ogling the gardener, I should think," he said, sounding chastened.

The surgeon, Dr. Cesar De Santos De Dios was a relatively recent arrival to Coventry. He had emigrated a few years ago from Mexico. He was elegant looking, with a precisely trimmed goatee, pencil moustache and bleached teeth. Outside the O.R., he wore starched white shirts with purple paisley ascots to protect his neck from the Canadian cold. He had a watch with a gold bracelet that hung loosely like a bangle around his wrist. Through the window in the door, I saw him put this in the pocket of his O.R. greens and cross himself for luck before coming in.

"Buenos dias Cesar," I said.

"Buenos dios Mateo. Cómo estás esta hermosa mañana? Estás listo para hacer del mundo un lugar más bello?" he replied warmly.

"Muy bien, gracias. Dos cervezas y dos chicas por favor." My Spanish vocabulary was limited.

The first patient was a thin, hard-looking woman about my age with a flat chest. She was a private patient and they are relatively scarce. They are prized because they can be billed whatever the market will bear. Since breast augmentation is a cosmetic procedure, it is not covered by government health insurance.

I grabbed her chart and approached.

"Hello Matthew," she said.

She was unfamiliar. "Hi." I glanced down at her chart. "Doris Delaney. This *is* a surprise. We went to school together, didn't we?"

"Yes."

"How *are* you?"

"Good."

"How's your brother Wayne?"

"Good."

"So, you're having surgery here." I glanced at her address on the face sheet. "And you still live in Scarborough. How did you end up at Coventry General?"

"It was the cheapest. Matthew, I'm sorry. I didn't expect to find you here."

"No problem, Doris. It's good to see you."

I filled the dead air with medical questions to cover the awkwardness until Cesar arrived. He chatted amicably with her until she was asleep and then personally scrubbed her chest with antiseptic solution before getting gowned and gloved.

As the surgery was getting underway, Sara, who was circulating, brought various sizes of implants in shrink-wrapped boxes, decorated with pretty, feminine logos for Cesar to choose from. "All tatted up," she observed, glancing over at Doris.

"Did you see the tramp stamp on her sacrum? It crawls half way up her back," Joanie, who was scrubbed, remarked.

"I'm too old to get a tattoo," Sara said.

"You are not that old," Cesar said. "I have some very mature ladies with a tattoo, and when you get tired, I can laser this 'tat.' It is very hard to see afterward."

"Do you think I would look good with a tattoo, Matthew?" Sara asked.

"I, ah, don't know. Sure, if it's discreet."

"Like on my ankle?"

"Sure. No nose rings."

"I am afraid these tattoos do look unfortunate after the bloom is off the rose," Simon said.

I peeked over the drape. "Why is she having the procedure? Did she recently get divorced and need a new husband?" I was hoping Doris wasn't carrying some sort of torch for me and wanted me to see her with new boobs.

"I don't know. I have stopped asking," Cesar replied.

"I want a new husband. I don't care whose," Joanie said, looking at Cesar. She was a divorcée with two grown sons.

"Yes of course, my lady. I could operate you. You could have many lovers, with my help." Cesar drew two curvaceous arcs in the air with his scalpel.

"Buy yourself a little black dress, Joanie. Most men like those." I was flattering her. Joanie's figure would not really permit her to carry that off.

"How much do you charge for this procedure?" she asked. "Do you have a nurses' rate?"

The men in the room surreptitiously examined the outlines of the nurses' breasts. This was not difficult as everyone was wearing O.R. greens. These are pyjama-like suits with deep "V" necks. Joanie's were middle aged and sagging. Sara was probably fifteen years younger. I didn't want to embarrass her by looking at her chest, surreptitiously or not. I knew from having looked previously that she didn't need improving. She was five feet four and everything was in proportion. Doris' boobs were perking up nicely.

"Yes, I do. I have, for one month, a special with the friends and family rate —50 per cent off." Cesar was not kidding.

"Buy one boob, get one free," I said.

"Do you think I need implants, Matthew?" Sara was blushing.

"No, you're perfect."

Sara looked pleased with the compliment. She did a little shimmy with her shoulders and blushed some more.

"You can watch this operation for real now on one of those personal makeover shows," Joanie said.

"Yes, and we will have one hundred of your closest friends and relatives waiting outside who are going to come in afterward to cry and applaud for you," I said.

She looked peeved. I should have been more sensitive. I remembered that one of Joanie's sons had been sentenced to jail time for cooking meth and would have to send regrets.

As Doris was waking up, Sara plopped an oxygen mask on her face for transport. "Nice big breaths," she coached.

"They're not bona fide," Simon said, wagging his white beard playfully at her like a horny Santa Clause. I gave him a stern look because he was an idiot who should keep his yap shut when my VIP patient was waking up.

Sara and I took Doris to the recovery room. As part of the hand-over, Sara reported details to the staff there. "This is from the manufacturer. It says what kind of implants she got." She handed a laminated card to the recovery room nurse. It was about the size of a business calling card. "She's going to keep that in her wallet to show policemen to get out of tickets. Her brand has the best mouth feel." Sara smiled at me. Doris made no comment.

The second patient of the day was scheduled for a breast reduction. Paradoxically, this procedure is covered by health insurance, if patients complain of back pain. They do, but they are coached. To my chagrin, it is far more common than augmentation. It seemed like women were lining up to have their breasts amputated because it was free.

I saw Cesar rounding the corner in the waiting area. He had a marker in his hand to put lines on the patient's breasts before she came into the operating room. These would guide his incisions.

"Matthew, where is this patient gone?" he asked, as if I were hiding her. I replied that she had just gone to the bathroom.

"That is so selfish and no considerate. She could have gone any-time when she was waiting, isn't it?" His tone had been far more solicitous with self-paying Doris.

"She probably has a nervous bladder." I had just finished inter-viewing her. She was a pretty 18-year-old.

"They will penalizate me if I run late you know," he fretted.

"Penalization is a bit drastic. Could you ask them to use a smallish dildo?" I suppose this was mean, but surgeons are always pushing. I was rewarded with a blank stare. English was not his first language.

After I induced anesthesia, one of the orderlies uncovered the patient and scrubbed her chest with antiseptic, smearing the lines into each other.

"I say, does this patient smoke?" Simon asked.

"You wouldn't do her if she smoked, right?" I said.

"You would not operate her, Simon?" Cesar asked.

"If making sweet love is an operation," I said.

Cesar and Joanie draped the patient with sterile green sheets, leaving only her breasts, framed in green, exposed.

Simon watched from the side. "My God! What you doing, man? I mean—I don't care about the old ones of course, but..."

"She's a little young for this procedure, isn't she? And how are you going to improve on that?" I said in a monotone. From a male perspective, she was strikingly beautiful.

"Well, I tried to talk her out of the surgery, but she has insisted," Cesar protested.

Apparently, he had no say as to whom he operated on. How could this girl really know what she wanted? She was so young. Some boys must have leered too long and made her feel uncomfortable.

"Let the record show that the patient had an operation, although the surgeon advised against it," Simon pronounced.

"Took a rather dim view in fact," I said mimicking Simon's English accent.

No one responded. Postoperatively, she would have scars, her nipples would be numb and her ability to breast feed or attract an alpha male would be impaired. We would all get a paycheque. I would be named as an accomplice at heaven's pearly gates. I wondered what I could do short of quitting my job to make my defence to St. Peter easier, but I couldn't think of anything.

"Do you know that if you put on the internet 'Coventry cosmetic surgery,' the first things are clinics in Toronto," Cesar said.

"That's a bit dodgy, those Toronto chaps intruding on your turf," Simon said.

"Well cosmetic surgery is not my favourite, but it pays. 'Oh my God! You look so great.' Yeah you have to do that," Cesar said sadly.

"My son is studying computer science. He would know how to get your name higher on the search, but he won't help you." I was projecting my biases. Cesar was a case study in how economic incentives shape practice patterns. He meant well but was helpless to resist them.

"It's rather unfortunate that women who don't have proper regard for their large breasts can't donate to their needier sistren," Simon said. "I say, whatever became of that fat girl whose nipples fell off afterward?" Simon had assisted Cesar with a breast reduction case where that had happened.

"I talked to her that this is a possibility and she is very happy. She does not miss them. She is not so sophisticate."

"Can she afford a lawyer?" I asked.

"No. She is very happy."

When we got to the recovery room, I went looking for Doris. She had already been discharged. I was going to wish her well. I was disappointed and relieved.

We had a little time left in our day, so I agreed to do an add-on case waiting in the emergency department. It was a tendon repair on a young man who had put his hand through a plate glass window. In addition to cosmetic surgery, plastic surgeons generally do all the reconstructive hand surgery. I felt happier doing this because it was genuine work that needed to be done.

I was less happy when I saw our patient waiting in the operating room corridor with an armed guard. He was lying shackled by his ankles to a stretcher, handcuffed for good measure. There wasn't any real estate left to decorate with ink. His tattoos celebrated snakes invading vacant skulls, which suggested he would be insolent.

I approached cautiously to take a history. Putting the policeman between the patient and myself, in case he decided to do a Hannibal Lecter on my face, I opened my mouth to start my line of questioning. I was abruptly interrupted by Joanie. Ignoring me, she proprietorially asked the patient to identify himself, checked his name against his identification arm band and launched into the standard nursing questionnaire.

When she had finished, she turned toward the cop. "Remove these shackles!"

He looked taken aback, but dutifully unlocked the shackles.

"The handcuffs too."

He meekly did as he was told. Joanie went back into the O.R. and I resumed my questionnaire. The prisoner-patient answered politely. There was no insolence left. He had done a break and enter a few blocks from where I live. I pushed the stretcher into the room and got him lying on the O.R. table. The cop waited outside, his framed face peeking through the face-sized window in the door. I assumed my position at the head of the bed preparing my drugs and equipment.

Joanie came over and spoke quietly into the delinquent's ear. I was close enough to hear her say, "If you make any trouble, I'll flatten you." He didn't, because of the maternal-son bond they had established. Our house has a burglar alarm that Katya, despite my admonitions, never turned on. I made a mental note to tell her about the case so she would take me more seriously.

When I got home, Katya was examining herself in the full-length mirror on the back of the hall closet door. She looked like she had gotten stuck there after hanging up her winter coat. I placed a supermarket bouquet and a card festooned with hearts on the hall table, and she blew me a kiss.

"You can stop looking in the mirror—your boobs are big enough."

She turned to face me. "My boobs aren't the issue. Who were you working with today?"

Sara would have answered differently.

"Dr. De Santos De Dios, a plastic surgeon from Mexico. Operating on boobs. He was selling dreams to suckers and I was helping."

"Is he good?"

"He's okay."

"How old do you think I look?"

"Really young."

"Do you think I should have my eyes done?"

"No! The laugh lines give you character, *old girl*."

"I was considering getting liposuction. How does that work?"

"You don't need that. A metal rod attached to suction is shoved under the skin of your offending part and rammed in and out in a circle. Undertakers use those too. You look like you've been mugged and get ridges like bicycle spokes. Better to ride a bike the long way to the gym. You could swim, but too much moisture can macerate your skin, and the chlorine might dry it out."

"Exercise is your answer for everything," Katya said. She really didn't look interested in my solutions. Talking about boobs made me forget to tell her about the tattooed break and enter artist.

Chapter 14

Having last choice of operating lists, I was assigned to do James' anesthetic when the day for his hernia surgery arrived in March, working with Angelo Amodeo. Angelo was making conversation with Isaiah, another Coventry general surgeon, across the operating table. Isaiah's was the only other signature on Angelo's petition against me. They assisted each other when they were short of work, even when there was no need for an assistant. Provincial health insurance paid for it.

Isaiah was a few years older than Angelo, but their residency training had overlapped. They were reminiscing about a house party hosted by their chief of surgery at his country estate. Their boss's dog had run away, and he had sent his residents out to look for it. When they triumphantly brought it back in the middle of the night, he produced a shotgun and blasted it for being disloyal.

"He was quite the guy," Angelo said.

"Taught me a lesson," Isaiah replied.

Shifting gears, Angelo said, "So I was showering this morning and my son said, 'Daddy, your penis is so big, much bigger than mine.' So I said, 'Go tell mummy what you just said, buddy.' And he goes, 'Mummy, when I grow up I'm going to have a big penis just like Daddy.' "

"Yeah, smart kid," his colleague said.

"Yeah, I'll have to remember that one," Angelo said. "Speaking of penises, Kristiaan is scrubbing the next case for us."

"He's the faggot, right? Not that there's anything wrong with that."

"Yeah, a fruit—not that there's anything wrong with that."

"How big is your penis anyway, Angelo?" I asked.

Angelo pretended I wasn't there and Isaiah broke the silence. "Hey, how many blondes does it take to screw in a light bulb?" I happen to have blonde hair.

"I don't know," Angelo said. "How many?"

"Two. One to screw in the light bulb and one to suck my dick."

"Ha ha," They both had a good belly laugh. I looked over at Joanie who was scrubbed and laughing too.

"On that same subject, with the addition of Kristiaan and excluding Joanie, we will have the two most experienced 'Kork-soakers' in the O.R. with us for the next case," Angelo said. Angelo and Isaiah turned and grinned at me. Then Angelo said, "This next guy is a friend of yours, isn't he? I didn't think you had any friends."

"I would say more of an acquaintance," I said.

When I met him outside of the operating room, James was beaming. He was lying comfortably on a stretcher, hair freshly coiffed, dressed in a blue hospital gown.

I picked up his chart. "Hi James. How are you doing?"

"I'm well thanks, Matt." His smile never dimmed. It was like we were getting married.

"You'll sail through this. You're young and healthy. You won't have any problems. So, what happened with the TV show you were telling me about?" I thought I would distract him with happy conversation, although it didn't seem necessary.

"Well, we filmed four episodes. They are going to be on TV sometime in the spring," he said proudly.

"Congratulations. You're on your way to becoming a household name."

"Thanks Matt. You know, I fixed it so that you would be the one doing my anesthetic."

"You're welcome, James." This seemed a little grandiose. I doubted that he would have been able to do that.

James had no health issues. I had no concerns about his anesthesia. He was just a routine case. I performed the usual induction sequence with the usual drugs, passed an endotracheal tube into his windpipe, turned on some nitrous oxide and Maxiflurane gas, and sat down to start my charting.

Once the surgery was underway, Eve came in and murmured into my ear that there might be a delay before we could start the next case.

"Great, I can get lunch," I answered.

"There's a bed shortage. They are trying to see if there is anyone they can discharge," Eve continued. Demand often outstrips supply with free universal health care.

"What about euthanizing a few?" I suggested.

"Got anybody in mind?" Eve asked.

"No, just whoever is oldest."

"Phew! That lets me off the hook. I won't tell Angelo yet. It will just upset him," Eve whispered, leaving the room.

Angelo had heard because I could see him silently fuming. His acne scars were glowing. Isaiah had left, so he had no wolf pack to commiserate with.

"I don't use this suture anymore," he said to Kris who was scrubbed, slapping his needle driver down onto the metal table. "I asked you to change my card last week. Am I speaking slowly enough for you? They could hire another nurse with the money you waste."

"You have to be nice to me," Kris replied.

"Why should I?" he demanded.

"Because Jesus loves you," I said.

Angelo was dumbstruck for a moment. I didn't know if he was religious, but it seemed so. I noticed him poking around, taking longer than usual. He seemed to be exploring, but not repairing anything.

"We need a special code of conduct for the operating room," Angelo said. "The O.R. is different. We tell off-colour, racist jokes. We use profanity. We have a different culture."

"We don't really like that," Kris said.

"I expect a lot of myself, so I expect a lot from you. It's all done in the interest of good patient care. You learn if you get slammed occasionally. We need a different code of conduct."

"No hernia?" I asked.

"No, I don't think so."

It was not uncommon for Angelo to operate on healthy people and find nothing. They say there is nothing more dangerous than a surgeon with unfilled time in his operating schedule. He was a good technical surgeon. The family doctors didn't refer to him much though, since he had had a public shouting match with one of their colleagues. This was in a hospital hallway over the appropriateness of a referral. I had heard that Angelo had to attend anger management classes.

"So, you are done then?" I asked.

"No. I think the lump I was feeling is actually a lymph node. I'm going to take it out and send it for pathology."

"I guess you heard there might be a delay before you can start your next case—until they can find a bed." We had physical beds on closed wards, but no money to staff them.

Angelo didn't answer, but Kris said, "I have an air mattress in the trunk of my car we could use."

"Anybody have a couple of lawn chairs we could put together?" I said.

"This administration is incompetent!" Angelo exploded. "It's the only department that's growing. They close beds and hire administrators. They need more and more administrators to manage fewer and fewer beds. They attend meetings and parade around in their party clothes. They babble about stakeholders and clients. We look after fucking patients, not clients!"

"Tell us how you really feel, Angelo." I had listened to the "Gospel According to Angelo" many times over the years.

"I should have gone to the States when I had the chance. They look for ways to do more cases there. They beg you to do more. Surgeons are revered because they bring work to the hospital. They bring in all the staff for you at a moment's notice. The ideal Canadian hospital does no surgery and the administration talks about all the money they saved."

"Sounds like you really should have gone to the States, where men with stethoscopes can steal more money than men with guns. They are looking for upstanding fellows such as yourself who would be pleased to garnishee Tiny Tim's crutches." I felt safe enough speaking my mind. He knew the legal ramifications of physically assaulting me. Anyway, it would be boxer versus bluster.

"Up yours. You are part of the fucking problem. You're always 'Korking' around, looking for ways to 'Kork up' and hold up my cases."

"That's all right. You have Tourette's."

"Fuck you."

The anger management classes hadn't worked. The lymph node attached to a clamp landed with a loud clank in the scrub nurse's kidney basin. One of the orderlies took it up to the pathology department for fixation, sectioning and microscopic examination. With the speed at which pathologists worked, the result would be available in a few weeks. I was envious whenever I saw pathologists chatting at their table in the cafeteria or out jogging on their lunch hour or lounging in the doctors' lounge.

I didn't hear the result until April, one month later. I had last choice of surgical lists again and found myself working with Angelo. He told me the diagnosis in the operating room. James had lymphoma—cancer of the lymph glands. This was not a death sentence. In fact, some types of lymphoma are completely curable with chemotherapy and radiation. James was going to be treated in Toronto and would probably do well.

"He asked me if I knew where you lived, so I told him," Angelo said in passing.

"You gave him my address?" There was an unwritten law prohibiting this. No doctor wanted uninvited visits from his patients after hours. He probably wasn't serious.

"Drew him a map on the back of an envelope. And your home telephone. I had to get it from the woman at switchboard. What? Did I do wrong? I thought he might want to give you a cheap bottle of wine for your shitty anesthetic."

"You shouldn't have done that."

"Why not? Also, the cell number of who to notify in case of emergency. That would be your wife, wouldn't it?"

"Because now I might have to kill you."

"How are you going to do that, tough guy?"

"I'll think of a special way for you."

As I was packing up at the end of the day, the phone rang in the operating room. I picked up and was surprised to hear my old friend Luke's voice. Being an operating room nurse, he knew enough hospital jargon to get his call routed through. Luke asked how I was and how was Katya. He inquired about Michael. I said everyone was well and what about everyone on his side, forgetting that he had recently traded his wife for a younger model. He said they were well too.

Luke told me that he was having some interpersonal grief at work. He had called me at the hospital so there was some urgency. He must have already tried me at home and didn't have my newest cell number. Luke asked if I could check into whether we had any vacancies in our operating room. It would be like old times. He added that he wouldn't embarrass me.

He had read my mind. I said that we were fully staffed and that part-timers at our place were looking for more hours. This was true, but I intended to put him off. He was my friend, but I didn't want to be stuck defending him when he inevitably provoked a fight with one of our big ego surgeons. Luke said that that was fine. Things weren't that bad. He was just inquiring out of interest.

I drove home again wondering whether I had done the right thing, and whether I would ever see James again in this life. A few green shoots with purple flowers at the tips were just poking their heads out of the soil in my front garden. Life is a precious and precarious thing. It can be interrupted for any number of trivial and incomprehensible reasons. Easter weekend was coming up. Perhaps James would be all right. His middle name was Jesus, and Christians believe Jesus was resurrected on the third day. Jeremiah Chang, who is no fool, also believes resurrection is possible.

I noticed that there was a page-long Easter prayer on our kitchen counter. It detailed an Easter blessing for each individual room of the house. Grampa must have brought that home from church. I saw him consulting it several times over the next few days. Finishing all the blessings could take a significant chunk of your time if you had a big house. I wondered how long a blessing was good for and when you had to start re-blessing.

"I have to have all my students dip their hands into a basin of holy water in class tomorrow," Katya said over a cup of tea.

"Sort of a team building exercise?" I asked.

"No. It's because of Easter. Easter is bigger than Christmas for Catholics. The school board administration came up with a new directive for us to follow."

"Are you cleared to recite incantations as they're dipping?"

"No. It's going to feel awkward," Katya said. "We've never had to do this before."

"Have them recite the alphabet backwards as they are doing it to increase the mystic power."

"The church is making a little progress. It is softening its stand toward homosexuals. Homosexuals are welcome if they don't engage in homosexual acts."

"That's funny because a large minority of priests are reputedly gay. It seems the Catholic Church is against cork-soaking, not cork-soakers." Katya didn't respond to this vulgarity. I found it clever, but then I remembered I had stolen it from Angelo who had stolen it from Isaiah. Pack mentality is seductive.

A small plastic bottle labelled "Holy Water" had arrived on the kitchen window ledge. It was another proof of Grampa's faithful church attendance. Over time this bottle was shifted along the ledge, so that it eventually ended up behind the curtain. Neither Katya nor I was brave enough to throw it out because of the potential for bad mojo.

Chapter 15

I walked through the doctors' parking lot toward the front entrance of the hospital, past the bundled up double lower limb amputee smokers in their wheel chairs. Smoking was not allowed on hospital property, but they still parked themselves just outside the automatic double doors. I passed the last one in the row, holding a cigarette to his tracheostomy stoma and he gave me a wink. For a split second, I registered a spent version of Luke. Entering the lobby, I noticed the coffee shop was bustling.

I was on my way to medical grand rounds before starting in the O.R. Grand rounds are usually only held in teaching hospitals. They are one of the nicer things about working at Coventry Hospital. Once weekly, from September to May most work stops, and nurses and doctors regardless of their specialty attend a one-hour lecture on a medical topic. The sessions are social as well as educational and a break from the regular routine. Some of our surgeons object because they would rather be working and making money, and these surgeons boycott.

A drug company often paid an outside speaker's honorarium and provided coffee and muffins. The speaker was not allowed to endorse any product directly, but might mention the sponsor's product in passing, as though incidentally. The sponsor was given the privilege of setting up a small display table at the back of the room and smiling engagingly at the doctors as they came in. I entered from the back after the talk had begun and scanned for a free seat. The drug company representative, who was blocking my path to the coffee and muffins, extended his hand for a heartfelt shake.

I found a seat beside Jeremiah Chang. I once asked him whether his parents had in fact named him Jeremiah. He smiled and said he chose the name himself when he came to Canada to attend university, because it sounded nice. He also has a Chinese first name, which I forgot right after he told me. He came to Coventry to practice because unlike most small cities, it has a Buddhist meditation centre.

"This will be quite interesting," he whispered. "I know these speakers."

The topic for today was antenatal screening for congenital disease. The talk was being presented jointly by an obstetrician and a geneticist from Toronto. A lot of the talk seemed to be focused on antenatal detection of Down's syndrome. The speakers were elaborating on a myriad of tests that were completely new to me. As I walked out of the meeting, I found myself shuffling lockstep toward the exit with Mark Vandermeer.

Mark is a large pear-shaped hirsute man. He has thick, black plastic framed glasses to correct his myopia. He smiled at me in recognition. I was collecting smiles today. Mark asked what I thought of the talk.

"I thought it was good."

He hesitated a moment and then said: "You know, the underlying assumption in what they talked about is that antenatal screening is useful for detecting fetuses that should be aborted. They never considered that these babies have a right to life. Some of the happiest people I know have Down's syndrome."

I knew that Mark held Christian fundamentalist beliefs, but I could forgive this. I had attended Baptist Sunday School as a child.

He was shy and a little socially awkward, but with undeniable integrity. I was empathetic toward him because I imagined that we shared not having been in the in-crowd growing up. He was an easy target for some of the other less enlightened members of the medical staff. By this, I mean surgeons.

"Well, it wasn't only about Down's syndrome. There have been a lot of advances in antenatal screening."

"Tell me, Matthew, what would you do if you knew your wife were carrying a Down's child?"

"I would want an abortion," I answered without hesitation. I didn't mind provoking Mark. Christians have to turn the other cheek.

"Do you really mean that?" he asked sternly.

I knew he thought that this was tantamount to murder.

"Yes."

"You know, Matthew, there is a book I would like you to read. It's only a pamphlet really. Can I leave it in your mail slot and get your thoughts on it later?"

"Sure." I still felt grateful to Mark for having gotten out of bed to see the patient I had called him about as a coroner.

Jeremiah was waiting in the hallway for a patient to arrive from another hospital. As usual, he seemed to have plenty of time to talk. Inspired by my interaction with Mark, I asked him what it was that Buddhists actually believed. I knew that Buddhists were supposed to be non-violent and didn't believe in a creator God, attributes with which I could sympathize.

He appeared reluctant, but when pressed, told me that there were five realms, four noble truths, four immeasurables and a noble eight-fold path. It sounded like complete made-up bullshit. This didn't detract from its optimism or his sincerity.

"Religions try to explain the origins of what we see around us—earth, sky, fire, water, life," Jeremiah continued. He extended a card inviting me to attend a Buddhist prayer meeting.

I hesitated to accept it. "Homer Simpson holds that they were just a bunch of things that happened. The simplest explanation is often the correct one."

"Homer Simpson is a very poor role model."

"If I had to choose a religion, I think Buddhists or Bahais might be the most logically consistent. Buddhists don't acknowledge God and Bahais magnanimously say all religions have the same one."

"There are differences, but all religions teach morality and we can learn from each other. We could offer you more lenient terms."

I accepted the card without intending to go. I didn't mind debating one on one, but didn't cherish the prospect of being the sole reincarnation denier in a roomful of disciples radiating inner peace. Jeremiah doesn't proselytize, but occasionally invites me to attend something. He holds out hope for me.

Discussing moral or philosophical issues makes you interesting to religious folk. They think that your soul is up for grabs. I'm not an easy mark for suburban missionaries leaning on my doorbell. I used to try to antagonize and confuse them, but less so now. They are just fellow travellers who have opted for the easy road. I subscribe to the standard moral codes. I don't regard them as absolutes. They don't survive emergencies.

I made my way to the operating room to start the day's work. My first patient was lying on a stretcher in the waiting area with his wife. He was having a total knee replacement because his knee was old, arthritic and worn out. The government had been rewarding hospitals for doing this procedure, so we did them a lot. Seniors have numbers and political clout. His name was flagged on the operating list.

I introduced myself and said I was going to read through his chart and then chat with him about the anesthetic.

"I won't accept any blood," he said before I had quite finished speaking.

"Are you a Jehovah's Witness?"

"Yes."

"We never need blood for this operation. It's done with a thigh tourniquet. What exactly does no blood mean?"

"No blood or products made from blood. I will accept substitutes."

"There aren't any. We won't need blood."

"Okay."

The orthopedic surgeon Josh Smith sauntered over, dressed in faded track pants and a T-shirt with a beer company logo. This was reverse chauvinism. He didn't have to dress up to prove his importance. He nodded to me, said hello to the patient and without further ado drew a giant black arrow on the operative leg with a felt pen. Operations done on the wrong side have been known to happen. He scrawled his own very large initials underneath and went off to change into greens.

I finished my questionnaire and told the patient what to expect. "The commonest anesthetic for this operation is a spinal. There is less pain afterward. I insert a needle between the bones of your lower back, near the waistline. Both of your legs will be frozen. You're going to hear some sounds, like in a dentist's office—some drilling, some hammering, loud rock 'n roll music, maybe some swearing."

He didn't laugh. "You can have sedation and ear muffs if you like," I said in consolation.

I wheeled him toward our operating room. The tunes were blasting joyously out from under the door. The orthopedic room is a happy room to work in. Orthopods enjoy their jobs. They are well paid. There are few diagnostic dilemmas. They do a lot of good. I looked forward to my days there.

Josh was waiting inside. The music was deafening now. He liked the volume on grampa max. I liked the festive atmosphere, but looking at the patient, I wasn't sure he did. This patient wanted to be asleep. I injected the induction agents into his intravenous and inserted a breathing tube into his windpipe.

"Yuk. I got some of his goober on my hand." Sara, who was assisting me, wiped a hanging teardrop of phlegm from her pinky.

"He's a Jehovah's Witness. Now you'll have to marry him," I said. "You'll have to tell his wife."

"Oh, I know. I saw them out in the waiting area."

"What do you mean?" I asked.

"They were holding hands and praying before you arrived. They had their minister with them."

"I guess they don't trust us."

"Did you see the Medical Directive for Blood Products form on the chart? They wrote 'NO BLOOD OR BLOOD PRODUCTS' in bright red capitals across the top. It's already written on the form."

"We never need blood for this operation," Josh said.

"Did they sign in blood though?" I said. "It would be funny if I found the wife after the surgery and told her, 'Listen, I forgot what you said for a moment about the blood. No doesn't always mean no, does it? I may have given him a couple of units, just to top him up a bit."

The orthopedic equipment company representative who had the contract for our hospital, Dave, was standing in the corner of the O.R. I knew him well because he played hockey with the doctors. Equipment reps are often hired for their golf and hockey prowess. He was a superb hockey player who knew to pass the puck when he should shoot. He was a nice polite man who might at some point have had dreams of attending medical school.

Dave came to the O.R. on most orthopedic days. He restocked our joint replacement supplies and offered token advice, which we didn't need since we had been using his products for three years. He paid for golf games and free trips to conferences for Josh, which was folded into the price. He was primarily here to protect his turf from any rival company reps.

"Did you go to grand rounds this morning?" I asked Josh.

"No," he laughed. "I only go to talks about bones. Did they say anything about bones?"

"No."

"That's why I didn't go."

"Are you ignorant or apathetic?" I asked. This was an oft-repeated setup line.

"I don't know, and I don't care," he said happily. "I do know some cardiology though, Matt."

"Go ahead," I said.

"The heart is the organ that pumps antibiotics to the bone."

"What would you do if a Jehovah's Witness was bleeding to death?" Sara asked.

"If it was a child, I would transfuse and take my lumps. If it was an adult, I guess I would let them die."

"If you said God told you to give blood, I would say I heard it too."

"I'm not willing to do jail time. If it was a child, I think the jury would be more lenient."

"They can't die in my operating room," Josh said. "I would sew up really fast so they could do their dying somewhere else." An hour later, Josh was sewing up.

"Perfect!" Like the creator on the sixth day, he had gazed upon his work and seen that it was very good. He was good at his job. He got a lot of practice. There was a never-ending supply of seniors.

"Can I buy you something for lunch today, Josh?" Dave asked.

"Sure—the usual. Good game everyone," Josh said.

"Thanks," everyone echoed.

"Let's give ourselves a round of applause," I said. To my surprise, everyone in the room began to clap. We had a collective appreciation for the absurd.

"Can I pat all the nurses on the bum as long as I say, 'good game'?" Josh asked cordially. No one objected to the suggestion.

I delivered the patient to the care of the recovery room nurses and reported that he didn't want any of their stinking blood products. I went back later to check how he was doing. He was looking sore, but extremely relieved. He didn't thank me, since it wasn't up to me. It was God who had spared him.

"Can I send you some publications written by our experts, Doctor?" he moaned through his drug haze.

"Do you mean The Watchtower?"

"There are articles and stories that show why God prohibits blood transfusions," he groaned. "There are strategies to conserve blood and information about alternate fluids you can use."

"Does the Bible actually say that blood transfusions are prohibited?"

"Blood represents life. Only God is authorized to give life. We are not allowed blood in any form."

"Are you allowed to eat meat?"

"Yes."

"Some of the pink fluid draining from a steak may be residual blood."

"God gave us animals to use as food."

"Can you perform combat duties in the military?"

"No."

"I guess asking you to murder my wife's lover is out of the question then."

"Yes." His expression didn't change.

"Good to know... Just kidding."

No response.

I wished him well. Jehovah's Witnesses were smart enough to have avoided the transfusion related AIDS and hepatitis C epidemics. Their morality was too inflexible though, bordering self-destructive. Jeremiah's and Mark's might be more flexible when it came to preserving the sanctity of a family unit.

Chapter 16

A booklet entitled Stones and Bones was waiting for me in my mail slot at the hospital the next day. It was authored by a "creation scientist," to rebut the other kind. There was a sticky note on the cover from Mark Vandermeer that read, "Let me know your thoughts."

I cracked it open during a long O.R. case. It had nothing to do with our conversation about right to life. Chapter one began at the beginning with a discussion of the origins of life, the universe and everything. God created species individually according to a literal Old Testament interpretation.

"Raise the bed please."

I looked over at the surgeon's progress. It was slow going.

...Mutation and natural selection could only result in loss of genetic information—incorrect premise. *Extrapolation backwards in time would reveal only more complex organisms. Complex organisms require a creator. The great flood drowned all creatures on earth. It was so cataclysmic and rapid that fossilized fish showed no signs of predation.* Flooding killed fish.

I wondered why Mark would think this was relevant to our talk, and then I understood. He believed Christian doctrine had to be accepted all or none. Mark was targeting me for full conversion and baptism.

The pamphlet ended with a Biblical quote warning of the wrath of God toward non-believers. There was advice to consult the Bible to see what form of vengeance God would seek. The implication was that Old Testament God, who drowned the population of the earth (not New Testament God, who forgave and rehabilitated sinners), would deal with heretics. It was stick, not carrot. Convert or else.

I didn't see Mark again for some weeks. We met by accident as we were passing through the doctors' lounge to collect our mail. We shifted around each other, awkwardly reaching for our respective mail slots, each considering whether we had time to engage. Philosophical disagreements can't usually be settled in time for the first morning appointment.

"I had a look at the booklet you left me. I put it back in your mail slot," I began.

"What did you think of it?"

"I left you some comments. I think it doesn't square well with mainstream science or fossil evidence."

"Is it possible your ideas are inspired by blind belief in scientific orthodoxy? Fossils do not themselves contain isotopes that can be dated by radiometric techniques. They are dated by their location next to rock strata that have been churned up. Religion and science aren't mutually exclusive. It is our job to figure out how to reconcile them." Mark had come prepared.

"I come from a value system that isn't religious based. If you think that fossils are incorrectly dated because of being next to the wrong churned up rocks, what about the rocks themselves? The earliest rocks are billions of years old. That should be long enough for mutation and natural selection of the strongest and smartest amoebae to make monkeys."

"You don't know that. How long would it take for a monkey to accidentally type a Shakespearean play?" Fundamentalists dislike fuzzy thinking as much as skeptics.

"The evidence seems compelling to me, unless the devil has placed false dinosaur bone clues."

"That's possible of course."

I saw an opportunity. "If you choose to believe that, then you don't need to counter scientific theories of creation with creation science. Invocation of demons or deities can explain anything. Natural selection occurs when the strong devour the weak. They do this because they are hungry, not because the devil inspired immorality." Mark's king was in check.

"The reason for ugliness and suffering in the world is Adam and Eve's disobedience, or original sin. Morality is a gift from God."

"Moral codes evolve. Original sin consisted of Eve taking a bite of forbidden fruit, which sounds minor and also very allegorical, snakes being metaphorical penises. The Old Testament God killed a lot of people—Philistines and such. God was taking vengeance on Adam's descendants. New Testament morality is different."

"We should accept the Bible in its entirety as a divine document and its teachings as a matter of faith. Not everything that is true can be directly experienced or tested. God's intellect is greater than ours. If God allows fetal anomalies, it is not our place to interfere with his will. Do you believe in the sanctity of life, Matthew?"

I decided it was time to wrap this up. "I don't know the answer. Is it murder to flush sperm down the toilet after you masturbate?"

A red flash of disappointment shot from his eyes.

"What if the devil seduced your wife and she was taking all eleven children to be with him? Would you use lethal force against him?"

"She would never do that."

"What if his personification were raping her?"

118

"Don't be ridiculous. The devil doesn't take that form anymore."

Of course Mark would and the devil might. We were done. We had debated religion and morality to an uncomfortable stalemate. I was breaking my rule, but Mark is more competent than the standard Saturday morning missionary. Is killing justified if it is well earned? The question is an important one. Countries with militaries subscribe to yes. The Bible is inconsistent. Fundamentalist Christians in past centuries found loopholes in the "Thou shalt not kill" commandment. "Vengeance is mine," Deuteronomy 32 and 35, is a useful mantra for agents of the Lord and others.

I like Mark. I didn't wish to undermine the faith that gave structure and comfort to his life. If I did, it was only a little. Mark is a happier, more optimistic person than I am. His life path has been set out for him by Jesus of Nazareth. He doesn't suffer from moral uncertainty. I think he decided there was no hope for me.

James Jesus reappeared unto me of an evening in early May at the Rec Complex. The devil sent him to undermine the structure and comfort of my life. James wasn't strong enough to devour me outright, but he was hungry and thirsty. I heard his mellow voice across the change room: "How about a burger and that beer you keep promising me, Matt?"

At the time, I was glad to see him, relieved that he was all right. He looked perfectly well. If his chemotherapy had caused his hair to fall out, it had all grown back.

"Well, tonight doesn't really work, but tell me, how is your health?"

"Good. I guess you heard I went to Toronto for some treatments."

"Were they rough on you?"

"Yes, but they say I'm probably cured."

"And how did your TV thing turn out?"

"Great!" he said, breaking into a broad grin. "I'm going to be on TV next month on the 'Home and Garden' channel. It will be on four consecutive Fridays. I'm going to be part of a panel of experts appraising and bidding on decorating jobs."

"I'm going to tune in for sure." I felt happy for him. He was on the road to becoming a TV celebrity.

"Come out for a beer and I'll tell you the details."

"No, I really can't tonight. I'll take a rain cheque though."

I wasn't in a hurry to take him up on his offer. I wasn't sure how I felt about it. Katya was at her book club, so I could have gone. He seemed a little needy. It might be uncomfortable talking about his illness when I wasn't really an expert on lymphoma. He seemed to think that we were blood brothers because I had given him an anesthetic. I was on call again in the morning, so I needed an early night to be alert. I had had my déjà vu of him with my wife.

I went up to the gym to lift weights for a few minutes before leaving. If I am physically tired, I fall asleep faster. Branko Markovic was across the room. He was a Coventry police detective whom I had met at some coroner calls. I was doing leg presses when he materialized beside me, jarring me from my reverie.

"Hey Matt."

"Hey Branko. Arrest any evil-doers lately?"

"All the time. You missed a good case last week. Were you away?"

"No. Maybe I was on call at the hospital. What was it?"

He paused before answering. It wasn't strictly professional to gossip, but we were in the same line of work and this could be considered educational, if you stretched the definition. "We couldn't find a coroner to answer the call. The regional supervisor had to do it over the phone. It was a guy paying by the minute for live sex on the internet—naked of course. Why are they always naked?"

"What's this world coming to?"

"I don't know."

"I had one like that. He was 400 pounds and covered with pop-corn and potato chips, but it was only an extra-hairy porno DVD."

"My guy was skinny," Branko said. "I had a really big girl last summer who checked herself into the Holiday Inn and put a 'Do Not Disturb' sign on the door so she could eat herself to death. The room was littered with candy wrappers. You know those chocolate cookies with marshmallow on the inside? I can never look at them again in the same way."

"Men like salty. Women prefer sweet."

"They need a dose of religion."

"What did the Regional do with the case last week?" I asked.

"He called it a heart attack. He found a family doctor to fill out the Death Certificate. I tell myself no matter how bad things get, at least I'm not *that* fucked up."

Branko drifted away. It wasn't my fault if the supervisor was forced to do a case because no coroner would respond. We had no call schedule. I signed out whenever I was on call at the hospital. The other two coroners were either away or wouldn't pick up the phone. It was a systemic problem in smaller locales. It was embarrassing though. I finished up at the gym and went home.

I checked my email as a last thing before going to bed. I was surprised to see one from Luke. It read, "Hey, what's up Mutt?" and that was all. I responded with a paragraph of pleasantries and was about to turn the computer off when his response came right back.

"Hey that's great. I'm keeping busy too. Had a few too many beers tonight, at least that's what my girlfriend says. Been doing that a bit too much lately. I guess no one likes alcoholics with drinking problems. Just going out for a few more. See ya."

I knew Luke wasn't an alcoholic. If he had become one, I knew that no one can stop an alcoholic from drinking until he wants to. I wrote back, "So what. You could quit if you wanted. Should get to-gether at your convenience, if you're not too drunk, weather permitting."

121

Katya was still out socializing with her book club friends when I went to bed. I needed to sleep well that night for the bleeding and screaming that goes with being on call and covering the operating and labour rooms. I slept in the guest room, so she wouldn't wake me when she came in. I made a mental note to watch James' television program, but preferably without Katya. Her next book club would be on a Friday in a month.

Chapter 17

A lot of Coventry doctors play hockey in winter and golf in summer. Since we are Canadian, we also play hockey during the two intervening seasons. This happens on Wednesday afternoons. We down tools and gather at the Coventry arena at 3 p.m. A similar ritual probably occurs in most Canadian cities where patriotic doctors ply their trade.

I thought that each year playing hockey might be my last. My legs were beginning to scrabble on the ice, like a dog on linoleum. But, there is nothing like hockey for experiencing the illusion of speed and freedom, and the dressing room camaraderie gave me a tribe. The game was strictly non-contact, but that didn't rule out incidental contact. Despite wearing equipment like a spaceman, every year somebody broke something.

It was the end of April and the last day of the season. I needed to get an operating list that would be done by 2:30 p.m. in order to get there on time. That meant choosing Angelo Amodeo's unhappy room since he also played and had booked a short list. I packed a bag lunch, so I wouldn't lose time buying one and arrived at work early. When I saw Angelo in the change room in the morning, I told him to hurry up and get into his "pyjamies," meaning scrub suit, so we could get going. Today, it was in my interest to expedite the list.

Angelo had a resident, a junior doctor training to be a general surgeon, assisting him. Residents were expected to work like dogs and in dog-like manner be obsequious, fawning and thankful. They depended on the goodwill of surgeons to be allowed to do more and more of the cutting. Until a resident was ready for additional responsibility, he or she would only be allowed to hold retractors and then sew up the wound at the end of an operation. I didn't especially like this development because having a resident would slow us down.

Angelo was only in his forties, but he was playing the role of stern, wise father-mentor. In fact, on one occasion he actually called the resident son, although their age difference was not more than ten years. Angelo was letting him do most of the first case, probably to annoy me. When the resident thanked Joanie, the scrub nurse, for handing him a suture, Angelo corrected him. "You shouldn't thank her. It's her job."

"Yeah, I remember back in the day when I was a resident," Angelo said. "We were on call one in two. We got up at five, if we got to bed at all, so we could round on our patients and get to the O.R. by seven thirty. It was good because when we woke them up, they were too groggy to remember the questions they wanted to ask. They could squeak in maybe one question before we were out the door and it couldn't be, 'Can I have more questions?' If they were slow to wake up, we would write, 'Resting comfortably, no voiced complaints' in their charts."

"Good one, sir," the resident said. "The problem with being on call every second night is that you miss half the good cases."

Toward the middle of the operation, Angelo took over. Whenever he pinched a bleeding point with forceps, he said, "Burn," and the resident would touch his forceps with cautery. This would pass an electric current to the tip of the forceps and coagulate whatever blood vessel was being pinched. Smoke would rise, and Angelo would say,

"Fire in the hole!" mimicking Hollywood military parlance for when a grenade is dropped into a bunker.

We were all expected to laugh. I had heard it too many times before. "Is that what your wife says when she visits the free clinic?"

I was undermining his god-like authority. He ignored me as if he hadn't heard, or I was too inconsequential to make a response. It was probably over the line, but I was annoyed that he was going to make us miss hockey. Luckily, one of Angelo's patients didn't show up and we did finish on time. I flung off my O.R. garb and rushed into the beautiful sunny day waiting outside.

The hockey change room was crowded with doctors and drug reps of all descriptions. The reps came as friends in blurry quotation marks. They never mentioned their products, but one would not refuse a friend an audience if he showed up later at your place of business pitching something.

"Hey Matt, there's room for your boney ass here," Josh called, shifting over and patting the bench beside him.

"You've got a nice ass too, Josh."

"Come on over and woo me. Spring is in the air. Last ice of the year."

I squeezed in beside him. "Fewer old ladies slipping and falling will hurt your practice, won't it?"

"I'll stand outside and trip them as they leave church."

From across the room, I heard Angelo saying, "Scored so many goals last week that I went home and did my old lady."

"By old lady, he means his right hand," I murmured.

"If he said 'my sweet young thang,' that would mean his left hand, 'cause she does it different,' " Josh replied.

After a warm-up, we split up randomly into two teams, trying to keep the skill level roughly balanced. I stayed on the ice to be in the starting lineup. Josh had taken the flashy centre forward position for our side. He was the best player on the ice. Most orthopods are naturally gifted athletes. Simon, the family doctor from England, skated around on his ankles. Adam, the Bajan gynecologist, was built for speed but couldn't skate at all, so he was in goal. I was playing defence in front of him. I skated over to whack his pads with my stick for luck.

"One love," he said.

"One love," I said back.

A few minutes into the game, I was looking down at the puck between my feet, trying to kick it up to my stick. I stared at it a little too long because abruptly I felt a heavy blow to the side of my head. Like a sack of manure, I went down and stayed down. I didn't pass out, but lay on the ice with a hand on either side of my helmet, stabilizing my head in case my neck was broken. I cautiously tried moving my legs. They seemed still to be working.

A crowd gathered around me. "Are you okay? Do you need help getting up?" I was a battlefield casualty who was holding up play.

When I had lain there long enough, I got up under my own power and limped back to the players' bench. I sat at the end and held my head some more, passing on my turn to play each time it came around. Josh came off the ice and sat beside me.

"Nice goal," I said.

"It's a team sport. I wanna thank my lord and saviour."

I didn't respond or look up.

"Maybe you should go home and live to fight another day," he said.

"I'm just waiting to see if I lose consciousness."

"If you can wait until the end of the game, I'll give you a lift home or alternatively to the hospital if your condition deteriorates sufficiently."

"Thanks. That's kind of you. I think I'm okay to drive now." I didn't want to strand my car.

"Somebody might be able to bring your car home."

"That would be a lot of trouble. Did you see who hit me?"

"Not sure, but it might have been Angelo. Someone built up momentum from the opposite side of the rink and put his shoulder into the side of your head."

As I got up, Josh smiled. "It's too bad it's not your leg. I can make lame people walk again." It was probably funny, but I was too perturbed to reply.

I skated past the opposing players' bench, scrutinizing the faces to see who looked guilty. I recognized Dr. Cesar De Santos De Dios. His name was his alibi. He could barely skate anyway. He was sitting beside Jonathan, a urologist. Jonathan was a really good player, but it wasn't him. We had a bond of trust because we played as defence partners at tournaments. He was sitting beside Kristiaan, the O.R. nurse. He met my gaze sympathetically. That excluded him.

I continued my slow skate back to the dressing room. Jeremiah Chang, the Buddhist pediatrician, who was in net for the opposing team, made a good save. Mark Vandermeer, the fecund family doctor, was playing solid defence in front of him. I didn't think it was him. I didn't exclude him entirely, but it was more likely to have been a forward. Angelo Amodeo was on the ice, but didn't look my way. I opened the gate and trudged down the concrete corridor, my clacking skate blades echoing under the overhead pipes and bare electric bulbs.

As I was changing back into my street clothes, I noticed that my teeth didn't mesh any more. I had blenderized bananas for supper and decided to go to the emergency department early the next morning to see if my jaw was broken or dislocated. The emergency department would be too busy in the evening, since it was Wednesday, and all the family doctors' offices had been closed that afternoon.

In the morning, the emergency clerk recognized me as she created my chart. I had a seat in the waiting room and after a few minutes she apologized for the wait. After half an hour, I had had enough of egalitarianism and wondered through the double doors to the nursing station inside.

"Are you very busy today? Who's covering 'emerge' today?" I asked the nurse conversationally.

"Yeah, really busy. We just had two ambulances pull in. Dr. Grigoriev is in with one of them."

"Okay, I'll go to another hospital then," I said. The closest would have been a forty-minute drive. I was serious, but the wait elsewhere would probably have been worse.

"No, don't do that. Have a seat in there," she said, indicating an examination room.

Thirty seconds later, Dr. Grigoriev was by my side, smiling like a good comrade. He extended his hand. I offered him a fist bump. "I'm afraid to think where your hands have been."

"Yeah," he laughed, making a fist. "Yours too."

"I heard two ambulances just pulled in."

"Oh well. That's pretty much always the case. What's up?"

"I got hit playing hockey and my teeth don't mesh any more. Could I get a Panorax?" This was an X-ray that displayed the whole jaw as if splayed and flattened into two dimensions.

He examined me. "There's no deformity. We don't have a Panorax machine."

"Could I get an MRI?" This was a magnetic resonance imaging examination for which there was a months-long wait list. There was no radiation associated with an MRI as opposed to the significant dose delivered with a CT scan, which would have been my alternative. You get the answer, but you get cancer.

"I don't think I can order that. I'll just sign an X-ray requisition and you fill out whatever you want."

I wandered over to the radiology department and found the radiologist who was the sub-specialist in MRI. I briefly explained my symptoms. "What diagnostic imaging test would you recommend?"

128

"MRI." This was the response I was looking for. He made a phone call and said, "How about next Wednesday?"

"I can't eat. I was hoping for today. If my jaw is subluxed or dislocated, I would like to get it put back."

He made another phone call. "How about half an hour?"

"That's great. Thanks." I didn't know whom they had to inconvenience to arrange this, and I didn't care. My needs trumped theirs. This sort of service was a perk of the job.

I used the half hour to call an oral surgeon, a specialized dentist, who used to work at our hospital. He retired early after a teenager suffered an anaphylactic drug reaction and died in his office operatory. This sort of career ending calamity was also an occupational hazard for anesthesiologists.

After offering condolences, I selfishly brought the conversation back to me. "My teeth don't mesh. My front incisors butt when I close."

"Did you get hit sideways, low on your chin?" His voice sounded different, aged and feeble.

"Probably."

"It could be a fracture of the coronoid process of the mandible, but it's probably just swelling. It should be better in a week."

I felt guilty bothering him because I hadn't called him when his name was in the newspaper day after day. I resolved to buy him a nice bottle of wine. Then I thought I had better not. If he had sought solace in alcohol, a pound of expensive coffee would be better. It would be a bother to do it if he lived out of town. I would have to find out where he lived.

After a few minutes in the MRI waiting room, the technician escorted me in, leaving the others in the room to use it for its intended purpose. The examination involved being in a narrow tube with earmuffs to dampen the thirty minutes of metal-on-metal banging noises.

I returned to the radiologist's office and lingered in the doorway for the moment it took him to notice me.

"This is really interesting," he said. "You've got an undisplaced fracture of the coronoid process of the mandible. You've probably also got a crack in the posterior maxillary sinus to go with it."

After seeing a maxillofacial surgeon that afternoon, I opted for conservative treatment, which meant a longer period of sucking nutritional shakes through straws to avoid surgery. I asked him whether he was able see any brain swelling on my MRI. He said they didn't take pictures of that and advised against more blows to the head.

Angelo never mentioned the incident, so I decided not to either. Knowing him, I didn't expect anything else. Everyone I spoke with said it looked like an accident. I doubted that. I would have to keep my head up better. Next time, it might be his car. My jaw was not quite right in the mornings because my face swelled lying flat. It was okay by the afternoon. Hockey season was over, and I would have a four-month break.

Katya asked if I wasn't ashamed using my connections to get faster service, what with my proletarian roots and working-class values. It is true that I have some of those. I said it didn't bother me. Retail clerks get ten per cent off things they buy at work. You can't be too ideological. You have to do whatever is necessary in the jungle. I had to get back in fighting shape for my next round with Angelo.

Chapter 18

In southern Ontario, winter can do a sudden frog leap into summer without much intervening spring. April could be cool, and May hot and humid. Weather patterns were definitely changing, and politicians were arguing about who was to blame. Many of the ducks and geese on the canal that runs through Coventry could no longer be bothered to migrate south. Evergreen trees were looking sickly. We might soon have to build a wall to keep out heat-crazed Americans.

May flowers were in flagrant premature blossom. Hockey season was over, and I needed something to look forward to. An opportunity arrived in the form of a phone call from Sean. He was my close friend and confidant in Coventry. Our two families had spent a good many school holidays together in sun or skiing destinations. He told me he had consummated a sailboat purchase. He was driving down to work on the boat.

It was 50 feet long, had cost almost 200 K and was docked in Maryland, in the U.S. of A. The price was discounted because it needed a lot of work. Sean was retiring from teaching. He had spent most of the lump sum payment he was receiving. Since he was interested in sailing it in off-season for his bed and breakfast hotel and eventually making an Atlantic crossing, there was no point in bringing it back to Canada.

Road trips are manly, so I jumped at the opportunity to go along. We gassed up his truck, bought some super-sized, take-out, high-test coffee and thought up talking points for the eleven-hour ride. The dashboard radio was calling for several days of rain. I was hopeful we might catch a break and still get a day nice enough to take the boat out sailing. I didn't think seafaring was the life for me, but I was curious about fresh perspectives.

We crossed the border and drove south through upper New York State and Pennsylvania. Sean told me about his plans. The boat needed a new dodger and Bimini canvas to protect the cockpit, a working refrigerator and updated electronics. Once that was done, he planned to sail it to the Caribbean in the fall. The Atlantic crossing would follow in two to three years when his daughter, his youngest child, would be finishing high school and moving out to attend university.

The miles droned past. We had no specific idea of where we were most of the time because we let the GPS pick the route. Both Sean and I were struck by the number of nameless towns in Pennsylvania, where people like us lived in parallel universes that would never intersect ours. The complete anonymity of these places made me consider their potential as hiding spots, if a worst-case scenario came to pass. Sean agreed that many men think in this way, but hypothetically advised against looking for anything but short-term sanctuary here. An ocean-going vessel would be better.

Sean had no police record as far as I knew. Moira's brothers knew him to be a crazy koont, likely an Irish term of endearment. I knew that a few years ago, Sean and his sons had driven to Toronto armed with baseball bats and balaclavas to deliver a warning to the material contents of a college fraternity house. It was the residence of a group of older students who had been bullying his youngest son.

They must have been quite astonished. It seemed out of character, but who knows what anyone is capable of if their family is threatened.

Sean had some previous sailing experience. A few years ago, he had rented a sailboat with his two brothers and they had island hopped in the Caribbean. The fun was not risk free. The primary hazards were weather and pirates. They were chased by a speedboat piloted by two young black men demanding assistance and permission to board. The sailboat had come equipped with a loaded revolver. When Sean held this up, and his brothers held up a flare gun and a winch handle for the pirates to see, they backed off.

We changed drivers. I asked what his next move would have been if they had attempted to board. He said that there was no question he would have had to kill them. He would have shot them and dumped their bodies in the ocean. They would have been eaten by sharks. There would have been no evidence of what had transpired. No local authority would have been too bothered about looking for them in international waters. That sounded about right. Anyone who chose sailing as a retirement lifestyle would have to be prepared to make the same choice.

It rained non-stop in Maryland. Sean did what work he could. I didn't know anything about boats, so I was his gofer. We visited the tradespeople that cluster around marinas, negotiating jobs and fees— new canvas, solar panels, new refrigerator. Everything was thousands not hundreds of dollars. Sean didn't seem discouraged by the expense. It was the cost of doing business. He was buying his freedom from a purely land based existence.

We used the marina facilities and slept on board the ark, pissing into beer cups at night to avoid dirtying the holding tank. Discharging waste into the water at marinas is prohibited, but not everyone abides by rules. Sean advised me never to go swimming anywhere near a marina. I considered the comforts of living on shore as warm nocturnal urine from an overflowing cup dribbled between my fingers.

The commonest way that men are lost at sea is urinating over the side in the dark. They fall overboard when the boat takes an unexpected dip as they are leaning forward. Even if you could find your boat, the ladder would be up and there would be no way to get back on board. It would be a stupid way to die. Depending on the water temperature you would have an hour or two of regret before drowning. There is no noteworthy allowance for slip-ups in God's great plan.

The sun came out on the fourth day and brightened our spirits. We went for a short sail to test our work. It took an hour just to get the sails and ropes ready, but I could see the appeal. We drifted with the wind for a while and then motored back to our slip. L. Ron Hubbard, the founder of the Church of Scientology, eluded his persecutors for years by living on the ocean. They can't arrest you for misuse of donations if you are not in territorial waters.

When we had done what we could, we drove back largely in silence, watching the trappings of lives lived in Pennsylvania. We saw clothes flapping on lines, but no people. They were trees falling unwitnessed in a deaf forest. Behind their locked windows and doors, they were as non-existent as a dead childhood friend. If Buddhist forces had reincarnated the friend, he could be lodging here.

Sean may have been auditioning me for a possible future role in crossing the Atlantic. If that were true, he never said so. On the plus side, no-one from work would be able to call me. I don't like confinement though. Also, there was no Rec Complex on board. The options for exercise were swimming in the blended urine near marinas or offering myself up as shark bait in open water.

We arrived home late on a Friday night to an impending tropical storm. High voltage flashes intermittently seized the sky. It was a tip-off to the heat and humidity waiting outside the vehicle. Sean dropped me in my driveway just as the rain let loose. Our farewells were brief.

I turned my key in the front door unintentionally locking it, and turned it back again. Katya had forgotten to lock up again. There was no warning buzz from the burglar alarm that Katya never bothered to turn on. Her father wasn't a cop. There was a note on the kitchen table. Katya had taken her father and the dog to visit her sister in Pickering. I left the unpacking for morning and walked through a deserted house to the living room.

Flicking on the TV, I got an earful of sound, the way grampas like it. The blue glow partially illuminated the chair I sank into. I was just in time for the beginning of James' program. After watching for twenty minutes, he hadn't made an appearance. The show was getting tiresome, so I tried something else. I tuned in again a little later to hear someone say, "Oh wow! Lots of closet space," but still no James. Perhaps I had just missed him. I went upstairs to bed.

Thunder pounded above me as I lay awake trying to make my teeth fit together the way they used to. The events of the week and the conversations of the day replayed in my brain. I had been looking forward to telling Katya about my trip, but now there was no one to tell. After an hour of trying to sleep, I decided to give up. I walked to the head of the stairs in darkness and heard the wind howling. Descending two steps, I saw that the front door was half open.

I must not have shut it properly. The storm had done the rest. Nevertheless, my recollection was that the door latch had engaged and that I had turned the bolt. Freezing for a moment, I listened for any extraneous sounds. I wasn't seriously worried but thought why not make a game of it? I went back to the bedroom and into the closet. That was where I kept my father's shotgun and some shells in a canvas bag on a high shelf. I hadn't looked at it since he had given it to me as a housewarming present.

The shells plopped easily into the two barrels. I unlocked the trigger lock, pulled on my underwear from the floor beside the bed, raised the weapon waist-high and touched the safety catch, trying to remember which way was on. Walking softly back downstairs, I felt cold-wet on my bare feet. There was a rippling lake blowing across the floor. A cold spray from the doorway lightly washed my face and prickled my spine. I scanned the street from behind the door and then closed and locked it.

It crossed my mind that the snakes and skulls housebreaker from the operating room might have made bail. I gripped the shotgun harder and waved it across the living room before turning on the lights. I systematically waved the gun behind every door and through every room. I didn't know how far to carry this drama but didn't stop until I had swept the house. Nothing was missing and nothing was out of place. It wasn't entirely pantomime. My heart was racing.

I propped the shotgun in the corner of the bedroom and went back to bed. It was too late to bother with the water downstairs. It wouldn't damage ceramic tile. I thought about what I would have done with a real intruder—shout, "Get on the floor or I'll blow your head off, fucker of mothers." What if they refused? I wasn't sure I could subdue anyone with harsh words.

What if the intruder were armed? If you have a weapon, you have to be prepared to use it. What if I shot a frightened unarmed teenager? I would have to explain why I didn't take him prisoner or give him an opportunity to escape. That would be the messy and troublesome part. There would be no sharks to eat the evidence, as they do pirates.

The morning broke sunny and humid. I noticed the shotgun. This observation dredged up memories of my prancing around the house in my underwear with a gun on my hip and my heart in my mouth. I unloaded the shells and tucked them away again in the canvas bag. I pulled the trigger. The firing pin clicked. My recollection was that the safety was on, but I was wrong. I flicked it back and forth several times contemplatively.

Some of the water by the front door had evaporated overnight leaving faint outlines of footprints that looked like running shoe tread. That was odd, but they must have been there already from whenever I was out jogging last. It was a new morning and I was done with paranoia for now.

Chapter 19

Scintillating jagged lights were spreading across my field of vision from left to right eye. This was either a detaching retina, or the aura before a seizure or a migraine. Both retinas don't detach simultaneously. Brain injuries caused by mean general surgeons can lead to epilepsy though. My best guess was optical migraine, my first ever, provoked by head trauma and the Home and Garden program I was watching on television.

The phone was ringing as the symptoms were subsiding. I didn't get up until it stopped. There was a message on the answering machine. It was Katya's twin sister, Magda. Magda claims vestigial guardianship over Katya. She believes that her responsibility supersedes that of a mere husband.

"Hi Katya. I'm calling to see you got home safely. Katya, I don't remember—did I kiss you before you left because..." Her voice was warbling with emotion. I deleted the message without listening to the rest.

I saw Katya's car through the window 20 minutes later as I was consulting Dr. Google about optical migraines. She came in through the garage with her dad in tow. I went to the kitchen to greet them as they came in. Grampa brought their overnight bags into the house in a gentlemanly and protective way. I watched him closely to make sure he didn't lose his balance. Katya wanted to tell me about family-in-law news, so I let her have the floor.

"Gabriela is finished school this spring. She'll be moving back in with Magda." Gabriela was Katya's niece. Magda got possession of the four-bedroom marital home in her divorce settlement last year. Gabriela loved animals and dreamt of marrying a farmer.

"She should apply for a husband on Craig's List," I suggested.

"She is applying to agricultural college."

"What do they teach there—plantin' and harvestin', knackerin' an' loppin' off chickins' heads?"

"General farmin' an' wife-in' I think."

"We should have had a daughter. Gabriela calls her mother all the time and tells her everything. Michael would never call unless you called him first." We only had one child. It was something we both regretted.

"We're too old now."

"You could have put ribbons in her hair and taken her clothes shopping."

Katya didn't respond.

"I got you a present." I brought out a parcel wrapped in brown paper. "It's Anne of Green Gables in Polish."

"How did you know that was my favourite book as a girl? Where did you find it?"

"In a Polish bookstore in Philadelphia."

"I love it. Thank you so much."

"You're welcome. I thought because of your red hair..."

Katya put her two arms around my neck and her cheek against mine. "How was your trip?"

"Good. We organized some renovations to the boat and did some male bonding."

"Did you get out sailing?"

"Just once. The boat wasn't really ready, and it rained almost every day. Did you get a storm in Pickering last night?"

"Yes. It woke me up at Magda's house around midnight. I had a hard time falling asleep after that. I was having terrible dreams."

"I'm sorry. What were you dreaming about?"

"I don't even remember now."

"Did you remember to turn the burglar alarm on before you left?" Despite my nagging, she hadn't even remembered to lock the front door.

"I'm not sure." She stopped hugging my neck. Security wasn't her thing.

"I think you should make the effort. I know you think I'm paranoid, but your father wasn't a cop. 'Break and enters' really do happen."

"Yes... What did you do today?"

"Nothing. I answered the door to some canvassers raising money for disease of the month. I'm not really in favour of heart disease or arthritis, but I did give them a few bucks because they were neighbours who looked vaguely familiar."

Katya returned to reporting in-law news. "Kristin told me that one of the boys on her best friend's cousin's boyfriend's hockey team committed suicide after he got his exam marks back." Kristin was another one of Magda's five daughters.

"That's tragic. Did he hang himself? Men choose violent deaths."

"Yes! What kind of God would allow that to happen?"

"Bruce Almighty."

As I was saying this, the floor began to shake. This normally happened whenever I lay down for a nap on the couch. Grampa was watching the big screen television below us in the basement. He didn't know how to switch the speakers to headphone mode. I had tried teaching him, but he wasn't capable of retaining the information.

Loud reportage of ramping amplitude greeted me as I went downstairs. Grampa was a news junkie. I offered him the headphones

140

as I turned the sound off. He was holding the remote with his index finger poised in mid-air, ready to switch between broadcasts.

"Are you getting every news analyst's viewpoint of the day's stories, Grampa?" I yelled into his ear.

"You know me, Matthias," he said sadly.

At 10 p.m. as usual, Grampa handed over the TV baton of power and went to bed. When Katya and I were lying in bed waiting for sleep, I heard: "I was talking to Phoebe who is married to that general surgeon. She was at a dinner party with a bunch of doctors last week-end. She said it was fun."

I was getting sleepy, so I didn't answer.

"We haven't gone out to a dinner party in a while. Wouldn't you like to go to a dinner party? I would."

"Very nice. Which one would you like to go to?"

"Well, wouldn't you like to do that?"

"Well, since no one has invited us, not really. You'll have to host your own dinner party."

"That's a lot of work."

"Okay then, nice talking to you." I closed my eyes again.

"Why don't we get invited to parties like that?"

"Well, because I am feuding with the general surgeons. Our interests are not aligned. That's why you weren't invited last week-end. I'm basically chained to a gas machine at work, so I don't get to mingle with normal doctors."

"Can't you just extend an olive branch and make up?"

"They would see it as a sign of weakness. They have a wolf pack hierarchy. I would have to be their bitch."

This theme of carping about surgeons would be familiar to Katya. "We had a bunch of those people over when we first moved here. Even Angelo Amodeo was here."

"That was before I knew how things stood."

"Who could we invite if we have a party?"

141

"The usual suspects I suppose—Sean and Sinead, Mike, Mike and Mike—you know, people of our quality or better." At least Sean and Sinead were real.

"I am serious. Would you like to invite people from your work or people from mine?" Katya persisted.

"I don't care. Are you trying to get me to organize it? It was your idea. You make the arrangements and tell me when to attend."

"You don't like many of my teacher friends. What about some of the members of your anesthesia department?"

"Yes, that's a possibility. Our department doesn't currently have much esprit de corps though. We went to the Christmas party. That was fun, right?"

"Why didn't we stay in Toronto? They offered you a job when you finished your training." Katya's tone was plaintive.

"I would have had to teach students and do research for free, so they wouldn't have to." I considered saying, "I am organizing a surprise birthday party for you though. Surprise!" Katya was turning forty-seven on July first. I had already called a caterer. I decided to sleep instead.

There was a period of quiet and then I heard, "Last night, I dreamt that we were breaking up. That's why I was so upset." I was jolted awake again. Katya likes to drop bombshells in bed.

"Don't ever think that or dream that, Katya. We have been through too much together."

I resumed my descent. Katya opened up another line of thought. "There is a student in my class who would like to interview you about euthanasia. He wants to make a video of you for his class assignment. Can I tell him to call you to set up a time?" Katya thinks that if she isn't sleeping, it's a husband's job to keep her company.

"Does he think I'm the angel of death? I'm not an expert and I especially don't want to be quoted or video-recorded. I don't think I want to talk to him."

"Don't you have a position on euthanasia?"

"It's still illegal. I might have opinions that don't bear repeating in public."

Although I couldn't see her, I presumed we were both staring at the ceiling from behind closed eyelids. I didn't know why I was so short with Katya. I thought about apologizing.

"My father told me that when the time comes, we should shoot him."

"Your father isn't that much trouble. It sounds like a cry for love. There are plenty of tall buildings and he has a full bottle of sleeping pills if he were serious."

"I think he was half serious."

"Philosophically, I am opposed to killing old people, but it will become more popular. There's a looming health care funding crisis."

"I am asking about ethics, not economics."

"What's the difference? Seniors are always falling over like old trees and breaking their hips. Orthopods insist fixing them is essential for pain control. I doubt they would operate on demented patients in India."

"Well, what else can you do?"

"Well, another treatment for pain is morphine. I see that as a coroner in nursing homes. Troublesome old people are given morphine for 'pain control' by their doctors in sub-lethal doses every four hours until they lapse into a coma and die. I suppose they die from fluid and electrolyte abnormalities, meaning hunger and thirst."

"That doesn't sound nice. So, we already have euthanasia."

"I don't find fault with that. No one gets out of this life alive."

Katya fell silent. My thoughts swirled past a lot of disjointed material. I thought about being nicer to Katya. I thought of all the elderly Rubies, Roses and Olives with hip fractures. When I arrived at the pre-loss-of-consciousness, sex-themed plane of somnolence, I remembered Sara and the penis.

143

Sara entered an O.R. where an older male patient was being catheterized. Pointing at his crotch, she announced, "What is that? Is there a penis in there somewhere?" Apparently, she didn't care for the uncircumcised variety. As she lip-read my animated, mouthed, "Patient is awake," she flushed from shoulders to scalp follicles and abruptly exited the room.

The following time Sara and I worked together, I told her, "This next patient is going to be awake, so no slapping the penis and saying you don't like foreskins." She laughed quickly, moved a step closer and tightly encircled my upper arm in her two hands, irises glowing neon green.

Chapter 20

July was as muggy as a Louisiana whorehouse on a really muggy day. Fish were jumping and the cotton was high. The Masters' Club at the Rec Complex was on summer hiatus. I was swimming more at the civic pool because it was outdoors. You could see a great big sky and make Rorschach interpretations from cloud patterns while doing the backstroke. I hadn't seen James in a while. He must have let his Rec membership lapse.

Katya's birthday was a steaming success. I told her I would just get her a cake with lots of candles, but I invited Sinead and Sean and Moira and her siblings and some other teachers and Katya's relatives, and Katya's urge to entertain subsided. The element of surprise went missing after Magda might have let the secret slip. The sisters were incapable of keeping anything from each other. I suspected Katya knew when she began hinting about details of how the party should be organized.

One hot Saturday, I cycled over to the civic pool for their lengths swim. As I was locking up my bicycle, I noticed an attractive young woman doing the same. I said hi to be polite and because she was pretty, but she didn't acknowledge the greeting. I changed into my trunks at breakneck speed as the minute hand indicated quarter past the hour reserved for lengths. The summer student lifeguards were strict with the schedule. Underprivileged feverish children without backyard pools had to be cooled off.

When I walked onto the pool deck, I noticed that the swim lanes were already overcrowded. There was one lane with a single swimmer. I got into that one and after ploughing back and forth a few times I heard an energetic, "Hi Matt."

"Hello James," I replied in recognition, doggy paddling momentarily.

I resumed my swim, thinking we could talk after the hour was up. When I stopped for breath, I noticed James speaking with a young woman over the buoy line in the next lane. It was the girl from the bicycle rack. I paused to eavesdrop, hanging off the side of the pool. James noticed me.

"Matt, this is my daughter Tuesday."

I said hi without a lot of enthusiasm because of her previous aloofness. Perhaps she was wary of Lotharios old enough to be her father. She returned the greeting warmly this time, turning talkative. She said she had just finished university and had been home for two months. She was starting a new job in Toronto. Her dad was moving her there next week.

To avoid being taken for a lecher again, I pushed off into the water. A few minutes later, I noticed James' daughter speaking with a woman in the lane one over from hers. I could see a world-weary, middle-aged face topped by a flowery bathing cap from which a few streaked strands hung limply out.

At my next pause for breath, James confided that that was his ex-wife. What was visible of her above the water line looked well nourished. Bathing apparel is unforgiving. She probably looked nice in business casual.

"Yeah, I thought so."

"I didn't know she would be here, so it's awkward." He sounded agitated. "I'm taking the high road though."

When I finished my swim, I noticed James hovering motionless above me on the pool deck. He wanted to talk some more.

"Yeah, I'm moving Tuesday into her new apartment in Toronto next week," he said.

"That's good James. That's a nice father-daughter outing to keep you busy—a labour of love."

"Yeah, I've been busy decorating my own apartment. It's a sublet I got from a teacher who is teaching in Saudi for a year and didn't want to give it up. It's pretty new, with a great ravine view."

"Sounds cool. I'd like to see it some time," I said. He needed consolation. I felt that I had been ungracious after James' surgery when he had invited me for a beer. I was curious to see what fate a 55-year-old divorced man faced. There but for the grace of God go any of us.

"Well, my stuff is mostly still in boxes, but come by for that beer," he said. "I was in a bit of a funk and didn't get around to unpacking."

James walked and I pushed my bike under the glaring sun. We crossed the bridge over the canal that bisects Coventry and I told him about my sailing trip and not to swim near marinas. We stopped at a burger kiosk to get some takeout supper. His place was only a five-minute walk from there.

James lived alone. The apartment was in a converted warehouse, overlooking a steep ravine, that housed a few shops and some unfinished space. It was situated above its own attached garage. We went in through the garage so I could park my bike, and then up a half staircase that entered into his living area. There was no relief from the heat inside. I complimented him on his apartment, but suggested he turn on the air conditioning before I fainted. He said he had become acclimatized and it didn't bother him.

The apartment had hardwood floors and high ceilings. Several unpacked boxes occupied the middle of the living room beside a leather couch. James had some antique-looking lamps and a beautifully carved sideboard. There were some paintings propped up against the wall that he had done as an art student. The apartment had lots of potential. I could see that through the disarray.

"I moved here after I left the farm. I'm travelling pretty light. I let my wife have everything after we split up," he said. "My lawyer told me to take the high road—be generous to a fault—give her everything if I wanted peace and move on."

If you engage in a conversation with someone for any period of time, they can't resist blurting out whatever has been foremost in their mind.

"Yeah, I've heard that's what you have to do. Aren't you a bit lonely here? You need a dog or a Filipino nanny."

"No pets allowed. I don't know about the other."

"Sorry about you and your fiancée. You were almost a country gentleman."

"That didn't work out, Matt. It wasn't because I didn't want it to. Her mother and I just didn't hit it off. I put a lot of my own time and money into improvements on the place too."

"I heard one of the neighbours didn't like you."

"That was a misunderstanding that we cleared up."

I got the grand tour. He had a work alcove with a desk covered with scattered stacks of paper and a computer. I admired the view of commercial rooflines from his bedroom window. There was a leafy tree in front of his living room window, but if you stood at a certain angle you could appreciate the coveted ravine view. The sightseeing ended in the kitchen.

"I'll take that beer you haven't offered me yet."

"Oh, sorry Matt," he said reaching into his fridge, retrieving two cold bottles.

"So, what happened to the woman museum curator who headed up the charity you were telling me about at the Christmas party?"

There was no place to sit. We stood uncomfortably, leaning against the counter, facing each other.

"Yeah, she was really nice. I haven't heard from her for some time now."

"I am dumbfounded. I would think women would be pursuing you willy-nilly."

On the surface, James seemed to be exactly what every woman would find irresistible. Yet his love life was difficult. Maybe he set his sights on the unattainable. The teenage lifeguards were too young, and the 1960's movie starlets were dying off. Art dealers and museum curators should have been attainable. Maybe they were already married. There was at least one woman who would know why he was not in fact irresistible.

"Why did you break up with your wife, if you don't mind a personal question?" I asked.

"No, I don't mind Matt, but I don't really know. Things seemed to be going all right in my opinion, but she asked me to move out."

"That's an odd thing to ask if things are going okay."

"She's already engaged to someone. She's marrying a doctor in Toronto. Maybe once our daughter became independent, she felt free to act on whatever grievances she had been nursing over the years."

What he said seemed insightful, and I didn't want to provoke a bout of melancholy. I could see this happening in any marriage, and since I am a man myself, I felt like James' ally. "Well, you have a beautiful daughter. I have been told that daughters are a great comfort to you in your old age. Since I'm not old, I don't know."

"Yeah, she's great. She really looks after me. She stays with her mother when she's home from university. It gives my ex more time to poison her against me. Tuesday wants me to text her more, and I would you know, but I've got an old cell phone, so it's clumsy. It takes several minutes to type one sentence. We send each other email and we agreed we really should Skype once a week."

"Speaking of screens, I looked for you on TV at the time you told me to watch, but I didn't see you."

"Yes, it was heavily edited, but I'm still in a few of the shows."

"Shit, I must have tuned out too early."

"I'm in there. You just have to watch closely."

So, he wasn't going to be an overnight media sensation. "You're looking really well though," I said.

"Thanks. I've been swimming a bit at the civic pool. I let my Rec Complex membership lapse for the summer. I'm recovering from DOMS."

"Never heard of that one. What is it?"

"DE-layed ON-set muscle SORE-ness. It's a well recognized syndrome. You haven't heard of it? My muscles don't get sore until a few days after a workout. Oil of oregano, ginseng and echinacea can fix it. I haven't been to the gym or gone out much at all lately. Still been getting a pretty good workout at home though."

"So, what have you been doing?"

"Well I've met someone new. I'm really getting a good workout."

I hadn't expected puerile bragging about shagging exploits. "I'm glad James. Who is she?"

"Oh, her name's Marina. I've just met her, but we seem to have a real connection."

"Is she working?"

"Yes, she, ah, makes submarine sandwiches."

"Well, I can guess how you met her. Does she have a work visa for this country?"

"Yes, we really seem to be hitting it off."

"Well it would be disloyal now to eat at any other restaurants."

"I mean really hitting it off."

"I get it."

There was a pause, which James filled. "So, what do you do for fun, Matt?"

"Well, not much actually—work, workout, eat, sleep, repeat. Friday seems to be our regular movie night. We either download something or go out to the movies."

He was curious about the nitty-gritty of what I actually did for a living, so I gave him a few gory details. He revelled in them voyeuristically like most non-medical people do.

"If I were in your position, Matt, I'd be afraid of catching CJA. Also, I'm very wary of MRSA and VRE, the superbugs. People just walk around with those and they don't look sick. They get isolated in hospital, but the moment they get discharged they're just loose again in the general population."

"Well, I agree with you there. That's exactly what happens. The isolation precautions in hospital are just window dressing for lawyers. I suppose it's also to prevent the carriers picking their noses and then pressing all the elevator buttons."

James looked satisfied with my answer. "What do you think of the DSM-5, Matt?" DSM-5 was the newest version of the Diagnostic and Statistical Manual of Mental Disorders. "Don't you think it's laughable that minor mood disorders are still included? It's a fact that of the panel members who authored the section on mood disorders, one hundred per cent have financial ties to the pharmaceutical industry, and if it's in the book it needs drugs."

"I didn't know that," I said. "I wouldn't be surprised though." For a layperson, James seemed to know a lot of medical jargon. I generally avoid those types. They tend to be the neurotics who spend their lives diagnosing themselves on the internet.

I didn't see a dining table, so his wife must have taken that. We sat on some unpacked boxes and had our burgers. I thought I might stick to the leather couch if I sat there. There was irony in an interior decorator living out of boxes. I thought of asking him to turn on the air conditioning again, but I didn't want to be mean. He didn't say he was economizing, but that was my inference.

151

"Wayne Delaney has something wrong with his white blood cells," James said casually.

"Is it leukemia?"

"No."

"What is it?"

"Leukemia."

"What type does he have?"

"I don't know. I'm keeping my distance."

"Leukemia's not infectious." I didn't feel like offering up any more health care insights. I asked, "Does the noise from the shops get bothersome?"

"No, not really. I don't even notice it. It's pretty well sound-proofed, and it's only busy during the day."

"It's a great apartment—too bad you can't get it long term."

"Oh, I wouldn't want it that long. I expect some big changes might be happening. I might be moving to Toronto, if I get some more television jobs. I have a good feeling about that."

James certainly had enthusiasm, but he seemed to lack focus. Maybe his TV appearance would lead to something bigger. We hadn't really talked about who we were or the meaning of life, although I am interested in that. The flow of the conversation never seemed to lead there. He offered me a second beer, but my butt was saying time to go.

We went downstairs to where I had left my bicycle and said our goodbyes. James let me out through the automatic garage door. He was a nice man. We didn't really have a connection.

Chapter 21

It was Friday night in Coventry, and Katya and I decided to see a movie. There weren't a lot of other entertainment options. You hear about people in Toronto lining up for popular new films and getting turned away. One of the benefits of living in Coventry is that never happens. You could leave your house fifteen minutes before show time, walk into a half-empty theatre and complain about being too early. The downside is that there is only one theatre. Another is that you have to behave well because people know who you are.

We were a few minutes late in arriving, and the lights had already gone down. Fumbling our way through the darkness, we found some seats in a middle row. I told Katya that we could still say we were too early because the previews for the coming attractions weren't done. The movie was about a man trapped in a lifeboat with a tiger. The tiger couldn't change its stripes and wanted to eat him. It didn't eat him because unlike most tigers you meet, it turned out to be imaginary.

When the lights went up, it was apparent that there was only a scattering of people in attendance. I stood up, relieved to be able to stop being on guard for hungry circus cats. As we filed up the aisle toward the exit, I heard a loud baritone, "Hi Matt." James was sitting in the back row with a young woman, clearly fifteen or twenty years his junior.

It had only been two weeks since my visit to James' apartment. Katya stood off to one side, while I made small talk. I was trying to see his girlfriend in the shadows. She was slim with shoulder length glossy auburn hair, freckles and a lot of teeth. She didn't say anything, but she had an engaging smile. We chatted for a few minutes as the theatre emptied out. It was time to either make plans or go our separate ways.

"How about that beer you owe me, Matt?" James asked. His smile was enticing.

I guessed I technically now did owe him a beer as he had supplied the beers in his fridge. I weighed the pros and cons of the invitation. I didn't want to appear rude. I was a little intrigued by the new girlfriend. Given their age disparity, I wondered how James had contrived to meet her. She didn't look Russian. He must have split up with his shag partner Marina, if she really existed.

This was Friday and I had the weekend off, so I really didn't have an excuse. It might be worthwhile. His forlorn quest of art gallery curators and auction house executives in Toronto demonstrated that he was capable of meeting, if not holding the attention of interesting women. I gave in to temptation and agreed. My misgivings had not disappeared. They were temporarily trumped by my curiosity to know whether this new woman was intelligent as well as attractive.

The four of us exchanged introductions and went to Amigos, the downtown tavern where friends love to meet and greet, and good food and drink are the law. It was a sticky summer's night. The outdoor patio was crammed with people thanking God it was Friday. We got a booth, which was nice because there was a throng of people waiting for service at the bar. A young waitress attired in shorts and prominent cleavage came over to take our order.

Katya, who had initially been less than enthusiastic, became loquacious and animated. She gets that way after a glass of wine if there is a subject she finds interesting. She enjoys stimulating conversation but feels shy about initiating. It may be the vestigial memory of nuns whacking her hand for talking in class. She had two months of summer holidays and freedom from workaday worries.

James was at his most charming. His eyes twinkled and his good humour was infectious. He let it be known that he was an architect, an interior designer and a freelance contributor to home improvement magazines. Although he seemed a little pretentious, he had the attributes that would make him a good television personality some day.

I could see that Katya had an immediate rapport with him. They were thick in conversation to the exclusion of the rest of us at the table. Katya drew on a store of knowledge of home furnishings that had been refined by decades of study. James demonstrated a depth of understanding that surpassed even hers. Having no insights into design trends, I was relegated to the role of disinterested observer.

I tried bringing the conversation around to James' girlfriend to find out who she was. "This is beginning to sound like an episode from the 'Home and Garden' channel," I remarked with exaggerated jocularity. "Are you involved in the home furnishings trade as well Candi?"

"No, I'm a hairdresser." She smiled sweetly. I noticed now that the tip of a tattooed rose rose from the top of Candi's blouse and that James had a very nice haircut.

"Is Candi short for Candice?" I asked.

"No. It's the name my mommy gave me," she said coquettishly. "It's different because it's with an 'i' instead of a 'y.' My middle name is Lila."

"Well, that must be short for Delilah," I said.

"Wait. What do you mean?" Candi asked.

James broke in. "Well, that might be enough genealogy. Matthew likes to investigate things, Candi."

Katya asked James where he was from. James said he was from Toronto but had grown up mostly in Europe. I hadn't known that about him. He was an only child. He had attended English language schools in Italy and France. His dad had been a consul general and was transferred every few years. He said he hadn't liked it at the time, but appreciated the advantages now.

I said my dad had been a cop in Toronto and my mother was a sales clerk at Sears. She really liked it because it gave her pocket money to buy Christmas presents for her children. This was reverse one-upmanship. It was to show that I had made it on my own merit.

"Why didn't you become a cop, Matt?" James asked.

"Cops are primarily hired as agents of the well-to-do to protect their property from the thieving less fortunate. Rich folks pay taxes to give the poor just enough to keep them from breaking into their houses at night and to pay for some solid police brutality."

"But you are a rich doctor, aren't you?" James objected.

"I suppose I would rather be a hammer than a nail. When my burglar alarm goes off by accident, the cops are at my door in five minutes. That's what higher property taxes pay for. I can't forget my proletarian roots and sympathies though."

"I should have married a doctor," Candi said. She crinkled her nose at me.

"So should I have," I agreed.

Katya didn't say what her dad had done for a living. He was a print press operator and her mum cleaned houses.

Katya asked James if he had gone to university in Europe. He said he had studied fine arts in France but had switched programs when his family returned to Canada. He had earned a Bachelor of Architectural Studies degree from Carleton University in Ottawa. Jobs were hard to come by when he graduated, so he had never worked as an architect, but he found his interior decorating and home inspection businesses to be very intellectually challenging.

"Do you think you'll go back to architecture some day?" Katya asked.

"Yes, I suppose I really should," he said. "What about this coroner work you're doing, Matt? How does it affect you when you have to see someone who has just died? Most people would find that stressful. Isn't it just sad and macabre?"

"It doesn't really affect me, as long as I'm not responsible. When you have a patient, what's the worst that could happen? The patient could die. Well, that's already happened."

"But don't you ever get personally involved?" he persisted.

"I have to say no, James. I try to behave sympathetically toward the relatives, but I have never sent anyone a condolence card. I don't see dead people in my sleep."

"Would it hurt to distribute cards inscribed with, 'My sincerest condolences on the loss of your beloved blank' and then fill in the blank by hand. You could get a good rate if you had a batch pre-printed with the same message." He was being clever at my expense.

"First of all, I wouldn't say loss of beloved. They know where their loved one is. I would use a synonym like obliteration or annihilation." No one cared to respond to that. I had decided I wanted the evening to end soon.

Then James said, "I'm really excited. They're running a TV pilot in September that I'm in. They're considering making it into a regular show. It's airing four consecutive Fridays."

Katya responded immediately, "That's amazing! What's it about?"

"Yes, well, there is a panel of design experts representing their visions for a space during each show. I am on the panel. The homeowners listen and then pick a designer they like best. If I get chosen, I take the homeowners shopping, advise them what to buy and coordinate the makeover."

"That sounds like so much fun!" Katya enthused.

"Is that the same show you were telling me about before, James?" I remembered tuning in but not seeing him in any of the frames. "It's like Makeover Mavens, Katya."

"Yes, they are running the pilots again. They are trying to decide whether to proceed with them as a series. I've got my fingers crossed."

"When is it on? What channel?" Katya was obviously keen to watch.

James gave her the particulars. Katya marked the dates and times onto a piece of paper, filing the paper carefully away in the zippered section of her purse. When he smiled widely, I noticed James was missing an upper bicuspid tooth. Either he forgot to wear his partial denture, or he was short of money.

It turned out that James' friend Candi had not always been a hair-dresser. She used to be a medical secretary. She had lost her job when the doctor had retired. She had two young girls. Both James and Candi had daughters. She was separated and fighting messy legal battles with her former spouse.

"You two are lucky you have daughters," I said. "Katya and I only have a son. We will have no one to push our wheelchairs or wipe our asses when we get old." Everyone laughed, but I had a feeling that this comment didn't play well with Katya.

Candi thought she might like to go back to school to become a nurse. It would be hard to do with young children. She was interested in what qualifications she would have to have and how long I had gone to school. I gave her the benefit of my knowledge, but I didn't think it was likely she could complete the course of study. Nursing requires a university degree now. She didn't seem to have any of the prerequisites to apply.

When it came time to pay, I offered to cover the tab. This was somewhat uncharacteristic of me. I was jealous of James' relaxed confident style and wanted to show off. Writers and artisans don't usually have money. I felt guilty that much of my conversation had verged on the negative. It had sounded belligerent and self-righteous. James accepted the gesture without the slightest hesitation. I even left an oversized tip in appreciation of the cleavage.

Driving home, Katya asked whether I had enjoyed the evening. She wanted to know whether we should arrange to go out together again as a foursome. I said I didn't think so, unless she really wanted to. She seemed quite impressed by James, and how could she help it? He was an architect. He was a genuine author featured in the kind of home decorating magazines that we had on our coffee table. Katya loved magazines and coffee tables. He had appeared on television. He seemed cultured, had a wonderful speaking voice and seemed generally wonderful. I felt like I may have been outsmarted by this man.

When we were lying in bed waiting for sleep, Katya said, "I still have this bump on my forehead from when I tripped over a curb doing my power walking. I was wondering whether you could notice it tonight."

"It's not really noticeable," I replied.

"It takes so long for me to heal. Maybe I got a concussion."

"A concussion is more of a brain injury than a forehead injury—you know—headache, irritability, memory loss."

"You have that!"

"I know."

"When Michael saw me the last time he was home, he looked shocked and said, 'What happened to you!'"

"You're lucky to be alive, I guess."

"Feel this bump on my forehead. What do you think of it?"

"The gypsy says you are going on a trip." I reached through the dark to place my index finger on her brow. "There will be a little bump in the road which will smooth out before you get to the scalp forest."

Katya laughed.

Chapter 22

I was having the kind of disturbing dreams where you are trying unsuccessfully to solve a problem, but it just keeps coming back in a frustrating circular way. Each night, I had to trek all over Coventry searching for a place to sleep or control a flooding basement with an old-timey wooden stick-handled mop. I was the sorcerer's apprentice being manipulated by an unseen vindictive master.

At work, I was exhausted from a night of walking and mopping. I kept my focus for eight hours, but when I got home I collapsed onto the couch for a nap. I slept deeply in the afternoons. Sara from the operating room was in today's couch dream, asking me if I wanted to be her husband. She looked really sweet and freshly scrubbed and I was tempted. "Could you have two husbands?" I asked her. "Sure," she said, "if you can do drywalling and plumbing. I would really like to get the renovations in my kitchen finished."

A loud vibration brought me rudely back. I groped over the coffee table beside me to see if my phone was there and in my confusion swept my watch and glasses onto the floor. I felt around in the folds of the couch but didn't find my pager or any other communication devices. Looking across the room, I thought I saw Sara. It was Katya, examining her cell phone.

"Was that your phone vibrating? It was so loud it shook the floor under the couch."

"It was my sister."

"What does she want?"

"Nothing important. I'll talk to her later." Katya slipped the phone hastily into her bag, snapped it shut and sat there avoiding my eyes.

"You always take your sister's calls. Did you just get home from work?"

"Yes."

"How was your day?"

"Terrible. I want a sales job at the mall."

"What happened? Discipline problems? Just send them off to the principals in charge of vice."

"I have a really disruptive student. He was in my class for two days and then disappeared for a month. I heard he was admitted to the psychiatric ward of the hospital. We have a new philosophy of full integration. All the psychiatric and mentally challenged cases are now in regular classrooms." It was the new fall term and Katya was just getting to know her students.

"Does he have a diagnosis?"

"It's a secret. They say he's manic-depressive, or bipolar."

"Bipolar affective disorder. What even is that? The whole classification of psychiatric disease is descriptive. There is no test you can do for it. Maybe he is schizoaffective or cyclothymic or has borderline personality disorder or is just very moody. My opinion is that it's mostly bullshit."

"The parents want integration and the school board gets extra funding. I am supposed to provide a meaningful teaching experience. They used the money to hire five educational assistants to take care of them, and now they fired three of them to save money."

"Is he violent?"

"I don't think so—maybe. I don't have a problem sending him to the office, but what's the use? He just comes back. They need a different solution for people like that."

"I guess politically correct pacifist female vice principals don't put the fear of God in him."

"Not like the good old days," she said.

"If he brings a knife to school, you bring a gun. Maybe you should take a martial arts course. Some psychiatrists actually do that. We had one psychiatrist who put a chokehold on a violent patient. I heard a 'code white' announced, meaning all the orderlies had to come help restrain him. The psychiatrist held it long enough that some minutes later, a 'code blue' cardiac arrest team was summoned. Fortunately, the damage wasn't that noticeable."

"I don't think that would help. Talking doesn't help either. Maybe he needs drugs."

"You're right. Psychiatrists found all that talking time consuming and not very effective. Now they just want to manage their patients chemically or have sex with them. Psychiatrists are always getting into trouble for that."

"You are so cynical, Matthew. I'm sure there is more to it than that. I want professionals to look after my manic-depressive student."

"Yeah well, here's how I heard a psychiatrist defend the shortcomings of psychiatry. Cardiologists' patients will die of heart attacks. Oncologists' patients die of cancer. Psychiatrists' patients risk dying of suicide, choking or being choked by and/or being molested by or having sex with their psychiatrists, consensually or non."

"It's easy for you to make jokes, Matthew. You don't have to deal with 16-year-olds."

"Don't allow yourself to be alone in the same room with him. I deal with all ages from zero to ninety-nine."

"Yes, but you just put them asleep. I wish my students were asleep." She looked away.

"Are you willing to consider all options?"

She looked back wearily. "Not all. I need a week off."

"You could call in sick. Teachers are known to have the highest absentee rate of any job."

"I don't do that—very much. Last week you said nurses have the highest absentee rate."

"Nurses say teachers. Can you just put your head down on your desk and tell the students you can't face them and you're having a nap?"

Because of my nap, I stayed up late watching television. I brushed my teeth, and then had to lick them to see if I had just brushed. That worried me a little. When I slipped into bed beside Katya, she turned and greeted me with, "Why do you make me go to bed so late, honey? I would never go to bed so late on my own."

I should have apologized for waking her up. After scrolling through my list of potential responses, I chose what I thought was the cleverest one. "Beelzebub laughs and claps his hands when he sees what he has wrought through me."

Rushing to work the next morning, I couldn't find my shoes. Grampa had gotten up early and reorganized the pile by the back door. He liked the shoe rack to be orderly and uncluttered. He was sitting at the kitchen table watching me.

Apropos of nothing, he read me a line from the newspaper followed by, "Vy is dat?" This was a ploy he used for engaging Katya in conversation. Grampa and I used to talk, but now we mainly shared brief opinions about the weather. I didn't have the time and he wouldn't wear his hearing aids.

"You're holding the newspaper, Grampa. You tell me," I answered as I found my shoes in the closet.

I was losing my enthusiasm for sharing my house with Grampa. He was just always there, watching. I missed my privacy. I alternated between feeling sorry for and resenting him. He didn't belong anywhere, and his health was slowly failing. On my "to do" lists I included "be good to Grampa," but there was no getting around it. He was a nice man who ate my food and kissed my wife.

I came home after a frustrating day at work. I told Katya, "I couldn't find the orange juice or a glass to drink it from this morning. Grampa reorganized the contents of the kitchen cupboards and refrigerator."

"He needs to feel useful."

"Did you tell him to stop double dipping into the food like we discussed?"

"No."

"That's too bad because yesterday I had to. He probably thinks I'm mean."

"What was he doing?"

"I walked in on him standing over the sink sampling from leftovers, and then returning them to the fridge."

"Oh well, didn't you ever drink directly out of the milk carton when you were a kid?"

"Yes, of course but that's different. Everyone was related."

"I know," Katya agreed.

"I don't want to share spit with him."

"Okay, I'm really tired from working all day. How long do you think he has left—maybe a year, right?"

I was silent. I didn't wish Katya's dad any harm. He was a good man. I had misgivings about adopting him. There didn't seem to be many options. Grampa wouldn't go to a seniors' residence or nursing home because he said that was where old people went to be ignored. He was right of course. I had visited several in the course of my work.

"My sister and brother are coming tomorrow," Katya said casually.

"Your sister was just here!" I said, exasperated. "She looks just like you, and I already know what your brother looks like too."

"Dad invited them."

I suspected that she didn't want to say her sister wanted to see her dad, because that would beg the question of why didn't her sister have their father living with her.

"Magda has been here three times since the August long weekend. Maybe your father would like to go on a little holiday to stay with her. They could visit to their hearts' content."

"Magda is starting to date again. She can't have dad there if she brings a man home."

I found this unreasonable. "Your father never washes his hands, and he touches everything. He reorganizes things in the drawers, fridge, dishwasher. I can't find the orange juice in the morning. He nudges up the thermostat. What happened to the bottles of hand sanitizer that I put in the bathrooms?" I had done this soon after Grampa moved in.

"I don't know."

I knew they had been safely stowed away in the cupboards under the sinks. "You know, in the hospital we wash our hands about nine thousand times a day. It's the easiest and most effective way of preventing infections. I watch the fluid levels in those bottles of sanitizer and they never change. I put those bottles out as a gage of personal hygiene."

"It dries out your hands."

I was beginning to get a little wound up. "All the things you said I did that your father wouldn't do because he is an old-world gentleman? He does them all. He eats standing up at the kitchen counter. He double dips into food. He farts."

"Matthew, stop! What do you want me to do about it? He doesn't know you're there. He doesn't hear you coming."

165

We stood glaring at each other in the middle of the kitchen. I modulated my voice to a normal tone. "I guess I'm just missing having some privacy. I think he needs that too."

"Did you order the takeout food?"

"And you need a pair of pliers to get his fingers off the TV remote."

"The food? Dad likes Chinese."

"Yes, I ordered it. I'm not hungry. The lengths swim is at 8 o'clock and it only lasts an hour. If you pick up the dinner, I'll join you later."

"We're hungry now. Can't you pick up the dinner? You could go to your new place later."

I had recently joined a weights only, 24-hour gym for when I was on call. It was inhabited at night by a few shift workers, an anesthesiologist and insomniac perverts.

"I'm on my way to the pool. Can I take the food swimming with me?"

"No."

"Would it make you happy if I got the food, brought it back and went to the grunt gym?"

"Yes."

"How long would that happiness last? Would it last past tomorrow for instance?"

Katya didn't respond.

"Okay. I'll do it."

I brought the Chinese takeout as promised. I felt ashamed of myself for speaking the way I did about Grampa. It was petty. I was going to tell Katya that her dinner had arrived, but I saw she was engaged in a telephone conversation with her sister. They were confiding the minutest details of their lives to each other. I left without eating.

When I got to the gym, there was a guy in his twenties standing beside the arm press machine. "Are you using this?" I asked.

"Yes." He sat down and started texting.

"Do you mind if I do a set?"

He was still texting.

"Okay, I asked you nicely. Now get up before I throw you off." He had a look at my face, got up and slunk away.

When I got home, they were still on the phone. It seemed impossible that Katya and her sister would talk so long. Spying the half empty sum-young-guy cartons, I suspected they had paused long enough to eat and then resumed their conversation.

We agreed to watch a movie as a threesome. I arrived with the leftover Chinese on a tray. Grampa and Katya had already settled on the sofa. Katya was cradling a glass of wine. Grampa made as if to get up from the couch to allow me a seat next to my wife. I let him stay where he was and sat down with him between us.

After an hour had passed, I paused the film for a pee break. When I got up, Grampa asked Katya whether he could get her another glass of wine. As a fallen Baptist and near teetotaller, I found it inappropriate that he would be procuring alcohol for his daughter, especially since it wasn't his booze.

"Do you have to have that second glass of wine?" I asked. "I think it may make you snore."

She didn't answer and had it anyway. After the movie, Grampa kissed Katya good night and said good night to me, forcing a smile. We went upstairs to the kitchen together.

"I've had a headache for a week. Is that okay?" Katya asked.

"Yeah, it's really okay. I'm glad I could resolve that for you."

It was bad temper disguised as medical humour. Katya used to suffer from frequent migraines when she was younger. She didn't laugh and just went up to bed. I went to the guest room to sleep. We had been sleeping apart more often than together.

Chapter 23

Katya announced that she was going to Toronto to attend a teachers' conference and would be staying three days. I was a little surprised by this because it was still September and the regular school year was just getting underway. She said she had told me about it weeks ago. I wasn't sure if that was true. I really had no recollection of it, but that didn't mean it hadn't happened.

I asked where she would be staying. She said at a convention hotel downtown. One of the other teachers named Aline from her school would be there as well. I didn't recognize the name. She said she was sorry to leave me to manage Grampa, but it would only be three days. I said that was okay—he was a self-cleaning model of Grampa. He was pretty much self-sufficient. We did leave him alone in our house for a week at a time when we went away on holidays.

Katya packed a bag and left that evening after the rush hour traffic in Toronto had subsided. She would have had to get up at 5 a.m. otherwise the next morning to arrive on time. She gave me a token hug rather than a kiss on the lips as she was walking out the door. I teased her that I had hired a private detective to check up on her movements while she was away. I also mentioned I didn't want her swanning around in Holt Renfrew, a luxury department store in Toronto.

The days passed uneventfully. I made a few rudimentary meals for which Grampa was profusely grateful. Madame Fifi peed on the living room rug. She liked Katya better than me and was miffed because Katya was gone. I cleaned it up but couldn't get the stain out completely. The dog barked wildly at people passing on the sidewalk outside. She was a burglar alarm that worked organically on sausages. She was compensating for her dereliction of duty the night I came home from Maryland.

I had another dream about Sara. Her eyes were luminous green, flecked with shimmering light. We were in a hotel room. I made a joke. She laughed quickly, moved a step closer and encircled my biceps with her two hands. I passed my free hand lightly over her blouse, bumping over two hard nipples, and she shuddered involuntarily. She turned to open a window, admitting the sound of jungle cicadas or an alarm clock set to 6:45 a.m. I lay in bed for a few minutes conjuring an ending, but it wasn't satisfying because it wasn't as real as a dream.

Grampa occupied himself with make-work jobs and sleeping in front of the television. When I left for work, he was in the front yard picking up tree branches that had come down in a recent windstorm. They were mostly spindly birch branches that you could break over your knee. He was carefully sawing them up into equally sized pieces and tying them into bundles for curb pickup. This would take him a long time. The cleaning lady was coming, so hopefully she could keep an eye on him.

It took eight minutes to drive from my house to the hospital. The breeze coming in the car window had a warm country smell. The farmers had been manuring their fields. Coventry was small enough that anywhere in town was only a few clicks from agricultural land. It was small enough that whatever was happening in its environs soon became apparent to everyone.

169

I finished my morning operating list and rushed down to the cafeteria to get something quick and portable to take back upstairs to our lounge. I met Jeremiah Chang in the cafeteria lineup.

"I was thinking about you. I was hoping to meet you today, Matthew." His 50-year-old face was as smooth as a baby's bum.

"Hello Jeremiah. How are you?"

"Do you have a few minutes to speak?"

I remembered he always had time for me. He made you feel like you were the sole object of his interest and attention. "I'm a little rushed. The surgeons are crying out in pain because I am breaking for lunch."

"Sit with me Matthew," he insisted gently. There was no way to refuse without being rude. We took a table together.

"So how are things up on pediatrics?" I asked.

Jeremiah responded slowly and methodically, but not to the question I had posed. "Matthew, there are some people who are carelessly trying to injure you and damage your reputation. You must fight a battle with them, I know. Try not to judge them too harshly. I realize that in a battle it is sometimes necessary to injure or kill your enemies. Do only what is necessary. Try to injure as little as possible."

I wasn't entirely sure what he meant. He was serious, so I had to respond in kind. "You are not wrong, Jeremiah, but this applies to almost everyone. Thanks for your advice. These things may be out of my hands. I don't know how they will turn out."

"Your enemies are suffering from greed and hatred. These emotions are spawned by ignorance."

"Okay Jeremiah. I'll try to kill as few as possible."

"You are mocking me, I know. I don't mind. These problems you are facing will pass. When that happens, you must let go of your resentments and return to a normal life. Katya is a wonderful, loving person. She has compassion for you and you for her. You are intelligent, so you understand the truth of this."

170

What did he know about my relationship with Katya. I didn't have the energy to discuss it with him. "Okay. I have to get going though. I hear the screaming of distressed surgeons."

"I wasn't talking about surgeons. They are not your enemies." He had barely touched his vegetarian meal.

"I know." I couldn't disagree without sounding paranoid. I gobbled the remains of my lunch and bolted back to the operating room.

Driving home in the afternoon, I saw an ambulance and a fire truck with lights flashing, pulled over, partially obstructing traffic. This was on a residential street a few blocks from my house. I slowed down and noticed a policeman next to the vehicles holding up his hand. I guessed he was stopping me to ask for my help as a physician, or if it was too late for that, as a coroner.

I eased the car forward slowly to have a closer look. When he pointed directly at me menacingly, I came to a full stop. He didn't look familiar. I rolled down my window.

"Is there something about this you don't understand?" he demanded excitedly, showing me the palm of his hand. "This means stop." He was a short, red-faced man. He might have been talking about my personal life. His words echoed Katya's.

"I am sorry sir. I didn't understand." I thought a dose of humility and military bearing might calm him down. He hadn't recognized me. He was alone, directing bi-directional traffic through a single lane past whatever had happened

"What is it about this you don't understand?" he said, berating me like a child. He held the palm of his right hand close to my nose. "When I hold a hand up with the palm flat, it means stop." He slapped his palm with his free hand and I felt the breeze on my face. "It means you stop where you are. Stop driving and freeze. There is a charge for failing to obey a police officer."

Cops are generally very polite to coroners. It might be because police consider us allies in law enforcement. The more likely explanation is that police need the goodwill of coroners, so they are not left waiting for hours at a death scene before the body can be released. They would also like prompt access to coroners' verdicts to expedite their form filling out. The universe was not unfolding as it should.

"I apologize. I thought you were waving me through," I lied. I had made a calculation that I didn't want to be involved. This was eating into my nap time. Cars were pulling up behind me and I was blocking traffic.

"You are lucky the paper work is more trouble than it's worth. Okay, get out of here," officer Mighty Mouse ordered.

I got along well with most cops. My dad was a cop before he shuffled off his mortal coil. I have cop genes. I resolved to remember this particular prick's voice and leave him waiting for his shift to end if he ever called.

The cleaning lady was just leaving when I got home. She told me Grampa had fallen outside again and had been unable to get up. He eventually wriggled close enough to a low tree branch to hoist himself onto his feet. She had found him sitting by himself in the basement. He had told her about it and they had had a nice talk. It had been a blow to his dignity, but at least he hadn't broken his hip.

Katya arrived home Friday evening. She noticed the stain on the living room rug almost immediately. "Did Madame Fifi pee on the carpet? You have to use the stain remover spray on that right away." She was standing in the doorway to my study where I was working.

"Well it's her rug too." Having deserted us, I felt Katya didn't have the right to complain.

It seemed like no time at all had passed during Katya's absence. I have heard that the way to slow down time is to travel. According to Einstein, time slows in accelerated frames of reference. When you are traveling, you do a lot of new things because time is limited and precious. You have new experiences that are recorded in unused parts of your brain. When you are living with a standard routine, nothing stands out.

I asked Katya if the time seemed to pass slowly or quickly for her. She was spare on details. The conference had been interesting. There had been a speaker from the Ministry talking about new trends and guidelines, and a motivational speaker talking about instilling Catholic values. She said I could ask Aline about it. I wasn't sure who that was.

I asked her what she had done in the evenings. Katya said she had gone shopping at the Eaton Centre and had gone to bed early because she was tired from driving. She went to the kitchen to pour herself a glass of wine. I got up and traipsed after her. She said she had some new ideas from a shop display to show me, producing some decorating magazines and catalogues, bookmarked with colour swatches.

"You are a slave to the trends in magazines. What we have is nicer than 90 percent of the population and it all works together. All you can think about is how to spend money to change it." I was sore about having been left alone with Grampa.

"You just don't like change. Living spaces need refreshing. I must have mentioned five times we need a new deck. One of the boards has rotted through." A red spot flared on each cheek. "If you had your way, we would never get anything new. You would be living with the furniture from your student days."

"You drag home new sideboards and étagères like a triumphant cat with a canary. There is nowhere to put it all without getting rid of something. We have a basement full of furniture that has fallen out of favour." I kept old furniture, hoping that a full basement would retard the pace of new purchases.

"That's why we need a cottage for our older furniture. You know I have always wanted a cottage." I knew that a cottage would give her an excuse to decorate two houses and that would be expensive.

"Can't you see the ideas you have are not original? They are planted in your brain by marketers and merchants who have to keep moving stock. If houses and furniture and appliances and clothing don't wear out quickly enough, they change the styles. They make you feel like you're in with the cool kids by calling every room a space. I'll be going from the living-space to the bath-space before I retire to the bed-space."

"Space is the final frontier. Please don't mock what I enjoy, Matthew."

"They should have a three hour 'best of' home renovation show, where all they do is the reveal. Reveal, reveal, reveal, reveal, reveal… Like a three-hour orgasm."

"Things get dated and need refreshing," she insisted sternly. "And don't rock on that chair. It loosens the glue."

"Can't we just pick things with a classic timeless look and be happy with them?"

"I know we could get a cottage cheaply designed by an architect. The market is tight for architects right now because of AutoCAD. It's a buyers' market."

"What's AutoCAD?"

"Design software for architects, I think. Anyway, I have some catalogues I brought from Toronto. I want you to look at them with me. I would like us to choose some new flooring and wall colours for the foyer together."

"My preferences serve as a guide for you to know what not to get. You've gotten rid of everything I had any input into buying."

"No, I like to hear your opinion. I want to be able to bounce my ideas off someone."

"Katya, you hired that decorator last year who helped you choose things for our living room. The two of you rolled your eyes and over-ruled everything I said I liked. There is no right answer to decorating. Everything is a matter of taste."

She folded her arms across her chest decisively like a lady rapper. "Most husbands don't care about interior design. They let their wives do it all. Why can't you just allow me to express myself and create a beautiful home for you?"

"Because I live here, and it's my house too."

"Most husbands are happy with working in the garage or the yard."

"Katya, you hired a landscaping company behind my back to replace all the work I had done in the back yard."

"That's because you wouldn't consider any changes. You always say no to everything. I asked you, but you didn't want to talk about it. You know it looks better now."

"Well, it does look better, but it's not what I created."

"Matthew, you don't even see what's here. You sit in your study, typing on your computer and shuffling papers most of the time. You ignore me. You don't share your feelings with me. I have to have something to occupy myself with. You don't know how many times I have thought of leaving you."

This was a much bigger gun than was necessary for the seriousness of our argument. I had heard this a few times before over the course of our marriage and never knew exactly what provoked it. Usually, I backed down and promised to change. Katya would look at me skeptically. I would try to give her a hug, which she might or might not accept. After a few days, she would forget the whole thing.

I considered my options and decided to make a half-hearted attempt to reconcile. Happy wife, happy life. "Katya, don't say that. No matter what we say in our arguments, I have never once said that to you. I just have to finish one thing and then we can look at your pictures."

"You really are a revisionist historian." She straightened a stack of magazines, tapping them emphatically on the kitchen counter. She wasn't pacified.

"Okay, can we look at the pictures together?"

She fell silent and then from somewhere found, "You are a pack rat. You never throw anything away. I would like you to go through your closet and give me the clothes you never wear. I get rid of things that don't bring me joy. I am going to Goodwill to take some of my things this week."

I caught myself just before I said, "Take your new clothes directly from the shops to Goodwill and cut out the middle person." She was right about my clothes. "Have you had dinner yet?" I asked, trying to change the subject. Then I heard myself say, "There is some double dip soup in the fridge."

Katya generally didn't mind eating food her father had sampled from and returned to the refrigerator. "Matthew, leave my dad alone."

"The cleaning lady wants you to tell Grampa to sit when he pees 'cause he's dribbling on the floor too much." As these words came out of my mouth unchecked, I knew I had gone too far, but for some reason I couldn't stop myself.

Chapter 24

I sleep terribly and have frustrating circular dreams after a fight with Katya. The second thing that goes out the window with marital strife, after sex, is sleep. I should just cave and agree with whatever she is saying or doing late at night. I should forget any principle that I think is important, and fall on my knees and beg forgiveness. Nothing is worth the agony of a white night. Who remembers what was at stake a few days later anyway.

At work on Monday, I finished my daytime operating room list and did one of the cases off the emergency list to help out. It was another demented nursing home patient with a hip fracture. When I interviewed her preoperatively, she generally gave me nonsensical answers. Then she reached over and pinched me very hard on the arm. I backed away and adopted a mock martial arts defensive posture.

There were so many patients like this. She reminded me of the demented, hip-fracture patient who had looked at me and declared, "Yes, I bought it and hid it!" In her delirium, she had mistaken me for a long-dead husband who had cross-examined her as I was doing. I wondered whether an older, confused Katya might say the same thing to an anesthesiologist one day. I resolved to be less critical of her love for shopping.

I generally got irritable whenever Katya brought up new decorating ideas. These were things I had not thought about, things she must have been thinking about for a while. She wanted me to have an opinion so we could talk about it, so she could refine her opinions and emerge triumphant with the correct answer. For her, purchasing something was progress. She got angry at my lack of interest.

I called up Sean because I needed to talk. I regarded him as an older, wiser owl, and he knew Katya. I could have called my sister, but I didn't think she would be objective. She knew me as her immature brother and would take Katya's side. I didn't have any male siblings and my parents were dead.

Sinead picked up the phone. "Hi Sinead. How's everything? May I speak with Sean please?"

I would normally spend a few minutes getting updated with her. She must have noticed something unusual in my voice because she summoned him immediately. After a while, I heard, "Hey Matt. How are you?" Sean had emigrated with his parents from Ireland at the age of five, but there was still a Celtic cadence in his speech.

"Good. How are you, Sean? Am I interrupting you?"

"No, no—of course not, Matthew. I was just taking a break. I was doing some work on the roof. You know these fucking old houses. I could spend my whole day, every day, doing repairs."

"It's a good thing you're handy, Sean." He had installed new ensuite bathrooms for each of the four bedrooms in his nineteenth century house to make it ready to receive upscale paying guests. He catered mainly to elderly couples, the kind who would break their hips at night looking for a toilet.

"You learn by doing, Matt."

"See one, do one, teach one. I suppose the second one is always a little better than the first," I said nervously, building up to the real reason for the call.

"Isn't that the truth. How's Katya?"

"Good. Gone shoe shopping I think."

"Matthew, as far as I can tell women aren't as interested in the big questions, like where did we come from and where are we going. They are more interested in family and relationships and shopping for shoes. They don't have the same conceit or delusions of grandeur as men."

"You might be right, Sean."

"What's new with you, Matt?"

"I'm losing a bit of sleep."

"When you get older, you start enjoying sleep more, and you crave more, and then you're on your way toward the light at the top of the stairs."

"I don't know how to say this. I called you because I value your opinion."

"What is it, Matt?" he said, sounding a little concerned.

"I'm pretty sure Katya is having an affair."

"What! No way. What makes you think that?" he snorted.

"Well, I don't have proof, but I know. There is a guy who any day now will ask me to step aside so that he and Katya can get on with living happily ever after together."

"Well, you're wrong. You've misinterpreted something. Or he's a head case. Who is he?"

"I know him from the Rec Complex. Katya and I went out to Amigo's with him for a beer once."

"I told you you worked out too much. That Rec Complex change room is especially noxious. I can guarantee you there's nothing going on. He's an idiot. Did you talk to her about it?"

"No. I'm afraid that saying it out loud will provoke a confrontation and she will leave...that saying it out loud will make it real."

"Tell the guy you don't want him to have anything to do with you or Katya. If it's true, which it is not, it's some sort of mid-life crisis. I could have Sinead talk to Katya to find out what's really going on."

"It may have gone beyond that. We haven't been sleeping in the same bedroom. He seems to be exactly what she would want if she were ordering from a catalogue."

"I don't believe that. Lots of couples don't sleep in the same room. I know for a fact that a husband's uvula thingy vibrates when he sleeps on his back, making it difficult for a wife to resist putting a pillow over his face."

"I can't get over that I introduced them."

"You can't prevent women from meeting other men, unless you're a Muslim. Men and women will always be tempted, but that doesn't mean they act on their impulses. Who is this guy?"

"He is an unemployed architect and a free-lance writer. He's sensitive and metrosexual. James is about to get a TV show about some sort of home renovation bidding competition in the fall. I think he may have had something to do with the death of his former future father-in-law."

"What?"

I was becoming more convinced that James was responsible for Mr. Anderson's death. Raven Anderson had said Jimmy made her dad take an extra blood pressure pill on the morning of the day he died. There were five pills too few in the bottle. Toward the end, James probably convinced him to take those too. This would have caused fainting with straining on the toilet. It would also explain the near stroke a week earlier.

"It's from a coroner's case."

"As you know, I enjoy reading. Does he write historical fiction, because I like that. I would hate to have to mess up a writer. What did you say about his father-in-law?"

"The guy was engaged to a farm girl with an old sick father. He was pretending to be a farmer. I suspect he convinced the old man to take some extra blood pressure pills, so he could inherit the farm sooner. A neighbour was suspicious enough to call the police. It would be impossible to prove. Old people are always getting their pills confused."

Sean grunted like he knew an old man who mixed up pills. "What makes you believe Katya is involved with him?"

"She's unhappy with me. We're not communicating anymore. I can't seem to stop the downward spiral. She knows that the market is tough for architects because of AutoCAD." The telephone receiver was damp in my death grip.

"This is sounding slightly more serious."

"He's exactly what she says she would like me to be—you know, like the person she was always destined to meet."

"No. There's no such thing. Well, if she leaves, she leaves. Marriages break up every day. It's not the end of the world. Good riddance and move on."

I fell silent.

After a pause he said, "Maybe you should get professional couples' counselling."

"Is, ah, is that what you would do?"

I waited while Sean considered.

"I would find out where this boyo lives and deliver a stern warnin'." Some Celtic menace had crept into his voice.

"You're joking, right?"

"Possibly. That's what my father would have done anyway. Growing up, we had family friends who my dad rounded up occasionally to administer rough justice when the situation called for it."

"I think he targeted me specifically—or perhaps it was Katya, through his contacts with tradespeople who have been to our house."

"I can't afford tradespeople. You need to get as much information about this man as you can, so we can sort him out. What do you know about him?"

"He seems to need money... Maybe if I offered him some he would go away," I said.

"You couldn't be sure that he would just take your money and not honour the bargain, or come back for more."

"I think he's already mentally dividing my assets. He's just come out of a divorce, so he knows how it's done."

"We could meet your writer together for a heart to heart, to see what the situation calls for."

"I don't think I could start all over again."

"Matt, look at you. You're a doctor. You're good looking. You're athletic. You wouldn't be alone very long. I wouldn't be worried in the least. You could get a trophy wife."

"This may sound awfully mercenary, but I don't have enough working years left to recover financially. I wouldn't be able to afford to keep a trophy wife in the style to which she would like to become accustomed."

"Yes, you would."

"I don't want to. I've fantasized a nice death for him, Sean."

"Don't do anything stupid. Actually Matthew, just get me his address. You don't have to come. It may be better if you aren't in-volved."

"I was more calling you for advice, Sean, but thanks."

"We should talk in person rather than over the phone. Come over for a cup of tea."

"Thanks for the offer. Let me think about it."

"What's the guy's name?"

"James Basciuseson… Mr. B."

Chapter 25

It often took a few days for points won or lost in the domestic quarrels between Katya and myself to lose their poignancy. A week went by and things had returned to more or less normal. As the weather was still warm, I decided to go for a run instead of swimming that night. The sun was blindingly low and beautiful on the horizon. I had looked up where Sara lived. I thought I might go jogging in that direction—to say hello if she were outside.

As I was setting out, I noticed a solitary figure walking toward me on the sidewalk. When I approached, I saw it was James, smiling a Mona Lisa smile. I was quite surprised to meet him here, since I lived on a residential crescent on the other side of the canal from his apartment. He was dressed fashionably in slacks and a crisp checked sport shirt. He seemed to be casing my house.

"Hi James! What are you doing here?" I asked. "Are you planning a break and enter?"

"Just out for a bit of a walk, Matthew. Haven't been to your neck of the woods before."

I had seen his condo, but it was true that he had never been to my house. I hadn't planned to take our relationship to this next level. After our previous visit, I hadn't exchanged phone numbers with him, so we wouldn't be arranging any romantic encounters. His smile broadened, as if encouraging an invitation. This wasn't in my plans.

"Well, I'm just out for a run," I said, avoiding the subject. I didn't apologize for my lack of hospitality, as this would logically require a rain cheque invitation. "How are you, James? No swimming for you tonight? Aren't you afraid of losing your boyish good looks?" I was looking for a way to escape.

"Ha ha. I'm doing pretty well thanks... I noticed there's some algae on your aluminum siding. Of course, your house faces north, but I wonder whether there's water leaking behind or overflowing your gutters."

"That could be."

He was still gazing toward my house. "Have you been doing some gardening?"

"Yeah, a little," I said modestly. The yard looked nice because my lawn service had just mown the grass. "Who would have thought I'd end up a grass farmer? And Grampa likes to keep his hand in."

"Who is Grampa?"

"Grampa is Katya's dad. He lives with us now."

James seemed surprised. "That's awfully nice of you Matt, to take him in."

"Well, he has his idiosyncrasies, but he isn't a lot of trouble. Do you know where your parents are, James?" This was rhetorical, mimicking the newscaster from Buffalo who opened by saying it was 11 p.m. and wondering whether you knew where your children were.

"Oh, my dad passed away years ago. Mum's in a retirement residence in Ottawa. She's still pretty good, but she needs a lot of help."

"That's nice. Are you doing any running these days?" I was eager to leave.

"Not that much, Matt. I was out with the group, cycling a few days ago. We went over 50 k's."

"Okay, see you later then, James." I began jogging on the spot to show I had a fitness agenda.

"We should get together again for a beer—or maybe as a three-some with your wife. There's something I want to talk with you about."

"You don't want your girlfriend there to take pictures?"

"What? Oh, no—we've both moved on."

"We'll have to do that some time," I said, meaning we should really never do that. I started to move away from him.

"Okay then, Matt," he said. I jogged down the street, but as I was turning the corner I glanced over my shoulder. He hadn't advanced very far.

I like to run on a road that parallels the canal a few blocks from my house. The rich folks have their houses there on oversized lots with nice landscaping and water views. On my way back, I run along the canal bank on a public access path behind their houses, waking up sleeping ducks and geese that squawk off into the water. I have a loop that takes three-quarters of an hour.

I had only been running ten minutes when a passing car slowed and began cruising beside me. The window rolled down and I heard a voice call, "Hey Matt, great pace. We really do have to talk. Can we go out for a beer after your run?" James was leaning out the window. He must have had his car parked around the corner from my house to have caught up with me so quickly.

"James—it's not a good time—some other time maybe."

"She's the love of my life, Matt. She's my soul mate," he blurted out.

I stopped moving and waited for what was coming. He had stopped his car. The next words out of his mouth were, "I've been seeing your wife, Matt. We're in love. No one is to blame."

I didn't say anything. I was too astonished. I stared at him. This had been pre-ordained. He was protected by the metal body of the car, so I couldn't get at him.

"I'm not sure I know what you are telling me, James." I was stalling for time, for negotiating room, trying to think over the noise of the blood rushing in my head. A lone car passed, and the sound of its motor faded away.

"I'm sorry, Matt. We didn't mean for this to happen. We just have this amazing supernatural chemistry and compatibility. We were meant for each other."

It sounded heartfelt. The scheming bastard may have convinced himself that this was true. Perhaps he did this subconsciously and for him it was.

"We should all sit down and talk in a rational manner, to try to sort out what to do next." James wanted to map out his future. His dream of becoming a gentleman farmer hadn't materialized. He was looking forward to becoming an urban squire and stamping my return address on his envelopes.

I heard myself saying, "I don't want to sit down with you, James. I won't be sitting down with you. I won't be talking with you."

"You are in shock now, Matt. I understand what you are going through. Okay. We will do this another time." His brows knit together in mock concern. "I will speak with Katya about it and then we will have to meet."

"So, she doesn't know you are here confronting me?"

"No. She wasn't sure how to handle it. I think it's better this way—to make a clean breast of it—to have everything out in the open."

I began to think that James might be pushing an agenda that Katya wasn't in on. Perhaps there was still hope.

"I think you should get out of here and leave me alone. Otherwise, I might have to kill you."

The street was suffused with gentle twilight.

"Okay, Matt," he said mournfully. He felt my pain. He pulled away from the curb and drove away slowly, as befitted the occasion.

I carried on with my run, running further and harder than ever before. I had limitless energy because I was fuelled by grief and anxiety. Home was no longer a sanctuary. My world was imploding. I was going over arguments in my mind that I had had with Katya—replaying them to see what I could have said differently that might have been less inflammatory, so the conversation would have gone a different path. We could have gone to bed at night still friends.

At the end of two hours of exercising flat out, I was finally exhausted. Walking down my street, I resolved a course of action. I would say nothing to Katya for the time being. There was nothing to be gained. I would be nice to her and try to win back her love. The alternative was a life of chaos and pain. If it was true that she had had a liaison with James, it was also true that I was not blameless. If I had been more sensitive to her needs, less quick to give free reign to my temper, this might not have happened.

When I first met Katya, she was a devout Catholic. We travelled to a weekend medical conference together because we couldn't stand to be separated. At my suggestion, we went to an historic Catholic church for the Sunday morning service, because we were tourists, and I was curious. To my surprise, Katya curtsied when she entered the church and again before she went down a row in the pews. Before she sat down, she did the sign of the cross—wallet, keys, spectacles, testicles—in her case ovaries. I don't think she would do that now.

I knew that whatever bad was in her, I had a hand in putting there. She had learned cynicism from me. She reacted to criticism with attack, the way I had taught her. For every action, there must be an equal and opposite reaction. She had witnessed my reactions and mirrored them. I lectured and attempted to dominate. She was the neurotic patient whose concerns I could minimize. I was the smart

187

guy who was always right. It was my job as a husband to protect her. I didn't think it would be from myself.

Katya probably believed that in James she had met a man for whom she could check all the boxes as her ideal. There might be a few people like that in the world for everyone. You were lucky if one of them was your spouse, or was really the person they seemed. You were lucky if your perfect love was not also a murderer. James was exactly the right wrong guy.

When I got home, Katya was watching television with her father. During the school term, she would normally mark papers or work on the next day's lesson plan in the evening. Like most teachers, her day didn't end at 4 p.m. I had been away for almost three hours. I didn't mention that I had seen James, because my tone of voice would have betrayed my extreme emotional state. I didn't want a scene before bed because then there would be no sleep for anyone.

We went to our separate bedrooms for the night. After Grampa had retired, I went into his bathroom as if to urinate, but really to steal one of his sleeping pills. I thought of all the grievances I had been nursing. None of them were important. Thank God Grampa lived with us. I didn't have to worry about James coming into my house with him there. I had to figure out a way for James to not be a continual temptation for Katya. If perfect love is blind, it is also ephemeral. That was my hope.

I waited a few days to see whether Katya had anything to say to me. There was no difference in her demeanour. I didn't know if she knew what had transpired between James and myself. Trying to sound casual, I asked her about her trip to Toronto again. She described meetings that began with a prayer and touchy-feely hand-holding. When I asked who was there from Coventry that I might know, she said just Aline. In the past, Katya could never lie to me without looking flushed and flustered. She must have learned to lie better.

Chapter 26

The days were still warm although we were well into September. Luke telephoned me unexpectedly and suggested a reunion. I hadn't seen him in over a year. He had broken up with the girlfriend who had replaced his wife. We both had personal problems to talk over.

He drove the two hours to my house on a Saturday. Coming up the sidewalk, just after noon and wearing a plus-sized grin, he called out, "Hey Corgi! How are ya Mutt? I suppose it's more properly Dr. Mutt."

He was dressed in white shorts, shirt and running shoes, carrying a tennis racquet and a new can of tennis balls. His gait was the same as his 18-year-old self. I went down the sidewalk to meet him. "No, it's still Mutt. I'm good! How are you, Luke?"

"Good! Where's Katya?" We enjoyed a man hug.

"Katya just left with her father to visit her sister in Pickering. I think she wanted to give the 'bro's' some space." Katya was not a big fan of Luke's.

"I'm disappointed. Never mind. Fuck her. We'll have fun anyway."

"Come into the house so we can catch up over a cup of coffee and make polite conversation."

We went in and he took a seat at the kitchen table in Katya's chair. He yelled over the din of the espresso machine. "So, you were saying you're a coroner now."

"I got a badge and a bag full of warrants, disposable gloves and toe tags."

He chugged his coffee and I started making another one. He shouted, "So, did you go to our high school reunion?"

"Yeah, I went. Do you remember Murray Moses? He became a bank manager and died of a heart attack while eating his dinner at the age of 42."

"I guess being a bank manager is a stressful job." He paused for a moment while we considered our own mortalities. Then he said, "If it seems like people are dying all around you, it only proves it hasn't been your turn yet."

"Wayney Delaney, the class clown, was there with his boyfriend before I arrived."

"I could see that coming."

"I guess I should have twigged when he always wanted to wrestle to see who could pull the other's pants down."

"Did you wrestle?"

"I'm afraid so."

"You also kissed his sister Doris and never called her."

"On the pool vent. Thanks for remembering. That psycho Wayney actually confronted me about it."

Luke chugged his second coffee, got up abruptly and said, "Let's go play with my fuzzy balls."

Women can meet with their friends just to have a conversation. Men have to interact with parallel play. This could be a vestige of caveman hunting days. Cooperation was necessary to bring down large prey, and communication was necessarily goal directed. I dug out my tennis stuff, and we drove to the municipal courts.

In the spirit of caveman cooperation, we hit the ball to within easy reach of each-other's racquet. We played a few real games as well but were too out of practice to sustain any long rallies. Nonetheless, it was fun to relive that part of our childhood. We quit after an hour and sat on a bench to watch the next players who had been waiting for us to finish.

Luke said, "This is how I envisioned our lives after I finished training as a first surgical assist. We would be united in any conflicts with the rest of the operating room and play tennis in our spare time. It's too bad you couldn't get me a job here."

"It would have been nice," I answered, but I wasn't sure if I really believed it.

"Maybe it's not too late?"

"Well, I can ask around for you."

"Well, it's okay. My life is pretty settled."

"It would be harder to see your kids."

Our relationship had evolved to where I now seemed to be the senior member of the team. We watched the tennis balls getting whacked back and forth across the net. "So how are things with you anyway?" he asked.

"Not so good. I think Katya's having an affair." I had nothing to hide from Luke.

He didn't look surprised. "As the grains of sand through the hourglass, so are the days of our lives, Mutt." It doesn't matter who you are or what station you have attained in life, you are still the same teenager inside and your friends from teen age know it. He looked at me sternly. "What are you going to do about it?"

"I can't just move on and start over again. I don't have enough years left."

"Has she admitted it?"

"No, I haven't confronted her. But her boyfriend has confronted me. He basically asked me to step aside."

"Do you still love her?"

"I couldn't imagine my life without her."

"Who's the guy?"

"A middle-aged Casanova. Most women would consider him attractive. I actually had a beer with him in his apartment. I think he picked me rather than her. He lost his shirt in a divorce settlement and is hoping to recoup by taking half my stuff."

"Possible." I liked that Luke didn't need convincing to see things my way.

We drove home and found our seats in the kitchen again. I put some lunch things on the table. "Have you heard of O. J. Simpson's book, *If I Did It, Here's How It Happened*? I have fantasized a nice death for him."

"Yeah, but O.J. didn't do it 'cause the glove didn't fit."

"I'll take a glove with me that doesn't fit." I poured us both some orange juice. "The mode of death would be one millilitre of succinylcholine deep intramuscularly with a long number 25-gauge needle. Succinylcholine is a muscle paralyzing agent used in anesthesia." I was kidding, but it was cathartic to be able to talk like this.

"I know. We studied anesthetic drugs. What about your dad's shotgun?"

"How do you know about that?"

"You told me."

"I didn't think I'd told anyone."

"Your father was a cop. You had all kinds of guns in your house growing up. You showed me unregistered assault weapons and machine guns behind a fake wall in your basement." Luke leaned back on the hind legs of his kitchen chair.

"He said they were a hedge against inflation. I sold them piecemeal so as not to depress the market. My father said most people would get nervous holding a gun and miss their target. A shotgun was more useful in a crisis for the common man, meaning me. I got mine as a housewarming present."

"A shotgun makes a big hole."

"He said to take it, even though I didn't want it. It was like an insurance policy. I needed it, even if I never used it." I didn't mention my midnight shotgun fire drill in May.

"Whatever happened to your dad?"

"He ate and drank himself to death."

"Yeah, I remember he was a big guy. Is that why you don't drink now?"

"He used to say you can't get fat on pizza or drunk on beer."

"That's only half true. You can get fat on pizza. You should probably stay away from guns, Matt. You're not going to commit the perfect crime with one. Stick with what you're good at."

"I first met James as a coroner. I think he may have had something to do with expediting the death of an old guy whose farm he hoped to inherit."

"Sounds like a real douche bag." Luke leaned back in his chair some more, magically balancing on the hind legs.

"Well then, 'sux' it is. It's broken down into two acetylcholine molecules, which are normal neurotransmitters. There is no chemical assay for it."

"You know this from being a coroner?"

"Not really. I saw it being injected with a long needle into the nasal mucosa of a sleeping victim by a Russian assassin in a spy movie. The actor pretended to fasciculate and die. It had to be succinylcholine."

"So, then it will work for sure. I meant about there being no test."

"In most people, it only lasts a few minutes. One in 2,500 people is a slow metabolizer, where there might be some present in blood for testing. I've never heard of a way to test directly for it. I asked one of the younger pathologists who does autopsies at our hospital, and he's never heard of a test either." My throat felt dry.

"That's good, but it's not good that you asked someone at your hospital."

He had identified a flaw. That's why you need co-conspirators. I wasn't ready to abort the plan. "James is too young to just up and die. I have to supply a credible cause of death. Women usually kill themselves with pills. Men choose violent deaths—most commonly hanging. The best place to hang yourself is from a girder. It supports a man's weight."

"Have you picked out a girder for him?"

"You do realize this is just fantasy, right? There is one in his garage supporting the track for the automatic garage door."

"Would anyone believe he was suicidal?"

"Suicide is a multifactorial and impulsive act, predictable only in hindsight." I was quoting in ironic fashion from my coroners' course.

"How do you convince him to hang himself?"

"Well, I've thought of that too. I know where he lives. I would visit him after dark—park my car on the main street and wear dark clothing—walk the two blocks to his apartment. I'd take a rope and a pre-loaded syringe of succinylcholine in my gym bag. He would be coming home from the gym. I'd pick a night when I saw him there.

I pried the caps from a couple of beers. "I would put on disposable gloves and as he was opening the door from the garage to his apartment, stick the needle through his clothes sideways into his ass crack and inject the sux—then ease him to the floor, so he didn't injure himself."

"He'd be paralyzed, but still conscious. Good." Luke's response contrasted starkly with my disapproval the day he told me about shooting starlings in his cherry tree.

"Yeah... That would be the hard part. I couldn't look at his face. I'd feel sorry for him if I saw his eyes."

"Fuck him." Luke said reflexively. "He's doing just the same thing to you. He's trying to destroy your life. He would deserve it."

"I'd take the rope out and throw it over the girder—take the keys out of the door lock and return them to his pocket—then pick him up using a fireman's lift, put him over my shoulder and hoist him onto the roof of his car. I'd tie a noose around his neck and push him off so that his feet dangled a foot above the floor." I paused for air.

"Is he big?"

"Tall, but I don't think too heavy."

"I don't know if 20 milligrams would be enough, Matt. Use 40 milligrams, 2 millilitres of succinylcholine."

"I've attended autopsies. The departed is naked on a metal gurney and they do a thorough inspection of the front surface before starting the dissection. They look at the groins and antecubital fossae for needle marks. They don't turn the body over for a rigorous back inspection. They might lift a shoulder to make sure there is no protruding knife handle. No one spreads the ass cheeks for a good look. Pimples or sores there would mean nothing."

Luke was watching me closely.

"Most men choose violent suicides," I said.

"Yeah, you said that. You've obviously thought this through."

"It would be easier to just put him in the bathroom, lock it from the inside and pull the door shut, but they would examine the body more rigorously. The bodyguard for Berezowski, the Russian oligarch, found him hanging in his bathroom in England. The Russian secret service tried to kill him lots of times, so they probably did it. People contemplating suicide don't need bodyguards."

"Those fucking Russians again."

"He had a post-mortem, but it didn't show anything. A majority of post-mortems show nothing so it might be okay, but James is youngish and healthy." I was rambling. "It would be better if there was a more obvious cause of death."

"It's better to tie the noose at home and have it ready. You might be too stressed and waste time if you tried to do it there."

"I would take off my shoes, go into his apartment, find his computer and type: 'I am taking the high road. Please tell Tuesday I don't blame anyone. I am sorry.' Tuesday is his daughter. I noticed a stepladder in the garage when I was at his house. If it's still there, I'd open it on the floor under him. I'd bring a feral cat to claw the body—although a cage might attract attention. Then I'd leave through the garage door and close it behind me. That's it. Any cat would do probably." It felt like I was practicing the allocution for my plea bargain.

"They might have some feral cats for you in Afghanistan, Matt. I like it. Make sure no light comes on when the door opens. Some of those automatic garage doors turn on a light. If he has one of those, replace the bulb with a burnt out one. Take a flashlight. Maybe you should go by bicycle so no one sees your car."

"Yeah. I didn't think about the light. Lots of ways to get caught. The hard part would be identifying with his panic, and seeing his eyes—because that would stay with me—maybe also hearing his neck crack when the rope pulled taught."

"At the risk of repeating myself, fuck'im! It's him or you." Teammates backed each other up without question.

"There's a surgeon named Amodeo I would like to do while I'm at it."

"Good. Let's do them both. I'll find him on Facebook. Beer me."

Luke had enjoyed the show. Freudians would call this dreamwork. It was achieving a level of reality that I hadn't expected. The room was revolving around me in slow motion. The odds would be against me. Not many people can commit a perfect crime.

"Thanks Luke."

"Never mind. You saved me from drowning. You dragged me out of the lake the day we hitchhiked to the Bluffs."

196

"Your teeth have grown back in nicely."

It wasn't until I'd finished pouring my heart out that Luke told me anything about his own grief. His personal situation was none too rosy either. He was no longer living with his girlfriend. They had bought a run-down house in The Beach area of Toronto. The area was trendy and even crappy houses cost a lot. She didn't have much money, so he had paid for most of it.

They spent the next several months fixing the place up and furnishing it. Luke wasn't handy, so they had contractors and workmen coming and going. He used up most of his money because he also gave his wife a big chunk to live on and pay for his kids' needs. He hadn't seen too much of his children recently because they had taken his wife's side. He intended to turn that around now that he had some time.

Luke and his girlfriend were happy while they were decorating the house together. Her tastes weren't expensive, but things added up. He insisted on nice things to impress her. Luke worked extra shifts and she started to complain about being alone too much in the evenings. She would spend a lot of nights with her children at her parents' house. Sometimes she would leave them there and go out with friends.

She got more secretive about where she was spending her time. She was critical of Luke's personal habits. She got shrill. His consumption of alcohol increased. Things deteriorated, and she asked him to leave the house he had paid for. She made it clear that it was over. I imagined that she must have gotten a glimpse of his real personality and perhaps didn't like it. Luke could be hard to take in big doses. He couldn't afford to keep the good times rolling forever by buying more furniture and major appliances.

She had a new boyfriend now who was a cop. He had moved into the house with her. Luke was trying to get some of his money back, but she wasn't being forthcoming. He would have to sue her. A lawyer told him that it would be difficult to force her out since she had children living with her. He posted nude pictures of her on the internet to coerce her into some form of restitution.

He tried to speak with her, to appeal to her, but she got a restraining order. He couldn't go to the house because of the policeman living there. Luke was staying in a motel room with her cat and cooking on a hot plate. He knew he had probably been bilked, but said that he still loved her. Luke wasn't too smart about women.

Katya arrived back home around 1 a.m. She knew Luke well and said hello and how are things. She was diplomatic enough not to bring up his domestic situation. She said she had left her father at her sister's for a while. She was tired and went to bed. I showed Luke to my father-in-law's bedroom. There were fresh sheets and a towel and some toiletries on the foot of the bed. Katya must have put them there. I slept in Michael's room, which we hadn't altered since he moved out.

Luke left early the next morning. He seemed brighter and happier. I had the feeling that our day together had helped. I walked him to his car.

"Yard looks nice," he said.

"Thanks."

"Your dad used to make you do all the yard work."

"Yeah. I used to cut the grass and spray the apple tree with poison. Who knew poison was bad for you."

"Yeah. Who knew."

"I have a service now."

"Right."

"I'm sorry our conversation took such a morbid turn last night. Are you going to be all right?"

"What about you?" he replied.

"I get by with a little help from my friends."

"Me too, Ringo…me too."

Chapter 27

A week went by and the sky didn't fall. Two members of my department were away, so I was working a lot. It was just as well, as I didn't feel much like going home. There was less tension at work. I was on call for anesthesia again, preparing to be slapped around by and absorb the occasional gut punch from my pager. I did a calculation: I had been in Coventry twenty years and on call every fifth night. That meant I had spent four solid years in this unfortunate state.

Amazingly, at the end of the operating day there were no emergency cases waiting to be done. I skipped dinner and went to the gym to clear my head with a workout. Five minutes after arriving, I heard my pager beeping. I called the number on display.

"You at the gym?" It was my urologist comrade-in arms Jonathan Fischer. I was too predictable. We were a defence pair at hockey tournaments.

"Just got here."

"Can you come in now?"

"Sure, I guess. What's up?" I wondered if there was room for negotiation.

"Jeremiah Chang is in emerge with a kidney stone, running a fever of 39 degrees. He's okay, but I think he's starting to get septic. I wanna do a ureteroscopy. When can we do it?"

I stopped changing out of and started changing into my street clothes. My workout was over.

Jonathan was waiting in the O.R. lounge when I arrived. He was tall, like most surgeons, with a long face and rimless glasses that made him look professorial. He was into his sixties now and taking more time off. Despite looking at or holding penises all day long for a living, he had a beautiful wife and two grown children.

"Sorry to call you back in."

"For a good cause. You been away somewhere?" I hadn't seen him for a while.

"Yes, I was at a conference in South Africa, one in Brazil before that—tax deductible holidays."

"How were they?"

"Good places to disappear. I was back at work today, doing vasectomies under local anesthesia with Sara. The men got all flustered when they looked into her emerald eyes and fainted when they saw the scalpel. Jewish girls don't often have green eyes. She's gorgeous, isn't she?"

"Yes," I said. "And nobody has."

"Angels might have eyes like that."

"I heard you had a fire, Jonathan."

"The patient must have passed gas while I was using electrocautery."

"Were his scrotal hairs sparkling?"

"Like a Christmas tree. I was pretty upset about it."

"You should go back to two bricks, or an angry ferret. Too much alcohol-based skin wash in matted hair can also cause fires, can't it?" This was more likely than the gas-passing theory.

"That's what his lawyers might say."

"Yeah—sorry. I'm an A-hole." It can't have been fun when that happened. "Where's Jeremiah?"

Jeremiah was waiting on a stretcher in the corridor outside the operating room. He looked pale.

"Hi Jeremiah. Heard you weren't feeling well."

"I'm okay, Matthew. How are your wife and son?"

"They're fine, but let's make this about you."

"Matthew, I had to put my cat down today."

"I'm sorry, Jeremiah."

"It was losing control of its bowels."

"Was it old and demented?"

"Yes. My wife couldn't do it. I had to drive it to a veterinarian."

"You can't have a cat shitting in the house, Jeremiah. You can get another one."

"I don't think that they are strictly interchangeable. I am a Buddhist, and it is a living thing, but it was defaecating in my family room. You can't have that, can you Matthew. This is a problem, as you know. It's better to get professional help with these things."

Well, I did know. I asked him all the usual questions in the usual sequence. "Do you have any heart or lung disease? Do you have any loose, capped or false teeth?" This was the way to remain detached and avoid mistakes.

"I have a partial denture, but it doesn't come out."

I was used to hearing this. He was embarrassed to be seen without it. "It has to be removed so it doesn't obstruct your breathing or get lost."

He hesitated. "All business now, eh Matthew?"

"Don't worry. Bruno, our orderly, might use it to have his dinner, but he'll return it before you get back from surgery."

He took out the denture and gave me a gap-toothed smile.

Working on colleagues used to make me anxious. I was mostly past that. I pushed Jeremiah and stretcher into the operating room and settled him on the operating table.

"Are those dead flies?" he asked.

I followed his gaze up to the fluorescent lights, and there were indeed dead flies trapped on the inside of their plate glass covers.

"This part of the hospital is ancient, but the good thing is that we have really nice windows with a panoramic city view. You don't get that in new operating rooms. It helps us stay upbeat." I was suavely changing the subject. I didn't like hearing anyone say "dead" in the O.R. It was bad luck. "What kind of music do you like?"

Our hospital had recently gotten Wi-Fi. I had taken to asking patients for a musical selection to set them at ease. It suddenly occurred to me the alternative inference they could draw was that it was a last request.

"I like anything," he moaned. He was getting sicker, as Jonathan had predicted.

"Okay, name an artist. I can get you almost anything with internet radio."

"Okay then, Toby Keith."

"Okay, sure." Poor Jeremiah was devolving into a gap-toothed country music fan.

Sara was waiting at the head of the bed. "How come you're still working today?" I wondered if she knew about my domestic situation.

"Doing a double, so you don't get lonely. Christina called in sick again at 5 a.m." Sara fluttered her long eyelashes.

"She must have set her alarm."

Sara held the anesthesia mask over Jeremiah's face. "This is just oxygen. Matthew is going to give you some really excellent medications through the intravenous. He is a fabulous bartender." With her free hand, she offered the female end of the injection port for me to insert the first syringe.

"Yeah, except this bartender serves you even after you're unconscious," Jonathan elaborated.

"I know you'll all do a good job." Jeremiah's face was covered by the mask.

"Money back guarantee," Jonathan said soothingly.

I gave Jeremiah some intravenous fentanyl. He mumbled something. Putting my ear next to the mask, I asked him to repeat it. I pushed propofol and a muscle paralyzing agent into the IV, and he quickly lost consciousness to Toby's jingo chorus.

"What did he say?" Jonathan asked.

"I'm not sure. It sounded like, 'I don't feel lucky.' He's feeling guilty about murdering his cat."

Jeremiah was prescient. He must have been more septic than he seemed, or I had realized. He dropped his blood pressure, and I brought it back with fluids and vasopressors. I started some gorilla-cillin. He had a run of ventricular tachycardia. It was unnerving seeing him lying there, ill and still. I put it out of my mind, as I do with most emotions, and reverted to autopilot.

Jonathan passed a flexible fibreoptic ureteroscope into Jeremiah's penis and bladder and up into the ureter, the passage between the kidney and bladder. This is where the stone was lodged. I watched on the monitor while he broke it up with a laser directed through the instrument. When he was done, he inserted a catheter to drain the urine into a bag. The three of us slid Jeremiah over a plastic board back onto his stretcher.

The urinary catheter running from his penis to the full urine bag that we had forgotten on the floor was stretched as taut as a violin string. This elicited a frown from Jonathan and a groan from Sara. Jonathan hoisted the bag onto the stretcher casually and said, "Add prostatic massage to the procedure list."

When we arrived in the recovery room, Jeremiah was fully alert. "Meet your new nurses, Karen and Sharon," I told him.

It was actually Olga and Char, the student nurse, who received us. Char asked, "Did he get a general anesthetic?"

Jeremiah's eyes were open and focused and sharing a confidence with me. I was proud that I had timed his waking to coincide perfectly with the end of surgery. The stretching his urethra got must have helped. His incontinent cat story had given me permission to deal with James harshly.

"Yes. You can't use hypnosis for this operation."

Char seemed suitably impressed. "How long have you been doing this?" she asked.

"Twenty years."

"Do you like it?"

"Let's say yes."

"Is it true that surgeons used to throw scalpels at the nurses?" She wanted to find out before she advanced any further in this line of work.

"Well, blunt instruments anyway."

"I heard surgeons used to smoke in the operating rooms," Sara said.

"They smoked, but in the lounge," I replied. The only person I could think of in the O.R. who still smoked was Joanie.

"And everyone was having sex in the closets..." Sara said, smiling provocatively.

"That part is true. That's why they have to build modern hospitals without closets," I explained.

"There was a doctor looking for you. He said he's an obstetrician," the student said.

There was a Cesarean section to do with Adam. Surgeons always trotted out one more case just when I had my heart set on being done. We did the section in the obstetric unit, and I sat down at the nursing station to finish my charting. The words wouldn't come. It was probably just fatigue, but I had no recollection of the last case. I had done it completely on autopilot. I went into a reverie. I could go home now. Grampa was back and we were keeping up appearances. Doctors often escape their marital problems with work. I seemed to be going down that same shitty road.

Adam interrupted my stream of consciousness. "Hey, did you know that guy on TV who killed his girlfriend?"

"What guy?"

"They said he was an O.R. nurse in Scarborough. You worked in Scarborough, didn't you?"

"No, I grew up in Scarborough. I never worked there. I grew up and left."

"It was gruesome, mon. He stabbed her in the heart and cut her throat. He made sure she wasn't coming back. They have footage on TV of him leaving the crime scene with blood on his pants and wearing leather gloves like 'O. J.' He cut her like a sacrificial lamb. He killed her dead, and then I think he killed himself."

"Scarborough is pretty violent now, like Barbados. They moved a lot of subsidized housing projects there."

"Naa. Barbados' not violent—that's Jamaica. Doh confuse us wid dem ruffians."

Adam had no one left to deliver. We walked together toward the change room to get out of our greens and into our street clothes.

"I heard you and your wife are back together," I said. "I'm glad."

"Ya-mon. Done wid all o' dat chasin' punaani shite."

At least Adam had his life back on track. I noticed he was putting a key into a padlock to open his day locker.

"I never lock my locker," I said. "I don't want anyone to think I'm stealing drugs. They opened the locker of a past president of the Canadian Anesthesia Society and found he was squirreling narcotics."

"In that case, I tink I you pretendin' you not stealin' drugs if you locker not locked."

"Well, you can open the door and see that I'm not."

Adam was layering a sharp outfit onto his trim frame. He had a grey flannel vest on over his checkered shirt. "Then I'll think you moved them to your briefcase."

"Don't say that. If you say it even once, it becomes the truth. People believe that the worse the crime that you are accused of, the more likely it is to be true."

Adam looked at me uncertainly. He looked like he was afraid I might tell him something personal that he would have to respond to. "Well, I always thought you had latent homicidal tendencies."

"Don't let my steely-eyed stare intimidate you." I showed him my stare. Adam squared a grey herringbone peaked dustman's cap onto his shiny brown bald head. He didn't look intimidated.

As soon as I got home, I turned on the TV news. The first item was a video clip of the Scarborough killer walking briskly past some plate glass double doors. They said it was taken by a security camera at the entrance of a veterinary clinic. The image was grainy, and his face was turned away from the camera. He was wearing a baseball cap. Nevertheless, I was 99 per cent sure it was Luke.

Katya came downstairs. She must have heard the television. We hadn't been talking much recently, but I told her the story. We turned the TV back on and they were replaying the video. They were also showing a video of policemen looking in the window of a parked car with their guns drawn. I couldn't see what make of car it was, but it was a black muscle car. I didn't need to watch any more. I was one hundred per cent sure it was Luke.

They identified him later that night. I suppose the cops must have smashed the window of his car with their night sticks or the butt ends of their pistols to pull him out. He was technically still alive, but comatose, with a needle in his arm. He must have injected propofol he stole from work, without adding a muscle paralyzing agent. If he had, he wouldn't have been breathing. He didn't want to risk being awake and paralyzed.

Luke was taken to hospital, attached to a breathing tube and ventilator, and shipped to an intensive care unit in Toronto. The reporters said he had spoken with his ex-wife on his cell phone from his car to say goodbye. She had known that he was serious and had called 911. I needed to speak with his wife, but I would give it a few days. I didn't know how she would feel about me.

Katya was flushed and teary-eyed beside me on the sofa. I hadn't realized she cared for Luke that much. Women will cry non-judgementally. Perhaps she had seen the good in him. I couldn't cry. What was done was done. The reporting was that his ventilator was turned off two days later and he was allowed to die in hospital after being declared brain dead.

I never saw Luke in his state of being dead because as far as I know he didn't have a funeral. If there had been one, press photographers would surely have been there to embarrass any would be mourners, and I hadn't seen any coverage. His wife was estranged. His parents were deceased and his girlfriend murdered. I didn't know how his children felt about him, but they would have been too young to organize a funeral. In my subconscious mind, there was therefore a small chance that he lived on.

I sat in my empty kitchen where Luke had sat, looking out the window at the expensive landscaping. I had failed him. If I had realized how serious his situation was, I could have intervened. I could have extracted him from the intensity of his situation by insisting that he come stay with me. He would have been unable to think straight as long as he was in Scarborough. He had visited me to say goodbye. I had been preoccupied with my own problems.

Murder is a heinous crime. Violence against women is especially heinous. No set of circumstances can excuse it, but I could see what led him there. In his mind, his girlfriend had played him. She may have initially liked him. The financial advantages he offered must have added to his appeal, and she had decided to keep them. She had picked the wrong mark.

Would it help to say he had redeeming qualities? Luke was certainly extreme, but he was always a loyal friend. He had been my staunch defender during our school years. He took my side regardless of any alternate viewpoint. His sense of right and wrong in this respect was rigid and dictated by the responsibilities of friendship—more rigid than mine.

When I lay down that night I began to hallucinate—dreaming to catch up on missed rapid eye movement sleep, without yet being asleep. Luke was still on this earth and in this country. His dark form was waiting quietly in the shadows of his hospital room. He wasn't asking, but he needed help. He had to find asylum, and I was obligated to seek out and shelter his spirit for a while. I might have to make a short trip to the dark side to get him until he could sort out his future.

Chapter 28

I was sitting in my study, looking at my computer. Katya was making clattering noises in the kitchen, emptying the dishwasher. A coroner's call was vibrating on my cell phone. I had already worked a full day in the O.R. I picked up on the fourth vibe, just before it went to voicemail.

"Can you take a case, Dr. Kork?" The phone digital display showed October 2, 10 p.m. Luke had died one week ago.

"What's the address?" After age, the second most important determinant of longevity is address. People with crappy lives tend also to have short ones.

"It's a residence in Coventry. That's where you're based, isn't it? It's a suicide—a hanging. Police are at the scene. Can I give you their number?"

"Okay then. Give me the number. What's the decedent's name and date of birth?" I kicked my door lightly shut. The identifying information belonged to James.

I logged on to our hospital web site from my home computer to look up James' medical history, which I could now legally do. He had not been treated for any major illnesses. I dialled the number of the Regional Supervising Coroner on call to ask whether, ethically speaking, I could take this case. I wasn't sure I wanted to.

I got the regional supervisor for Central Ontario region. He was the same, older, plain-speaking gentleman I had gotten advice from when James' almost father-in-law died on the toilet. A lot of coroners in Ontario were older. An older coroner had won a lawsuit contesting mandatory age-based retirement.

"What's the problem, Matt?"

I described the situation and then said, "I knew the decedent a little socially."

"Was he ever your patient?"

"No—wait. I gave him an anesthetic once for an inguinal hernia repair."

"Are there any other coroners in town?"

"One more in Coventry, but he's away in Florida for the winter."

"What winter? Okay, well then, you're it, Matt. It sounds like a clear-cut case. You can't do everything the same way as they might in a bigger centre. Call me from the scene if you have any problems."

I called the police number to let them know I was on my way. Although I knew them already, I listened passively as Officer Mighty Mouse gave me directions. James had a respectable address, but he was dead anyway.

Coroners are reputedly immune from traffic tickets. As it would be potentially embarrassing to test this premise, I was used to exceeding the speed limit by only a comfortable ten clicks. Today, I barely touched the accelerator. It had nothing to do with my promise to make this cop wait. I was in no rush to get back to James' apartment. I wondered whether I had killed him and somehow forgotten about it.

There was a police car on the street and another in James' driveway. The engine of this car was running and one window was half open. No one was inside. I could hear lonely staccato chatter from the dispatch radio. Officer Mighty Mouse was waiting beside the garage. After a flash of recognition, inhaling, exhaling and calling me sir, he escorted me through the building entrance to the second floor. The chief investigating officer, Detective Sergeant Branko Markovic, was waiting outside James' apartment.

Branko and I had worked together before. I saw him occasionally at the Rec Complex. He was lanky and middle-aged, with a nose like a can opener for sniffing out perps. He wore a loose-fitting suit as plain clothes cops do to hide their guns. He was as jaded as anyone, but I knew him to be diligent and forthright. He was a younger version of my father's cop friends.

"Hey Matt. Good to see you. Sorry to get you up."

"That's all right. My sleep is screwed up anyway. I don't go to bed this early."

"You might want to smear some Vick's VapoRub under your nose for this one."

"I knew this guy," I said. "I used to see him at the gym."

"No kidding? Small world."

The coroner is in charge of a death scene unless there is any evidence of criminality, in which case the police take over. From his attitude, I presumed I was in charge. As Branko opened the door, we were met by a wall of heat and the odour of decomposition. A cat exited past us and raced down the corridor, disappearing down the stairs.

"The neighbours called it in because of the smell," he said. "They reported that there had been a stray cat hanging around. He must have adopted it because there's a bowl on the kitchen floor." We went through the hallway into the living room. "The apartment's a little messy, as you might expect from a bachelor lifestyle."

James' artwork was now up on the walls. It was abstract, modern and attractive. There was still a lot of stuff in boxes. As the coroner, I was entitled to look through his private effects. I opened a few drawers and made a display of looking in his medicine cabinet. A few bottles containing giant herbal and vitamin supplement capsules decorated the shelves.

"Did you find any prescription drugs anywhere?" I asked.

"Just some Tylenol and Pepto-Bismol on his night table. Can that combination kill you?"

"The Tylenol can kill you if you can afford to wait three days."

We began walking back toward the living room passing the work alcove.

"There's a suicide note."

"Where is it?"

"It's typed on his computer."

"Relatives like to destroy suicide notes," I said, and we stopped walking.

"No relatives around… I had a constable go through the garbage in case he printed a first draft."

"Where's his next of kin?"

"He has an ex-wife and a daughter who the note is addressed to. Their numbers were on his cell phone. I was talking to them just before you got here."

"How were they?"

"The daughter was broken up. The wife was angry, like my ex-wife. That outlasts an average lifespan." Branko's face was dead-pan.

"We can go view the body first."

"I think that's where the money is. You can see the note when we come up for air. We kept the outside garage door closed to be mean to gawkers. Brace yourself."

We went down a set of stairs. I let him show me the way to the garage, although I knew it. The door was open. A terrible weight at the end of an extremely taught rope was suspended from a girder. It seemed to be James, but he was not at his best.

"Not a very good-lookin' corpse," Branko volunteered.

James' head was torqued at an unnatural angle. It was bloated, blistered and oozing, nearly black in colour. The lips and cheeks were missing, exposing dental sockets and cheekbones. Newborn flies were testing their wings in a cloud around his head and little white maggots wriggled in his eyes. His pants had multiple small rips and puncture holes.

"It seems the cat climbed up his legs to get at his face. It's been up there more than once. What do you think, Matt?"

"I think he's been up there a week or so—maybe less. The heat would have accelerated the decomposition."

"Yeah, that's what I thought too."

The body was dangling a foot off the ground and a foot from the side of James' car. There was an open stepladder askew on its side on the concrete floor, as if kicked there. A police photographer, who was with us in the garage, was packing up a professional-looking camera.

"Matt, meet Caleb, our new 'ident' officer."

"Hey," I acknowledged the fresh-faced photographer. I didn't shake hands because I wasn't sure where his hands had been.

"I think I've got enough shots now. Okay if I go?" Caleb asked. He was a constable, so he needed permission. The stench was over-whelming.

"Did you get some good shots of the rope around his neck and the ladder position?" Branko asked.

"Yes, I did."

"Okay. See you back at the ranch," Branko said.

I put on two layers of disposable gloves and walked up to the body with my pen and clipboard to take notes. I laid them on the floor, pulled up his shirt and undid his pants to pull them down. The discoloured wet skin began coming off in sheets, so I stopped. There was nothing really to examine. I peeled off the top layer of gloves before grabbing my clipboard again. I was never sure of the etiquette of where to dump used gloves. Branko watched as I awkwardly placed them in a corner.

"Do you want to read the note on his computer now?" he asked.

"Yes, I'd like to see it," I said, modulating my tone to a matter-of-fact pitch. I'd been to scenes with decomposition before, but not this gruesome.

We went back into the apartment. Branko jostled the mouse for James' desktop computer and it sprang to life. The open page read: "I am taking the high road. Please tell Tuesday that I love her. I don't blame anyone. I am sorry." Life imitates art.

"Do you think she was born on a Tuesday?" Branko asked.

"I don't know."

"Must have gotten teased a lot, about being Tuesday every day, crap like that," Branko said. "I wonder if she was mad about it."

"Better than Moon-Unit."

"Please tell Moon-Unit that I love her, and Major Tom... So, can I call the body removal service?" The funeral homes did body removals as a side business. Branko must have been there a long time already, and he wanted to get the wheels in motion.

"Yeah, give me a minute." I needed a better look at the computer.

"Are you going to want a post?"

If I ordered a post-mortem examination, the body was going to a hospital, not a funeral home. Our hospital, like many community hospitals had recently stopped doing coroners' autopsies, so the body would have to go to Toronto. Forensic pathology was being centralized in major cities.

"Every suicide has to have at least an external exam," I said. "I have to phone the pathologist on call to let him know."

"Can we call the body removal service?" Branko persisted. "Who do you like—Schade's or Christobel's? Christobel's is quicker." Competition for business was cutthroat.

"Yeah, go ahead. I don't care who. I'm going to make a few calls," I said, not leaving my chair. Branko went into the corridor to tell the constable to telephone. The air was better out there.

I opened James' email program and scanned the "In" box. There were at least a hundred messages. As I had feared, there was one from Katya that was a few days old. Without reading it, I highlighted it and pressed delete, and then deleted it from the deleted emails folder. I didn't see anything else from her, but I couldn't spend more time at the computer without arousing suspicion.

Branko came over to see what I was doing. "I was looking at his most recent emails and internet searches," I said.

"What did you find?"

I opened the browser and the search history. "There are no 'how to commit suicide' web searches anyway. Maybe you should take the computer as evidence."

"Yeah, I suppose. The ident officer did a screen capture of the note—took a shot of it. We don't really need the computer. We'll take his cell phone. It's lighter to carry." For him this was an open-and-shut case.

"Yeah, okay. Was there anything else on his phone?"

"There were some texts from his daughter. There were some pictures of houses. It's just a shitty old flip phone, so there won't be much on it. The records of calls older than two weeks are automatically deleted on most of these."

I suddenly realized that when I was hatching my plans with Luke, I hadn't considered that there would be cell phone records with service providers that could be subpoenaed. These might show calls from Katya.

"Let's see the photos," I said.

Branko scrolled through them and I was shocked to see a photograph of my own beautiful house. Then he brought up a photo of the interior of my study. James must have been planning some renova-

215

tions. He must have been in my house the night I arrived home from my road trip with Sean. James probably left without closing the front door completely, so I wouldn't hear the latch engage. I could have shot him and had a plausible defence. I thanked Branko and he flipped the phone shut again without comment.

I said, "I still have to phone the pathologist and next of kin."

I retrieved the pathologists' call schedule from my bag and dialled the number in the self-important city of Toronto. I chose my words carefully while Branko listened beside me.

"Hi. I'm sending you a probable suicide from Coventry. There's been a lot of decomposition, so he has been here for a week or so. You could just do an external exam and some toxicology, but because of the state of decomposition I think you should probably do a full exam." Hanging victims didn't necessarily require a full autopsy.

"I always do a full autopsy, especially in 'decomp' cases. What if I were to just do an external and then some question cropped up in a week when the body had been released? We only get one chance at this."

I had only dealt with this guy once before, and he didn't know me. He was a forensic pathologist, which is a sub-specialty. His society had recently launched a campaign to wrest control of death investigations from coroners. They felt their expertise trumped ours. There might be more glory in a medical examiner system such as exists in the United States. There were plenty of examples of crusading forensic pathologists on the silver screen to emulate.

"Okay, sure, do a full autopsy." This included a complete gory evisceration of abdominal and chest organs and sawing open the skull to remove the brain.

"Did you get a positive ID?" he asked.

"I think so, but he's pretty disfigured."

"Was the apartment secure?"

"What do you mean?"

216

"Were the doors and windows locked?" This fellow was in the forensics trade and he was using the lingo.

"He was found in his garage. I believe the doors and windows were locked, but I suppose people with universal remotes can open any garage door." I didn't know if there was such a thing as a universal remote. I had heard of thieves trying all the possible frequencies that garage doors use.

"You don't need a remote to close a garage door. We would have presumptive ID if he had locked himself in with a dead bolt. Could you check whether there are any dental records and issue a warrant to seize?"

"Sure." I didn't tell him that the real James would have a missing right upper bicuspid.

"Did he have a criminal record? We might be able to match a fingerprint."

Branko overheard and shook his head.

"No."

"Do the police want to attend the post-mortem?"

"I'll ask."

Branko didn't look enthusiastic. He would have to get up early the next day and go on his own time. He hesitated and then said, "Yeah, all right."

"Okay, tell them to be here at 9 a.m. tomorrow. Have them bring the dental records. Are you working tomorrow? I'll call you around noon with the results. Make sure your phone number is on the warrant."

The warrant for a post-mortem examination is a four-page information sheet that I had to complete for the pathologist and send with the body. I used to fill these out in expansive detail before I realized that writing less took less time. I didn't leave any white spaces today. My handwriting was shaky and barely legible.

As I didn't think an estranged wife qualified as next of kin, I dialled James' daughter's number. She answered on the first ring. She was very weepy, so I gave her the facts and as much professional sympathy as I could muster. Although I had met her at the civic pool, there was no sign of recognition in her voice. I didn't think she would remember me unless she saw me again in person.

"Okay, I think I'm done." I looked at Officer Mouse. "You can take the body down." There were three policemen present, but none of them moved.

"The body removal people can put him in a bag first," Branko said grimly. They were waiting for the undertakers to get slimed.

Chapter 29

The call from the pathologist came through the next day when I was in the O.R.

"Didn't find too much," he said. "His neck showed a rising abraded furrow of course. There were lots of scratch marks and predation of the face, as you noted. Fluffy must have gotten hungry." He seemed friendlier. I suspected he had found nothing more than the obvious and was considering letting me into the club.

"Bad kitty."

"I see on your referral note, you wrote that he had been treated for lymphoma. There was some scarring from radiation therapy, but no obvious signs of lymphoma. I can't be definitive because of the decomp. Oh, he had prostate cancer. It wasn't invading capsule and I didn't see any mets." "Mets" were metastases or distant spread of cancer.

That must have been a new diagnosis. Prostate cancer didn't appear anywhere on James' hospital medical record when I looked him up. Prostate cancer at that stage is often just an incidental finding. Most men who die of old age have it if an autopsy is done. In the late stages, the treatment for it includes castration.

"Did you do any toxicology?" I asked.

"No blood left. No vitreous either." Vitreous was fluid in the eye. "Too much putrefaction. Global warming, I suppose. We could send a piece of liver if you have any special concerns. I don't think he had a 'psych' history or any history of drug abuse, did he?"

"No special concerns," I said. I had recently stopped liking myself.

"Okay then, Matt. I'm going to do some sections and you should have my final report in a month or two."

"Thanks." The average time was closer to five or six months. No one knows why it takes so long for autopsy reports to be completed.

"Have a great day."

I called Branko to give him the result of the post-mortem. Emailing was easier than telephoning the initial pathology reports to investigating officers. It was hard to know what shift they would be working. Branko would probably already know the result if he had attended the autopsy, but I wanted to hear his voice. I wanted to know if he had developed any misgivings about a suicide verdict.

There was no note of caution in Branko's speech. He wanted me to call him with the toxicology results when they became available. He would keep the file open until then. His friendliness, and the pathologist's, made me sad. I hoped there was a way back for me across this bridge. I said that there might be some toxicology from liver or urine, but that the result might take months.

On an impulse, I looked up my notes on the Anderson case when I got home. I wanted the name and number of the neighbour who had reported James to the police. He had said that if anything ever happened to Mr. Anderson, they should suspect James. I got the neighbour on the line, told him who I was and asked him to recall the events surrounding the death.

"Yeah, I called the cops," he said. "I had to talk to the answering machine. I seen them shouting at each other in the bank."

"Did you know Jimmy very well?"

"No, I didn't know him *very well*. I known him to see him and I heard him yelling at my dog over the fence one time."

"What were they arguing about in the bank?"

"Oh, I don't know. Money probably. Jesus, they were both furious. Jimmy especially."

"And then you called the cops and recanted."

"Recounted?"

"Recanted."

"I never heard tell of it."

"What do you mean?"

"I never called anybody back. I got a call from the coroners to tell me they had investigated into my complaint and there was nothing to it."

"Who did you speak with?"

"I don't know. I think he was Dr. Kork. That's you—or is that your brother?"

"I didn't call you. Okay, thanks. I think I know what happened... Was there anything else that made you suspicious of Jimmy?"

"He didn't like country people nor country life. I heard him yelling at my dog over the fence. My dog took sick and died, but *he* didn't know about that."

"Thanks for your time."

"Is that it? Is everything okay?"

"Yes. Sorry about your dog."

I called the Warwick Ontario Provincial Police detachment, identified myself and asked to speak with the duty sergeant. It was still early enough that they had staff there.

"Can you give me the name of the female officer who was involved in the Anderson case from last November?"

After a few minutes, he came back on the line and said, "That would be Constable Gupta. You're in luck. She just came in. I'll put her on."

"Constable Julie Gupta here."

"Do you remember I spoke with you back in November about the Anderson case? He was an old farmer who was found without vital signs on his toilet. You spoke with a neighbour who advised you to be suspicious of the daughter's fiancé."

"Yeah I remember. It wasn't my case. I was just covering for the investigating officer who was off duty. There was nothing in it though."

"Did you speak with the neighbour in person?"

"I don't think so. I guess I should have. He telephoned the next day and got me. Why?"

"What did he sound like?"

"Very mellow. Like an actor."

"Okay. You were probably speaking with the fiancé."

"Really? That's embarrassing. I guess we should take a little drive out there and talk with the fiancé again."

"Too late. He's dead."

This was an interesting situation. James had impersonated me to the neighbour and the neighbour to police to subvert an investigation. Coroners' cases are confidential, but I would often discuss some details with Katya. I could trust her not to repeat anything. I didn't mention this one. We weren't on good terms at that time. We danced around each other in the house like shadows. I felt she could barely stand to look at me. When our eyes did make contact, something like accusation or blame glistened in hers.

New deep vertical lines were forming between Katya's eyebrows. I needed to rest my finger over the lines and smooth them magically away. I needed to tell her about James, but I couldn't because you can't speak ill of the dead. He was a martyr and her lover. Married people know that couples go through cycles of apart-and togetherness. This was one of those apart times—the most severe one we had ever had.

PART 3

October 2018

Love can never be, exactly like we want it to be. —The Mamas and the Papas

Chapter **30**

I came home from work four years to the day after James' death with the subpoena unopened in my briefcase. "The anesthetic given by Dr. Kork was of the type that was known or should have been known to cause immune suppression. This caused Mr. Basciuseson's lymphoma and prostate cancer to progress, which in turn resulted in his committing suicide. Alternatively, if it did not cause Mr. Basciuseson's cancer to progress, it caused an exacerbation of his bipolar affective disorder, which led to his suicide. Dr. Kork had a conflict of interest in acting as the coroner investigating Mr. Basciuseson's death in that he both gave the anesthetic that led to his death and was in a position to cover up the actual cause of the death."

Morality. It gets complicated when happy endings must justify unhappy means. Most people are capable of terrible things, given the right set of circumstances. There is an American attorney hawking his wares on television who says sometimes good people make mistakes. That didn't exactly describe me, but I think the spirit of it is correct. All's fair in love and war. None of the usual rules apply.

What happened to Mr. B? Although my colleague Zack was taunting me with the question, I think that he, like most people, is searching for what is true. The truth is that I had a temporary but necessary moral lapse, or more exactly, a devolution to a more primitive biological rather than religious based morality. Modern concepts of human morality evolved from the animal instinct to preserve family and tribe. A monkey will kill for this. Pushed to the extreme, I would as well.

I am not a religious man, so I have no fear of punishment in the next life. Religion died for me as an eleven-year-old boy, the day my mother died. I sat by her bedside, holding her hand and she called me Matthias. I prayed fervently for God to let my mother live. I begged with the force of a thousand starving, maimed children in India. I promised every concession, but I didn't pray hard enough because she died anyway. I grew up to be a passably moral person, but not without some bitterness.

I'm not opposed to religion. It makes many people happy. The moral latticework of religion provides a justification for behaving well. Is religion a necessary prerequisite for good behaviour? The prospective, double blinded, randomized, placebo-controlled study has never been done. There is ample evidence to the contrary.

Jeremiah Chang would have been a good person whether or not he had religion. Inner peace cannot be learned. His wistful, philosophical personality was refined, but not inspired by his spirituality. Mark Vandermeer is a good person too. For him, human life is sacred. If he had lived in the Middle Ages, he might have sternly been prescribing corrective beatings to maintain religious orthodoxy. He lacked the power and numbers that religious authorities historically had.

Jeremiah and Mark were interested in my soul. Baptists and Jehovah's Witnesses had kicked the tires. I suppose the Catholics wanted it too. Catholic nuns, not so long ago, whacked my pretty

226

six-year-old wife's hands with a ruler for speaking to the boy seated behind her in class. Nuns had power and numbers over six-year-olds. In this context, I am a saint.

A monkey will become distressed if it is shown a picture of a decapitated fellow monkey. Because I have been desensitized by my work, I am not appalled by the sight of a dead body in that way. Of course, this would not apply if the corpse belonged to someone close to me. I didn't view either of my parent's bodies when they died. The macabre image of their death masks would have stayed with me. I don't know what happened to Luke's body, but I wouldn't have looked at it. James' was just business.

I hadn't known about James' "bipolar affective disorder." It was on the subpoena I was served with, but it hadn't shown up in our medical records in Coventry. The diagnosis was doubtful. It was probably just a convenient label someone had used once for whatever personality disorder he had that defied categorization. He wasn't taking lithium, the standard treatment. Actually, he wasn't on any medications, so maybe he had decided to stop taking his drugs. Being manic occasionally probably felt good. He was a genuine television star in his manic phases.

Like most corpses, James had been completely gone and almost forgotten. He never visited me in my sleep the way Luke did. He was a calculating, interior-designing opportunist, and that couldn't be excused by dint of mental illness. Armed with his internet medical acumen, he murdered Mr. Anderson. He also fed a poison steak to the neighbour's dog. I'm fond of dogs, so I would say his fate was karmic. But James couldn't stay dead.

I met with the lawyer assigned to me by the Canadian Doctors' Defence Association about a month after calling the CDDA to tell them I had been served. It was November, and every day the calendar shaved the daylight by a fraction. It was 6 p.m. and already dusk. As I drove downtown, a light rainfall was making halos around the streetlights. I pulled into the parking lot of the best hotel in Coventry, where we had our annual Christmas party, and took the elevator to the top floor. I was looking for the penthouse suite.

My new CDDA lawyer opened the door and introduced himself in a perfunctory way. Richard Chrétien was a man in his forties. He had fashion plate good looks—impressively lean and clean. Despite the late hour, his cleft chin was freshly shaved and shiny. His longish thick dark hair was greased and combed back. He was dressed in a sharp suit, which he seemed very comfortable in. His attitude was business-like.

I entered a large sitting room that contained nice furniture and smelled of new carpet. Wide city-view windows revealed blackness streaked by undulating trickles of water. There was a small suitcase in the corner, designed to fit into the overhead compartment of an airplane. Otherwise, nothing of a personal nature was visible anywhere.

There was another person in the room, obscured from me, sitting in a winged arm chair. Mr. Chrétien gestured toward a chair across a coffee table from him. Angelo Amodeo had arrived ahead of me. He was also involved in Mr. Basciuseson's care, and it dawned on me that he was being sued as well. He was sitting very still, his round face expressionless. He looked at me dully, like a cow at a passing train, but pulsating acne scars betrayed his mental state. His chin moved a slight nod.

Our lawyer asked Angelo to give his version of events first. Angelo spoke slowly, maintaining control, carefully enunciating every syllable. "I am a surgeon. Surgeons operate. I have nothing to do with anesthetic choices or conduct. Dr. Kork was in charge of the anesthesia, and I would always defer to Dr. Kork in that domain. I operated on Mr. Basciuseson to confirm the diagnosis of lymphoma. The treatments for Mr. Basciuseson's lymphoma were all decided by the cancer clinic in Toronto. My only job was to operate when and where I was told, and I did that."

Mr. Chrétien commiserated with Angelo, saying that the lawsuit must be an annoyance. He said that Angelo was being sued because it was standard practice to name everyone in order to not have to refile a claim later. Defendants would fall off the claim as it became more focused. He would see if Angelo could be let out of the action. He would still probably have to attend a few more of these meetings.

The lawyer turned to me and asked for my version, as if that's all it was. "What about this allegation that you were using outdated anesthetics?"

"I wasn't using outdated agents. I was using the agents I trained with. The safest anesthetic is the one you are most experienced with."

"So, the drugs hadn't expired?"

"Absolutely not. It's about marketing. New drugs are introduced when older ones lose their patent protection and cheaper generic versions become available. I am still using some of those."

"Which one did you use?"

"Well, there are probably a dozen different drugs I use during a standard general anesthetic. The primary agent was a volatile gas called dexaflurane. The trade name is Maxiflurane."

The lawyer raised an eyebrow and looked at me quizzically. "Perhaps you should switch to the newest agents."

"They are more expensive."

"So, you are saying that there is nothing to these allegations?"

"That's what I am saying. There might be something to the thing about suppressing immunity. There is some new evidence, but it hasn't really affected anyone's practice significantly. All general anesthetic agents are implicated. The bottom line is that nerve blocks lower the stress response and might depress immunity less than general, or sleeping-type anesthetics."

"What about causing mental depression and suicide?"

"I doubt it. They just pulled that out of their asses. The drugs are gone in a couple of days. They are mostly exhaled with a small percentage metabolized by the liver or excreted by the kidneys."

"And this thing about you being in a conflict-of-interest position in being the coroner investigating the death?"

"Well, I definitely considered that before accepting the case. I ran it past the Regional Supervising Coroner on call and got clearance."

"Is it ethical, or at least acceptable practice that you could be both anesthesiologist and coroner for the same patient? Could the same thing happen on any given day in another municipality?"

"Yes," I said, although I really wasn't sure. "I can give you the name of the guy who was covering that night. Is he being sued too?"

"No. We'll keep his name out of it for now. We cover all the doctors in Ontario, so we try to limit our liability. We'll bring him into it later if we need to."

Mr. Chrétien turned to address Angelo, who had been sitting so quietly I had forgotten he was there. "Does all this jive with your understanding?" he asked. This agnostic attitude was hurtful.

"Yeah, I guess so. Like I said, I'm a cutter. I can't control what the anesthesiologist is doing. I have to trust that he knows his job." Angelo was speaking at a normal pace again, feeling good enough to let some irritation show.

"Well, I'm sure you must be very busy, Dr. Amodeo," Mr. Chrétien said. "There is no need for you to stay any longer."

Angelo fixated me with a narrow squint and then made quickly for the door, brushing past me without saying goodbye. That asshole gave James a roadmap to my house.

After he was gone, Mr. Chrétien asked me to provide more details to help him understand my version of events more clearly. The meeting lasted about two hours in total. I had worked that day, so I was tired and a little disoriented. My explanations didn't elicit the endorsement or approval that I craved.

I knew that Mr. Chrétien didn't have to be my friend, but I would have preferred knowing that he was in my corner. It crossed my mind that he could only serve one Lord at a time, and that was the insurance company. I consoled myself that he must be good or he wouldn't have been given my case.

After we were done, Mr. Chrétien put his feet up on the coffee table. "You know, I prefer working with surgeons. They don't get overly emotional about getting sued. They look at it as a cost of doing business. They know their job and leave us to do ours." He seemed to find playing the role of father confessor to stressed, cry-baby doctors a little boring. As I was leaving, he picked up the television remote and turned on the hockey game.

I thought I would ask him a hockey-related question to get on a friendlier basis. "Hey, is it assault in Canadian law if someone intentionally hits you in the head during a game of recreational hockey?"

"Generally, not. I think that being there implies consent."

"Do you think that we should be on a first name basis with each other?"

"That would be all right," he replied, with what sounded like indifference.

Chapter 31

James was coming back like a whack-a-mole phoenix. God has an unfortunate sense of humour. One day he just reaches out and says, "Let's mess with Matthew a bit—send him James, allow him to be killed off, resurrect him—see what happens." Maybe I was being given the punishment for heresy that had been foreseen in Mark Vandermeer's pamphlet. Maybe it wasn't really God's will that James Jesus should do my wife. Perhaps he was operating independently. In any case, he had to disappear again.

James was not someone that I obsessed about, but he was there like a festering abscess that needed surgery. My life was in limbo while I waited for this drama to play out. I spoke to my lawyer about the case, but no one else—not even Katya. It was a depressing subject anyway. I was strictly heeding the admonition from the CDDA. Richard Chrétien had become my primary confidant and email pen-pal. James was our dirty secret.

The two of us met again a few months later, in a restaurant in Coventry to discuss the hearing for discovery. It was to take place in June in the offices of the lawyer representing James' family. This was a proceeding where lawyers met to disclose their evidence to each other and see what facts they could mutually agree on. Richard said that after the hearing, it was possible the opposing sides could reach some sort of settlement. He said that this was the most common outcome.

The lawyer for James' family was a Mr. Caine. The lawyer acting for the hospital would be Mo Khaliq, whose specialty was defending hospitals. Richard didn't know the lawyer for the drug company. I had never heard of Mohammed Khaliq, but I knew Caine's name from a high-profile wrongful death suit in the newspaper. Richard told me ominously that Mr. Caine had poured a significant amount of his own money into this case, paying for research and expert witnesses.

Richard ran through a list of rapid-fire instructions, as if reciting disclaimers at the end of an infomercial. He told me to answer only the question being asked and to answer briefly. A long answer might provide the plaintiffs' lawyer with new ideas for questions. He said not to answer any questions that required me to venture opinions on areas where I wasn't an expert. If I did so, the opposing lawyer could undermine my credibility by contradicting me later with a real expert. He told me to review my notes before the hearing but not to place them on the table in front of me. I wasn't allowed to consult anything that everyone else wasn't also entitled to examine.

Our meeting was over in half an hour and there were no plans to meet again. It was up to me now to perform. I felt like a Christian about to be ushered into the lions' den, where Christians have to fight on their own, and the lions usually win. Richard Chrétien was a Roman, not a Christian. Adam, an obstetrician with some experience, told me that these hearings have nothing to do with finding the truth. They are about posturing and gamesmanship. He said I would be a tennis ball for the lawyers to bat back and forth. This was marginally better than dead Christian.

Lawyers were also busy on other fronts at our hospital. A class action lawsuit had been launched over an allegation that colonoscopes had been incompletely sterilized between uses. About 2,500 patients were affected. The hospital sent letters advising them to return for testing for hepatitis and AIDS. This had caused such an uproar that we were featured as the lead story on the evening television news out of Toronto.

The young lady newscaster dutifully reported, "A colonoscope is a long black snake that is inserted through the anus into the colon to look for cancer. A camera at the tip transmits the image to an external monitor. Experts now advise mass screening of the population over age 50." This represented an excellent revenue stream for general surgeons and gastroenterologists. The Coventry general surgeons used their influence to make sure no gastroenterologist got privileges at our hospital.

Patients were fasted and purged for three days before the procedure, but the colon can never be completely clean. It appeared that the irrigation channels in the newer scopes used for flushing liquid faeces out of the operator's line of sight had themselves not been properly flushed with disinfectant when they were sent to the cleaners. I could well believe this. I had overheard whispers in the endoscopy suite that we had used the *same* colonoscope on two consecutive patients. The cleaning staff on that occasion had not performed any disinfecting procedure at all. If colonoscopes were white, the shit might have been more easily visible. My impression then was that everyone involved just instinctively agreed to keep silent.

The newscaster showed a clip of the Vice President of Client Experiences reading a statement in our hospital lobby: "Experts have informed us that the risk to clients is extremely low. Nevertheless, in the interests of full disclosure and the historical trust relationship that we have with our clients, we have decided to notify everyone who had colonoscopy during the past year. We are facing this problem head on and along with all of our stakeholders are leveraging this opportunity on a go-forward basis to foster strategic expectations for actionable process improvement and continually refine our mission of exceptional client-centred caring and family relationships." Then, blinking back tears, "Thank you for understanding."

Colonoscopes all look alike. The newer ones had an extra channel. No one at the hospital had any idea which scopes had been used for which patients. All of the general surgeons were implicated. In one of his last reports to the medical transcriptionists, Angelo dictated, "The stupid bitch who cleans the scopes and the stupid whore who hands them to me failed to rinse the shit from the irrigating channel. I then proceeded to do my examination in the usual fashion..."

The scandal broke exactly one month after news of the lawsuit against me became public. The endoscopy suite was shut down until officials from Health Canada had finished their investigation. Dr. Amodeo was so angry at this development that he refused to dictate the backlog of charts for his most recent colonoscopies. With no reports, they had to be repeated at a different institution. Then, he disappeared. Rumours circulated that he had taken a forced leave of absence to regain his composure.

The general surgeons at our hospital had extra time on their hands. Isaiah, their highest biller, was enjoying the fruits of his labour. He was witnessed racing from the scene of a hit and run accident. A police chase ensued. They apprehended him inside his Porsche, which was wrapped around a tree. They found his zip-lock bag of cocaine on the passenger seat.

Isaiah was the senior "aggressive-aggressive" surgeon who had helped refine Angelo's "agg-agg." Who knows how long he had been putting sugar on his boogers. The defendant surgeon's superior agg-agg was partially drug fuelled. These events were disconcerting. If I ever needed an operation, I would have wanted Isaiah to do it— probably still would.

We were having a run of bad luck. Church congregations prayed for us. The Catholic bishop for our diocese called, wondering whether he should get an old priest and a young priest together to perform an exorcism. The Catholic and Protestant hospitals in Coventry had amalgamated some years ago in the interest of getting more public funding. The bleeding Jesus-on-the-cross icons had come down, but the bishop felt he still had jurisdiction. Something had to be done before it began raining frogs. No one was sure what that was.

Doing nothing is sometimes a good option. It can't rain frogs forever. Sometimes you get by with a little help from your friends. In my case, help came from the cleaning staff at the hospital. The colonoscopy crisis diverted attention away from me by giving people something juicier to think about. It made for a better story. People were more able to grasp the concepts when they involved faeces.

Chapter 32

June, the month for my discovery hearing, arrived. I had been nervously awaiting the date. It seemed a long time since Zack wanted to know what happened to Mr. B. It had been eight months.

Things were returning to normal at the hospital. General surgeons were back scoping for dollars. I had been in the newspapers on and off for a week, but this was fading from public memory. Patients asked me to repeat my name when I introduced myself. They didn't really remember the name of the guy from the newspaper who was being sued. When I freely enunciated it syllable by syllable, they were reassured that I wasn't that guy.

I got up early and drove into Toronto along the Gardiner Expressway, an elevated highway that parallels Lake Ontario. It was 8 a.m. on a Saturday, so there was very little traffic. The downtown core was already oppressively warm. I cranked the windows down a little and sipped a breath of dank air from between skyscrapers. I was looking for the Empire Trust building, which housed the offices of Bartholomew Caine LL.B. He was the Basciuseson family's lawyer, who had arranged for my name to be featured prominently on the front page of the Coventry Herald.

I rode the high-speed elevator up and passed through the double glass doors of Suite 4000. Caine Law Group, which seemed to occupy the entire fortieth floor, was hosting the hearing. I saw my lawyer across the large foyer, looking relaxed in a beautifully tailored suit, chatting amiably with a tall man in his fifties. From his tailored suit, I guessed he was another lawyer.

When they finished their conversation, Richard came over and without preliminary niceties handed me a bound volume of several hundred pages. He said that this was evidence that each party involved in the suit had surrendered as voluntary disclosure, and that we would be starting in about fifteen minutes. He shifted his gaze and told me that he probably wouldn't interrupt or object while I was being questioned. The idea seemed to have just occurred to him.

I leafed through the volume sitting by myself in the waiting area. It looked like reams of useless material meant to make the reader give up reading. There was no way I would have time to digest it. One of the pages in the middle, an extremely bad photocopy, appeared to be about James' lymphoma pathology and his response to chemotherapy. It was impossible to decipher. It looked like the copy machine was almost out of ink and only printing partial letters.

After a few minutes, I was ushered into a boardroom with a panoramic view of the lake and white sailboats polka-dotting the blue distance. My lawyer was making small talk with Mr. Caine. He was in his early sixties, corpulent, peering over half glasses, looking proprietorial. The glasses were attached to a gold chain slung around his neck. He was wearing a crisp blue and white striped shirt with a navy tie boasting a symmetrical full Windsor knot. His suit jacket was off, revealing wide matching navy suspenders and sleeve garters. With his shirt cuffs suspended at mid-forearm, he looked ready for action.

Caine walked over confidently to introduce himself and shake my hand. This was done in a friendly fashion, and I suppose it was a strategy to disarm me. I had seen Caine's name in the newspaper in connection with high-profile cases. It was strange how mine had attracted this shark. The potential payoff wasn't huge. He must have smelled my blood in the water. Maybe he divined that the story was newsworthy and saw an opportunity to advertise a nascent medico-legal business.

We were seated around a long rectangular table. It was polished mahogany and could have accommodated two dozen people, although today there were only eight. Caine was seated at the head with an assistant on either side, managing his papers. It appeared that Caine was to be master of ceremonies. He formally introduced each lawyer as his friend or his learned friend and established the order in which they would question me. I was seated in the middle of the table with my back to the view of the lake. I didn't protest. I was in no mood to enjoy it.

Seated across from me was the lawyer for the hospital. Beside him was the lawyer for the manufacturer of Maxiflurane gas, the anesthetic agent I had used. This was the lawyer I had seen speaking with Richard in the lobby. Both the hospital and the anesthetic manufacturer had been named in the suit as well. Richard was seated far away at the head of the table opposite Caine. Angelo Amodeo wasn't present. I hadn't seen him in a while.

I had prepared some handwritten notes with talking points about the three principal allegations. The first was that the primary anesthetic agent I had chosen had suppressed James' immunity enough to cause a recurrence of his lymphoma. The second was that the anesthetic had exacerbated his depression, leading to his suicide. The third was that I had a conflict of interest in acting as both his anesthesiologist and coroner. I didn't think I could remember to emphasize the most salient points without help. I slipped the folded piece of paper out of my pocket and laid it near the edge of the table. If my lawyer noticed this, he didn't seem to mind.

Mr. Caine had assigned the lawyer for Maxiflurane to start. I initially felt a kinship toward him. His company was being unfairly victimized. The evidence that anesthetic agents suppress immunity was very preliminary and was non-existent at the time that James had his surgery. Maxiflurane was certainly under no more suspicion than any other newer agent in current use. In fact, his company produced many of these agents as well.

This lawyer evidently felt no special affection for me as he made his eyes into hard, blank discs. He asked me about current evidence that anesthetic agents can suppress immunity and when this evidence was published. I said that the evidence was preliminary and not specific to his drug. I thought it would make him like me, but this wasn't noticeable. He asked me what I knew about anesthetic agents exacerbating depression. I answered that I wasn't aware of any evidence of long-term mood changes, but that I wasn't an expert in the field.

He produced the product monograph for his drug from the year in which I had given James the anesthetic. He had me read the relevant sections out loud. I was his agreeable puppet, emphasizing the line that "small changes in mood could persist for up to six days post-operatively." He asked me whether I was aware of this fact. I answered that six days was probably the outside limit of how long it took to clear Maxiflurane completely from the body. The Maxiflurane lawyer asked me how long after his anesthetic James had died. It was six months.

Next up was the lawyer who represented the hospital, Mr. Khaliq. He was a short man with a scholarly demeanor and a chin beard like our Somerset county Mennonites. He must have attended better schools than they did because when he opened his mouth some upper crust English jumped out. Despite the warm weather, he was wearing a tweed jacket with elbow patches. He asked me whether I was a hospital employee. I said no. He asked me if I was in fact an independent contractor. I answered that that was what I was.

Mr. Khaliq inquired whether any hospital employee had advised me about which anesthetic agents I should use. I said no. I said that we, in fact, advised the hospital pharmacy which agents to buy for us. I added that naturally the administration was happy when we used less expensive agents. I had selected the agent I did partly because it was economical to use. His attitude changed immediately to one of combativeness.

He asked me whether I had in fact not chosen it because it was the only agent I was familiar with. He said that a member of the operating room staff had suggested to him that I was uncomfortable with newer drugs and techniques. I stared at him incredulously, but he met my stare full on with what looked like righteous indignation. I answered that this wasn't true. I knew how to use newer drugs. I just often chose not to. I had my favourites. If they were older and cheaper, they worked just as well. Everyone benefitted. I realized I might be talking too much.

Mr. Khaliq wanted to know whether I had used nitrous oxide during Mr. Basciuseson's anesthetic. I agreed that I had. He said that a member of the operating room staff had told him that I used this drug routinely. He asked whether it was true that this drug was being abandoned in the modern practice of anesthesia because of its detrimental effects. I remember thinking he was either an idiot or pretending well. The question had nothing to do with any of the allegations. Nevertheless, he had me a little rattled.

I replied that it might be harmful with prolonged exposure, but that Mr. Basciuseson was only under anesthesia for one hour. Mr. Khaliq said he had information that my colleagues rarely used it any more. I said that nitrous oxide was still used fairly commonly. He shook his head dubiously. He wouldn't know anything about nitrous oxide. He had paid an expert for these questions and had a confidante in our operating room.

241

His next question was whether I had specifically checked the expiration date on the Maxiflurane that I had used to anesthetize Mr. B. I said probably, but I probably didn't. It wasn't as if these agents would spoil overnight. It wasn't relevant, since nobody was contending that an outdated drug was responsible for James' death. He said an operating room employee told him that I didn't routinely check expiration dates on anesthetic drugs. He said it went to the root of whether I was a sloppy doctor. I said I was a very good doctor, but no one looked convinced. Negative advertising is powerful.

Mr. Caine was next. He was the only one who looked at all friendly. He remarked on the beautiful weather outside and asked politely if I was ready to continue. He lobbed some softball questions to me about my qualifications. Then, without changing pace or tone, he asked if I routinely examined medical records of patients before giving them anesthetics. I answered that of course I did. He said in that case I must have been aware of Mr. Basciuseson's manic-depressive illness.

I answered that this information was not present anywhere in the medical records available to me in Coventry. He asked whether, if that information had been available to me, I would have chosen a different anesthetic. It was possible that one of Caine's staff had found James' psychiatric history in an archived chart, but I didn't think so. James spent a lot of time growing up in Europe. I said it would have made no difference. Anesthetic agents were not known to cause or exacerbate depression.

Caine inquired whether anesthetic agents put people to sleep, and if so, was this not a form of mental depression? I said that anesthetic agents depressed all cerebrocortical functions to achieve loss of awareness but were not known to specifically affect mood. I added helpfully that these agents were known to cause depression of cardiovascular functions and respiratory drive, and was that what he meant?

He looked over at his assistants who were shuffling papers and not able to tell him anything useful. He pretended not to care, but it was obvious he did not like being defeated on any point. He asked me what was on the piece of paper I had under my left hand. I answered that it was just some personal notes to help me organize my thoughts. He asked whether he might see it. I looked over at my lawyer for help. Richard said, "Give it to him." It was the first time he had spoken.

I handed the paper over. Caine made a show of scrutinizing it, holding it up with his fingertips like a shitty diaper. Then he handed it to his assistant, and that was the last I ever saw of it. After some thought, Caine asked me whether anesthetic agents ever caused long term confusion in elderly patients. I agreed that they could, but didn't offer any more information. My lawyer had advised me not to give him ammunition. He had received plenty by seizing my notes.

Caine wondered next whether I thought a recurrence of cancer might provoke a manic-depressive individual to become depressed. I answered that I wasn't an expert on psychiatric illnesses. He said, "Be that as it may, wouldn't this just be common sense?" I didn't offer a reply. I looked over at my lawyer for approval. I had had the benefit of his wisdom. He wasn't invested anymore.

After a pause for dramatic effect, Caine asked whether I should have used a nerve block technique rather than an immunity suppressing general anesthetic that might provoke a cancer recurrence. I said that the evidence for suppression of immunity was preliminary, and that there was no cancer diagnosis when James received his anesthetic. Caine said that James had both lymphoma and prostate cancer, and it was lucky only one of them had progressed.

Caine paused again, seeming to collect his thoughts, and then abruptly changed course. He wanted to know whether it was ethical for me to have acted as James' anesthesiologist and coroner, especially as I was acquainted with him socially. I responded that I wasn't his physician for more than the anesthetic intervention. My supervisor had given me permission to act as coroner. Being acquainted with patients socially was almost inevitable in a small city.

Caine asked what my relationship was to Mr. Basciuseson, and could everyone agree that we could just henceforth refer to him as Mr. B. Everyone murmured yes in a jocular tone, as if this was a piece of devilish cleverness that had escaped them all. I said I had been his anesthesiologist for his lymph node biopsy and had seen him a few times at the gym. Caine asked whether I would say Mr. B. was my friend, since I had seen him socially. I said he was no more than acquaintance. I wasn't sure whether Caine had a witness placing us together somewhere. He seemed to know more than he was saying.

Caine inquired if I had requested an autopsy for Mr. B. because I had doubts about the cause of death. I said that an autopsy was mandatory for suicides. He asked whether I had considered any causes of death other than suicide. I said that I always try to keep an open mind. Mr. B. was found hanging, so suicide was the likeliest cause. The autopsy had uncovered no other trauma and the toxicology was negative.

He asked if I really thought it was possible that Mr. B. was suicidal. He said that Mr. B's daughter, with whom I was also acquainted socially, had noticed nothing but optimism. She told police that he had a new girlfriend and was looking forward to a career in television. Quoting from coroners' course notes, I answered that suicide was multifactorial and impulsive and predictable only in hindsight.

Caine stated that the body was in an advanced state of decomposition, was it not? Since this was the case, was it possible that signs of trauma could be masked, or indeed, that signs that the body had been moved could be masked. He was dancing dangerously close to a version of the truth that I preferred not to discuss. I said yes, they could be masked, but not trauma sufficient to fracture his skull or a long bone.

I could see where things were heading. This was going to be a circus where I would be in the newspaper every day as the star performer. James' daughter had remembered me. Caine may have had another witness placing James and me together socially. I was getting tired. Caine wasn't letting up. These tennis-playing jackals intended to consume the ball, me, the racquets and net.

I looked over at my lawyer for guidance and got a blank stare. I needed for this to end. They didn't yet know how well I or Katya knew James, and I couldn't afford for them to find out. Adultery is a fine motive for murder. Try to put that jack back in the box. I swallowed hard and made admissions that I didn't have to make. I said that I had neglected to give James the option of a spinal block. I should have done a freezing type anesthetic because it is less immune suppressant than a general anesthetic. I agreed that, in retrospect, I should not have acted as coroner in this case.

Caine relaxed. A partial smile flickered and disappeared. He had recovered from the earlier setback and saved face. His diligence and skill had paid dividends as usual. He nodded knowingly to his assistants and wrapped up his examination. Richard rose from his vantage point at the opposite end of the table. The other lawyers had objected to various things to slow down each other's momentum, but my lawyer never found anything worth objecting to.

Chapter 33

Life returned to normal. I still had a job. I hadn't heard anything from Richard Chrétien or the CDDA. No trial date had been set. It was as if it had all gone away. If people behind the scenes were deciding my fate, they didn't tell me.

After my fifteen minutes of fame, Sara became protective of me, shutting down conversation about my legal woes amongst the nurses. Our flirting at work was becoming more serious. We were toiling shoulder to shoulder in the O.R. again, getting a patient to sleep.

"Did you go out on the weekend?" I asked her.

"Yes. I was at a party Saturday night. I may have been singing 'warm kitty, soft kitty' to a few people."

"That's funny."

I turned my back to discard some used syringes when I heard her whisper, "I'm as wet as a teen-age girl on prom night." She didn't say it to me, but I was meant to hear. Everyone else was at the scrub sinks outside washing their hands. I turned, and we locked eyes momentarily before she looked away.

"Matthew, if there is any chance you are interested in me, I want you to know that..." She didn't finish. The rest of the staff came back in and we resumed our day.

Sara's shift ended before my list did. I wasn't sure what to do about her. She was brave enough to show her cards while I was still holding mine. I was moved and flattered.

As I was leaving the building, I got a coroner call to a county road about 30 minutes from Coventry. There was a single car on its roof in the ditch with a deceased driver. I examined the scene and organized an autopsy. A curious thing happened on the way back. It began raining golf balls—big chunks of freak, freezing rain in July. There was a thin layer of snow on the highway. I had to remind myself to be careful of my brakes, as I had just had them fixed.

A raccoon ran across the road in front of me, trying to keep up with its scavenger family. I touched the brakes lightly and began to swerve. My SUV did a 360-degree spin helplessly down the middle of the road and ended up facing forward again. This seemed lucky, but I still had momentum. My vehicle slid sideways to the edge of the median ditch dividing traffic directions. The top-heavy truck hovered for a moment and then capsized, sending me diagonally head first into the roof.

I watched as a car on the opposite side of the road came to an abrupt stop. The driver's door sprang open, and a man in a full-length leather coat sprinted into and up out of the median ditch toward me. I heard him pulling open the upper door of my SUV just before I passed out.

Sitting in the passenger seat of a car with black leather seats, my eyes rested on a black dashboard and a manual gear shift stick with a custom chrome knob. Its big noisy engine was propelling us down a county road. A pair of truck nuts dangled from the rear-view mirror.

"I guess it wasn't your time. Looking out your windshield at me, sandwiched in your seat, you looked like my mutt Corgi. It's a good thing you didn't break anything."

Startled out of my haze, I tried to focus on my saviour speaking next to me in the driver's seat. His wide-brimmed leather hat

247

matched his dark leather coat. He was staring through the windshield between the wipers down the highway. It was hard to see his face clearly.

"I don't have a cell signal here," he continued. "There's a Tim Horton's down the highway. I'll take you there so you can call a tow truck."

"Thanks. I have an automobile club membership. Maybe they'll come out."

"Okay. Good. It'll be nicer for you waiting in Timmy's."

"Thanks. Where did you come from? I mean where were you heading? There's almost nobody on the roads right now. It's lucky for me you happened by."

He made no response.

"Did you pass two police vehicles beside another car in the ditch?"

"Yes."

"How did you get me into your car?"

"I carried you on my back about half way before you perked up. You managed the rest by yourself."

My medical training was not to move injured people in case they had a broken neck or a lawyer. Maybe he was a paramedic or a fire-fighter. "So, what do you do?" I asked.

"I'm in the service industry."

I waited in vain for more information. "What do you service?"

"More like an event planner."

"Like surprise parties?"

"It's complicated."

"Have we met before?"

"Just moved here from Calgary."

"You look like Clint Eastwood."

"That's a coincidence. The coffee shop is coming up now. You should be able to make a call here. Do you want me to come in with you?"

I felt shaky but didn't want to impose. "No. I'm all right. What's your name? I'd like to thank you somehow."

"It's Clint. Take care of yourself."

"What's your surname?"

He was already driving away. "Bye Matt."

I don't think he heard me. I don't think his surname was Eastwood. I would have liked to have been able to look him up to send him a gift or something.

After getting a tow out of the ditch, I drove home. The vehicle seemed fine. The weather was normal again. There was a note from Katya waiting for me on the kitchen counter. As I reached for it, the telephone began to ring. I peeked over at the call display to see who it was. Ordinarily, I don't even bother to do that. Digits without a name. I lifted the receiver, thinking it might be Sara.

"Hi. It's Mark Vandermeer."

"Hi Mark. What's up."

"I thought you should know I have been praying for Angelo to leave Coventry. I know you are no fan of his either."

"I'm not sure that will work, Mark. Maybe we should just kill him."

"Don't worry about Angelo. Whatever one sows, that will he also reap. Judge not, lest ye be judged. His bullying days are over."

"Mark, you're creeping me out. Did you see him? I haven't seen him for months."

"Whatever you ask in prayer, believe that you have received it, and it will be yours. I think with our entire congregation praying, we're going to get some results. Talk to you later."

As soon as I hung up, the phone rang again. This time, the call display recognized the caller. It was Katya's sister. Our billing plan allowed her to call our home phone long-distance without charge. I listened to a few more rings before answering.

"Hey Magda. What's up?"

"Hi Matthew. Is Katya there?" We didn't normally engage in much small talk. Our personalities were temperamentally mismatched.

"No, she's out running errands. She should be home in a couple of hours if you call back."

"Is my dad there?"

"Yes, he's sleeping in front of the TV. I'll wake him up."

"No. That's all right. Don't wake him. I'll call back later."

"Magda, there's something I would like to talk to you about. What do you know about Katya and James?" I knew she knew everything there was to know.

"James who, Matthew?"

"James Basciuseson. He was a local guy who died five years ago. He liked interior design a lot, just like Katya. They had a lot in common. I suspect he may have been irresistible."

"Matthew, don't go there."

"Let's go there, Magda. I need to know the truth. I know you are party to most of our personal affairs." This was not the way to get information from her, but I felt like being blunt. My latest head injury had disinhibited me. Third concussion's a charm.

"It would be disloyal to Katya for me to talk about it."

"Katya and I are currently a family unit. You might say your father is in that unit as well. If you are interested in preserving that, you need to air the dirty laundry. It's time for some old-timey Catholic confession."

"There is no dirty laundry, Matthew. Katya says you live too much in your head. You don't go out socially a lot. You are away too much. You are stressed out and angry, and only really nice when you're away from home on holidays."

I stopped talking to reflect on her accusations. I believe in cause and effect. There must have been some truth to them. Why else would these events have come to pass? It's difficult to say whether being an anesthesiologist and a coroner made me more introspective and remote, or being that way already led me to those professions.

"So, Katya didn't tell you about him?" I asked.

"I met him once. Katya just knew him socially. She invited me to join them in Toronto for dinner. He was working on a TV show."

"When was this, Magda?"

"I don't know—five years ago— just shortly before he died. You were going through some difficult times." I had known that those times were difficult, but I resented Magda knowing that. Naturally, she was obligated to defend her sister. Katya was seduced by Jesus, as have been many others.

"Was Katya attracted to him?"

"Yes, obviously. Who wouldn't be? He was compelling... Katya never had sex with him."

"She told you that? How do you know that?"

Magda paused. "Because, I did. Katya invited me to chaperone, and I was attracted to him. She said that I could have him. We played a little trick on him."

"And you never told him it was you?"

"I decided I didn't want him calling me... Matthew, don't judge me. I would have gotten around to it."

So, there it was. Jesus died for nothing. He died for our sins. He died because husbands and wives will always keep a few material facts from each other. The email from Katya that I deleted from James' computer may have been an explanation of the sisters' deception.

"What about Wayney, Magda?"

"Wayne loved James."

"James was gay? That makes some sense."

"James was bisexual. He loved everyone equally."

"How did *you* know Wayney?"

"Wayne was James' roommate in Toronto. They shared an apartment."

"Okay..."

"Katya didn't know he was bisexual."

"Why did Wayney run his bike into me?"

"He said you killed James. He was letting his imagination run rampant. Maybe he had been following you. He was very distraught."

"Did Wayney have AIDS?"

"Why?"

"I nearly gave him mouth-to-mouth. There was something wrong with his white blood cells."

"I don't know."

"How could James have met someone from my street?"

"They both had sex with men in Toronto. That must raise the odds. They had you in common. There is a maximum of six degrees of separation between any two people."

Magda was still talking. I tuned back in mid-sentence, "because she was married to you and she loves you. She wanted to give your marriage another chance. She also blew him off for practical reasons. Dad needs a place to live, and we couldn't be sure that he would fit into James' plans. It would be too stressful to change everything at our age."

Chapter **34**

I woke up on the couch from a profound sleep. Katya was sitting across the room in an armchair with her legs crossed, reading the newspaper. She was wearing freshly laundered blue jeans and a white cotton T-shirt that outlined her breasts. Both garments held soft, ripe femininity. The effect was startling. She looked happy. She was a pleasure to behold.

"What day is it? Is it a day ending in day?" I asked. "What time is it?"

"What time do you want it to be?"

"I don't know."

"It's August 2019."

"I slept so deeply. I fell into a black hole, and then I was back."

"We are such stuff as dreams are made on, and our little life is rounded with a sleep, etcetera."

"What do they say the weather will be like today?"

"The 'they-sayers' say it was pretty nice—birds singing, sailor's delight. Poor baby. It's almost dinnertime." She was studying me closely.

I propped myself up on one elbow. "A day without pierogis and pickled herring is like a day without sunshine. Pass the kielbasa."

We went to the kitchen to look for something to eat. We were cooking together again.

"We're running low on groceries." I was rummaging through the refrigerator. "My mother used to make hot dogs roasted in Cheez Whiz on white bread, skewered with a toothpick."

"What? No lard in that sandwich? We always kept bacon drippings for spreading."

"Us too! See—Ve da same," I was mimicking Grampa's accent. "Where's the cup o' lard, hon? I can't find it." I fished out some freezer burned steaks that I had bought on sale. "What if I toss these on the barby, hon? They say charred meat will kill you, but they don't say when, hon."

"You could use a non-stick pan on the stove. It won't be as tasty or kill you as quickly."

"They look pretty good. I wonder why they were discounted, hon."

"Does it say imported from Eastern Europe? Could be horse."

We assembled at the dinner table. I positioned myself beside Grampa and across from Katya. I didn't like to sit facing Grampa because he didn't often speak. I thought perhaps I made him self-conscious, but Katya's brother had told me that it was the same when he lived with them. It had upset her brother's wife and made her feel that he harboured some resentment toward her. That was just the way he was now.

"How old was your dad when he got married?" Katya asked.

"Twenty-two or three. You know my mother was pregnant, right? My father needed to weigh the pros and cons before doing the right thing. Grampa, how old were you when you got married?"

Grampa livened up as if he had been waiting for his cue to speak. He said he got married at age 36. His life had been unsettled until then. He had been forcibly conscripted into the German army. Having carried a secret stash of civilian clothes as they retreated from the Russians toward Germany, he shed his uniform and changed into civilian dress when the opportunity presented. The war was ending, and Europe was in chaos. He lived with a false identity until the Americans arrived.

After the war, he came to Canada on a contract that required him to work in a northern gold mine for two years. The underground drilling ruined his hearing. After he had satisfied the terms of his agreement, he moved to Toronto. Tens of thousands of young Polish immigrants had gathered there. There was a euphoria from surviving the war and an anything goes attitude from being young and rootless.

"You vant short and happy life or long sad?" he asked. Katya's mother, who was less facile in English, used to ask, "You vant long happy life, or short sad?" Easier choice.

He met her in a Polish dance hall. He didn't say it, but everyone knows what dancing leads to. Katya's mother was a pregnant bride too. Katya said her dad smoked, drank and danced like there was no tomorrow. When he discovered there would be one, he stopped drinking and got a job as a print press operator for the Toronto Star newspaper.

I hadn't heard Grampa speak this much in a decade. He told us about getting his driver's licence and in the spirit of camaraderie, taking the driving test for all his friends. "'Polack DP's all look same to Canadian people." "DP" was the epithet hurled at the new arrivals to Canada. It stood for displaced person. It was nice to see him smile.

"Good girl. You cleaned off your plate. You are quite the carnivore," I said.

"I do love meat. Do you think that's hereditary?"

"You were definitely a carnivore in past lives. A few incarnations ago, a girl would have to give her love to the Polish prince who was most likely to provide her with woolly mammoth."

"I know."

"Have some sour cream, a favourite of Polish princesses."

"Okay, but pass the diet Coke," she joked. "How is your dinner, dad?" Grampa hadn't cleaned his plate. He had been too busy talking.

"Delissiouws," he said pronouncing every letter in the word.

"Finish your horsemeat. How ken ye have any puddin' if ye don't eat your horsemeat?" I teased him. He didn't get the Pink Floyd reference and fell silent.

"What's the weather for tomorrow, Grampa?" I encouraged him. Grampa always knew the weather forecast because he watched TV news all day. There was no answer. After his dinnertime loquaciousness, he was returning to his usual state of pensive. The dog was flashing her winning smile, so I gave her the rest of Grampa's food.

Katya said she would take Grampa for a walk in the mall. It wasn't good for him to be stuck in the house all day. He was more of a free-range Grampa. He couldn't manage the indoor track at the arena any more. His health was declining steadily. When he first moved in with us, he used to take half hour walks to the canal by himself to feed the ducks.

"If they had opposite walking directions on alternate days on the track, Grampa wouldn't have ruined his knees," I said stridently. "Who makes these decisions? The seniors need to organize a demonstration outside the hockey arena demanding action. Or go to the top. Picket the mayor's house. Hold up their X-rays and present their physiotherapy bills. That's the way to quick action!"

"We might stop at Marks and get a few things. Dad needs some shorts for the summer—and then to the drug store. Dad needs his prescriptions renewed. Do you want anything?"

"Just a big bag of drugs."

"Any particular kind?"

"Just you know, all different colours."

"Okay, hon."

"Good hunting!"

"Happy trails."

Katya scootched in beside me on my kitchen chair like a little girl and reached her arms around my neck. I felt her weight and her lips against the side of my face. Her affectionate nature superseded any postural challenge.

I felt energized by my nap. I cycled over to see Sean at his house. During tourist season, the front foyer and living room were often in use by guests. I wheeled my bicycle around to the back, climbed the stairs to his deck and knocked on the frame of the screen door.

I heard Sean's Irish lilt. "Come on in, Matthew." He seemed to be expecting me.

Entering the kitchen, I saw Sean sitting beside a commercial sized, red enamel gas range on a black and white checkerboard tile floor. He was in an armchair with his back to me.

"How did you know it was me?" I asked.

"I heard your bicycle coming up the walk."

"How did you know it was my bicycle?"

"You were due for a visit."

"I thought I should come over before you left—to, ah, inventory your belongings."

Sean, his sister and his wife Sinead had attempted an Atlantic crossing that had not gone smoothly. They set out from Elbow Cay in the Bahamas and encountered a serious storm with house-high waves. Sean was forced to stay awake for a continuous three-day stretch at the wheel. The two women crouched in the tiny cockpit beside him. Going below deck would have provoked violent seasickness. They abandoned the boat in the Azores in the mid-Atlantic. They were flying back there to complete the crossing.

"Have a look around. Take whatever you like," he said.

"It would only be to console me and to remember you by."

"We leave in two weeks. We'll see our last guests off then."

"How does Sinead feel about it?"

"She says she's coming. She doesn't want me to meet my fate alone."

"I'm going, but there are only two things I don't like, Matthew." Sinead was standing in the hall doorway.

"What are they Sinead?" I asked.

"Wind and water." She laughed nervously.

"You're the Viking wife who has to be buried at sea with her husband."

"We'll have help this time," Sean said. "My daughter and son-in-law, who is an experienced sailor, are coming." Sean's daughter was now a newlywed.

"It's good your sons aren't coming," I said. "There will still be someone to carry on the family name. Maybe you should take separate flights. Sorry, I'm being glass half empty… Go and kick that ocean's ass."

"Don't think I wasn't aware that if anything happened to Sean, we were doomed," Sinead said.

"We have to get the boat ready to leave. It's been on Terceira for a year and the Azores customs inspectors will come to visit soon," Sean said.

"Too bad. Maybe they'd take a bribe and leave you alone. That is one of the most beautiful places on earth." Katya and I had flown out to visit them during March school break. Terceira is a world heritage site, Ireland with palm trees.

"They won't take a bribe, but they are very disorganized. They may not find us for a while. We won't leave until the weather conditions are right."

"Terceira is one of my favourite places on God's blue earth—which we wouldn't have discovered without your sea-dog pioneering." We had travelled by air to bypass the wind and water.

"Hey Matthew, have a look at this," Sean said, holding up his hand. "I've had surgery. Getting all my ailments tended to before we leave. I was having some tingling and weakness."

I saw from the scar he had had a carpal tunnel release, which is a minor procedure for releasing an entrapped median nerve at the wrist. I examined his palm like a fortune teller. "The wound looks well healed... You still have your appendix? Astronauts have that out before they boldly go anywhere. Who did the surgery?"

"Dr. Amodeo."

"No one's seen him lately."

"My thumb is better, but my palm is still numb."

"Well, that's not coming back," I informed him. "He probably cut the palmar cutaneous branch of the median nerve. It's a well recognized complication. It's not serious, but it happens if you make the incision too far medial."

"He seemed to know what he was doing. He said he had done hundreds of these."

"Yes, you should lawyer up and sue his ass—if you can find it. You might get twenty thousand bucks. What ye have cut, so shall ye reap." I said this as a devil's advocate, but I didn't really care what trouble I caused for Angelo, or his heirs.

"I could never do that. He's a good man."

Sinead excused herself to look after a guest.

"Suit yourself. Maybe it's not enough money to bother. I never properly thanked you for helping dispatch Mr. B. to the nether-world."

Sean walked to the sink and turned the tap on full blast. "He was already dead when I got there, Matthew. The less you know the better." He filled the kettle and turned the water off. "Cup of tea, Matthew?"

He methodically brewed and doled out the tea and then resumed sitting where I had found him. He said, "It's convenient to have an

259

armchair in the kitchen, when there are paying guests in the living room."

I returned home to find Katya and her father sitting together on the deck in the dark. Katya said, "You missed the sunset."

"There will be another one tomorrow, I hope."

"The sun's moved. The sunset was over there last month." She was pointing at the horizon.

"It is the earth that moves, not the sun. Catholics are always making that mistake."

"Where were you all this time?"

"I cycled over to visit Sinead and Sean."

I could see that she was jealous. She wanted to know when they were leaving and whether there was enough time to organize a farewell party.

"We had a false alarm farewell dinner for them last year," I said. "They came back. You invite the Buckleys and I'll invite the Bennetts for next Saturday. If anyone cancels there will still be enough noise to keep it lively. Invite your sister too." I thought, why not? She sacrificed herself to save our marriage. Magda was my new favourite person.

In bed that night I heard Katya say, "I guess we were meant to grow old together."

"I guess so," I answered.

"That's it?"

"I do try to follow Danny DeVito's advice in *War of the Roses*. He's a divorce attorney, but his advice to the husband is to remember something positive about his wife from when they fell in love, because the alternative is so catastrophic. When we have a disagreement, I travel back and remember why I fell in love with you. I chose you for a reason."

"I know. Thanks."

"Only please never say, 'Yes I bought it and hid it.' "

"Okay."

"Those whom God has united, men must not divide."

"I thought you weren't religious."

"Score another victory for Baptist Sunday school... I envy your father."

"Really, why?"

"He has two doting daughters, a live-in doctor and a reservation in heaven."

"You have a son."

"It's too bad we didn't have any daughters. Sons aren't reliable. There will be nobody to care for us. I'll be strapped into a chair in a nursing home, trying to grab visitors as they walk by."

"Where will I be?" Katya asked.

"I don't know. Maybe down the hall, trying on other people's clothes."

"Matthew, I'm sorry you didn't get the life you wanted."

I took her in my arms in the dark and kissed a salty tear. "It's close enough."

I lay awake in bed holding Katya until after my lower arm went numb, waiting, sensing that she was still awake. After half an hour, when her breathing finally became rhythmic, I relaxed and stopped guarding her, reassured that she had let go of the day and I could sleep.

Chapter 35

Adam was moving fast. He had to be in Toronto that evening to catch an early morning flight. We finished the first case, a hysterectomy, in forty minutes. The standard time for this operation is an hour and a half. There were no wasted movements when he operated. We had started another hysterectomy.

"How old is this patient?" Sara, who was scrubbed, asked. "She looks really young." She was about the same age as Sara.

"She's 35. He's already taken out all the 36-year-old uteruses in town," I said.

"What's the youngest you can have this operation?" Sara was standing at her instrument table in full O.R. garb. Large jade green eyes glowed between her mask and bouffant cap.

"No lower limit, mon. I'm doing her because she has chronic pain." Adam sounded defensive.

"We're going to cut out her pain you see." Simon was pressing a sponge on the edge of the incision.

"No upper limit either," Adam said. "I may give the 80-year-olds magic pills instead."

I stood up to look over the drape. "Magic pills sound good. Do they work?"

"Only if you truly believe."

"I heard you were in last night at 3 a.m. for a section," Sara said.

"Ah, yes... the bleeding and screaming ward. Did you know that most human babies are born at night to protect them from predators?" Simon said. "It's not foolproof of course."

"Did you get some sleep after that?" Sara asked sympathetically. I liked Sara. She was nice.

"Ya-mon. I had a fine two-hour sleep."

"Luxury! We used 'a dream a' two hours' sleep," I said, affecting a Monty Python Yorkshire accent.

"Do any of you lot know anything about how the colonoscopy law suit was settled?" Simon asked. "That's all died down now hasn't it. That must have been jolly expensive."

"I think it was settled with the terms to be kept secret," I said. "If I sat on any committees, I could tell you. We do have to chant, 'clean scope, every patient, every time, that will be our goal,' in the scope room."

"Admirable optimism. The hospital's defence should have been that dirty colonoscopes can be good for you," Adam said. "You might get a better class of E. Coli in the transplanted faeces."

I was waiting for insensitive Simon to ask about my lawsuit next, but along with everyone else he seemed to have forgotten about it. "Yes of course. One must remember to request the class that doesn't make you fat or give you fibromyalgia," he opined.

The uterus was out. Simon dabbed away a few drops of blood. Sara handed Adam a needle driver clamped onto a large suture to begin closing.

"Adam, you are such a slick surgeon. You could slip into a lady's boudoir late at night when she is asleep, and she would wake up in the morning with her uterus gone," I said. "The only evidence that you had been there would be your calling card on the night table."

He looked like he didn't know whether to be pleased with the compliment. "Any retirement plans yet, Matthew?" he asked.

"Why should I retire from this sweet gig? I might need more money. I still don't know how long I'm going to live. Maybe Simon will bequeath his assisting job to me."

"I should say not. You have not always been kind to me," Simon said.

"I intend to mend my ways," I promised.

"I'm thinking about a job with the College of Physicians and Surgeons or the CDDA someday," Adam said.

"I don't think I would be an empathetic enough person to deal with cry-baby doctors," I said. "Where are you going on holiday, Adam?"

"A second honeymoon in Costa Rica. My wife picked the resort—all private suites with their own infinity pools."

"Just you and your wife?"

"Yes."

"Do some excursions—you know—zip-lining amongst the howler monkeys in the jungle canopy and so forth. One doesn't want too much time alone together while reconciling," Simon advised.

"I was a little worried about that. I am not sure this is such a good idea," Adam fretted.

"Do you have a kitchen where you're going?" I asked. "If you cooks together, you stays together."

"I wonder how old Amodeo is liking his new job in America," Simon said.

"Probably earning the big bucks, but he has to live in a backwater in Arkansas," Adam said. "He could only take a job no American wanted. There's a new surgeon here today, looking around. He was swapping recipes with the nurses."

"His prayers were answered! Mark was praying for that. I hope they do a 'Deliverance' on Angelo's ass."

"Surely Matthew, you can't mean torturing and anally raping him?" Simon asked jovially.

264

"The procedure should be familiar from his residency. I hope he likes banjo music."

I delivered my last patient to the recovery room. A young man came over with his right hand extended enthusiastically and introduced himself. He told me what a relief it was to have passed his exams and called me sir. He was Angelo's replacement. He was looking forward to working with me. Times change.

Returning to the O.R. to collect my briefcase, I found that everyone had cleared out. The computer terminal had been left on. Signing in wasn't required here. I pulled up James' chart. This was technically illegal because I wasn't involved with his case any longer. I was surprised that they hadn't quarantined the record somehow. A report dated a few weeks before James' death showed that his lymphoma was in complete remission. It was the same page I had seen as an illegible photocopy, buried in the disclosure notes that Richard Chrétien had handed me at the hearing for discovery.

This evidence didn't support the contention of the litigants that an anesthetic had depressed James' immunity and caused a recurrence of lymphoma, which made him depressed, which made him dead. It didn't support anyone's version of events. I emailed Richard about it, but he didn't respond. It was around the time when terms of the settlement were being finalized. It would have been an unwelcome disruption if Richard was in the process of recommending terms to the CDDA and if he was complicit with arranging the bad photocopy.

I know that the CDDA never settles frivolous lawsuits, but they do sometimes act expediently to limit their losses. A few weeks after the discovery hearing, the CDDA informed me that although in the broad sense there was no merit to the case, their experts had told them there was one aspect where the defence would be problematic. They weren't concerned about whether I had exacerbated James' depression or suppressed his immunity. While there may have been some truth to those allegations, the "dinosaur anesthetics" James received were still in use in many Canadian hospitals and widely in other countries where cost containment is more of an issue.

The problem was that I had admitted to knowing I shouldn't have acted as coroner in this case. The Regional Supervising Coroner who gave me the go-ahead was by now retired. He was also suffering from early dementia and was unable to corroborate my story. Consequently, the CDDA settled the case against me for the sum of one million dollars. The settlement stipulated that there was no finding of fault, no one could disclose the terms of the settlement and no one's relatives or heirs into perpetuity could revive the lawsuit.

The anesthetic drug manufacturer also contributed a million loonies and withdrew Maxiflurane from the market. They held their nose and paid because they had deep pockets. The business was diverted to nearly identical anesthetic agents that were more profitable because they were still under patent protection. The hospital paid four hundred thousand to be let out of the action before its resolution. The total was worked out according to a formula that took account of how many productive years were stolen from James.

Even though there was a tacit admission of some responsibility on my behalf, I needed peace. Two point four million was the price. I had helped my side realize that the case was not worth fighting. Learning how the game is played is part of survival. I have to thank the CDDA and their contributing members for the favour. It meant that my name was out of the news. The police wouldn't be investigating Dr. Kork for conspiracy in the murder of his wife's or her sister's lover.

Two point four million was not large as settlements go. It was enough to add to Caine's notoriety and establish his winning record as a medico-legal attorney. I never saw or heard from my lawyer again. I was looking at a brochure for a medical conference in a holiday destination some months later and noticed that Richard Chrétien was a featured speaker. I Googled his name and was floored by the first item. The Caine Law Group was pleased to announce that they had taken on a new partner specializing in medico-legal matters and that henceforth they would be known as Caine Chrétien LLP. Caine at least must have liked Mr. Chrétien's work.

Eve, the operating room head nurse, told me she had been required to attend meetings with the hospital lawyer before the hearing. Joanie had also been present since she was the scrub nurse for James' surgery. Eve intimated that Joanie had been talking a lot with the hospital lawyer and may have been impugning my honour. I heard that Joanie got a generous retirement package a few months after the settlement was announced. I didn't attend her farewell party.

It would seem that Richard Chrétien is a specimen of opportunistic jackal or vulture as forecast by the prophet-pediatrician Jeremiah. Joanie is only a parasite. Her son's legal expenses probably made a dent in her savings. They are all God's creatures. It's not that I forgive them their trespasses. I am as indifferent as a Buddhist. Vultures and parasites are part of any ecosystem. They clean up the detritus after you can't fight any more.

Did James kill himself because Magda blew him off? Maybe his love affair with Katya had been part of a grandiose fantasy, where she was the key to his entire future. In my report five years ago, I ruled that James' death was a suicide by hanging. I don't believe that anymore. It is trendy nowadays to medicalize personality flaws. James was a narcissist. Balls or none, on or off his lithium, that would be my diagnosis.

In the coroner business, the cause and manner of death is decided on the balance of probabilities. Although it might be self-deception to elevate Luke to an evil sainthood, and three concussions can cloud your judgement, I prefer this version of the truth. Luke did an altruistic killing to atone for a vicious one and was reincarnated according to Buddhist precepts. He is serving his penance in an anonymous town in Pennsylvania or has a job in the service industry in Somerset county. He executed my fantasy killing, just the way I described it to him. The proof was the cat. James didn't have a cat.

Tainted Jesus is still dead either way and so is Luke, probably. Wayney is riding a heavenly Harley. They will stay that way until they are reincarnated. Luke considered it a mark of friendship that he did James first. It was a goodbye present. He must have thought he had nothing left to lose, since he was doing one killing anyway. The subtle distinctions between murder, suicide and accident will lose importance and disappear before many years have passed.

Luke was my friend, and I should have tried harder to help him. I could have shown him alternatives. I might have prevented the savage exit that I helped inspire. On the day after a blinding snow-storm, after the traffic accidents have been towed away, the sun will be shining disingenuously. You have to wonder why the casualties didn't wait a day before undertaking their journey. I didn't predict this outcome, and it bothers me that from a selfish perspective I still can't think of a better one. I never spoke with Luke's wife. I sent her a condolence card with a long message about remembering the good times. It came back unopened.

At one time, Katya may have thought I had something to do with James' death. Now, she likely believes that my code of ethics is the same as hers—that I am not capable of murder or arranging one by proxy. I can almost convince myself that I am innocent. James was less so. No doubt the situation is rife with moral ambiguity. Religious folk might say that God's will had been done. God works in rounda-bout ways. Ours is not to question.

Sean and Sinead cast off from the Azores, bound for Spain, and hit another storm. After fighting it for two days, they detoured south and made it safely to Madeira, which was serendipitous as it too is uniquely beautiful. To this day my wife and I have not discussed the sequence of events that led to the death of James Jesus Basciuseson.

She may not even know that I know she was involved. My feeling is that time is a better healer than open and frank discussion.

Postscriptum

After completion of this manuscript, Sinead and Sean embarked on their return voyage, crossing the Atlantic from Madeira to Martinique. It took four weeks. Sean said the crossing was 95 per cent boredom and five per cent terror. That is comparable to the practice of anesthesiology. Sinead said it was 50–50, referring I believe to sailing.

It was Sinead who confirmed my suspicions about Luke. She said that in an idle moment at sea, Sean told her that he had arrived at James' apartment in time to help Luke, whom he had never met, hang up James' corpse. It would have been difficult for one man to do alone.

Grampa died of pneumonia in his ninety-second year. Pneumonia is potentially survivable. He refused antibiotics, and his doctor facilitated his passing with morphine. Medical assistance in dying had become legal. I was sad and conflicted. The manner of death was not completely natural.

IF YOU ENJOYED THIS BOOK and would like to receive notification when the next in series becomes available, please go to www.petertinits.com and fill out the contact form. Click the Free Content tab and scroll down to read previews of works in progress.

Please also leave a review on Amazon and/or GoodReads.

MORE BOOKS by Peter Tinits

An UNDETERMINED MANNER of DEATH: The attractive beneficiary of a new life insurance policy promotes a homicide verdict to the coroner investigating her father's apparent suicide. This second-in-series Matthias Kork novel, published in 2023, features a humorous blend of lying, cheating, killing and domestic drama.

A HOMICIDAL MANNER: Dr. Kork's inquiries into a death on a passenger train attract attention from domestic and foreign intelligence services. His efforts to discover the cause and manner of death do not go smoothly or unpunished. The third Matthias Kork novel, published in 2024, showcases travel, romance and assassinations.

MILLENNIUM LAMENT: Rupi Kaur for your father—a collection of darkly humorous, illustrated poetry, published in 2022.

Reviews for *A CAUSE and MANNER*

Bloody good —SEBRINGVILLE STAR

Effing great —MENNONITE GAZETTE

You have to read this one. Very effing great — MITCHELL TIMES

It changed my life —13th DALAI LAMA

So-so, if you've seen everything on Netflix —CAL MALINKOWSKI

Strong writing, if you like that kind of thing —CHARLES HAMILTON, HAMILTON HOUSE

Pretty darn good —NIJOLE TINITS

Passable first effort —LILA COOK, NIJOLE'S SISTER

Not that bad —PETERBOROUGH ANARCHISTS MOTORCYCLE CLUB

I liked the hockey chapter —FATHER O'BRIEN, COACH, COVENTRY MINOR BANTAM HOCKEY

No blood or blood products —THE WATCHTOWER

I would rather have a root canal —MARK STRAUS DDS

I'm a better writer —HAWTHORNE DIDIER

It's no Duddy Kravitz —YALE ERENBERG MD

Smut and filth —SMITHS FALLS LITERARY REVIEW

www.ingramcontent.com/pod-product-compliance
Lightning Source LLC
Chambersburg PA
CBHW020419260626
47156CB00007B/2469